JORDAN'S
CROSSING

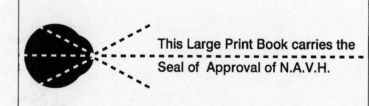

This Large Print Book carries the
Seal of Approval of N.A.V.H.

JORDAN'S CROSSING

Randall Arthur

Thorndike Press • Waterville, Maine

Published in 2005 by arrangement with Multnomah Publishers, Inc.

Thorndike Press® Large Print Christian Mystery.

The tree indicium is a trademark of Thorndike Press.

The text of this Large Print edition is unabridged.
Other aspects of the book may vary from the original edition.

Set in 16 pt. Plantin by Elena Picard.

Printed in the United States on permanent paper.

Library of Congress Cataloging-in-Publication Data

Arthur, Randall.
    Jordan's crossing / by Randall Arthur.
       p. cm. — (Thorndike Press large print Christian mystery)
      ISBN 0-7862-7502-2 (lg. print : hc : alk. paper)
      1. Clergy — Fiction. 2. Europe — Fiction. 3. Missions — Fiction. 4. Professional ethics — Fiction. 5. Large type books. I. Title. II. Thorndike Press large print Christian mystery series.
PS3551.R77J67 2005
  813′.54—dc22   2005000017

DEDICATED . . .

to Sherri, Heidi, Shanda, Flora, and Jan —
the five wonderful ladies in my life
and to the people of the BIBC,
who actively encouraged me
during times of uncertainty.

A THOUSAND THANK-YOUs . . .

to the Multnomah editors for their
editorial artistry; to the several test readers
of the first-draft manuscript who provided
objective criticism; to the various Atlanta
hospitals and law enforcement agencies for
helpful information; and finally,
to Bill and Marian for their special favor.

OF INTEREST . . .

Flint Konserne in Bad Tolz, Germany,
officially closed on July 15, 1991.
McGraw Konserne in Munich
closed in the summer of 1992.
The Bad Aibling station in Bad Aibling
closed on September 30, 2002.

As the Founder/CEO of NAVH, the only national health agency solely devoted to those who, although not totally blind, have an eye disease which could lead to serious visual impairment, I am pleased to recognize Thorndike Press* as one of the leading publishers in the large print field.

Founded in 1954 in San Francisco to prepare large print textbooks for partially seeing children, NAVH became the pioneer and standard setting agency in the preparation of large type.

Today, those publishers who meet our standards carry the prestigious "Seal of Approval" indicating high quality large print. We are delighted that Thorndike Press is one of the publishers whose titles meet these standards. We are also pleased to recognize the significant contribution Thorndike Press is making in this important and growing field.

Lorraine H. Marchi, L.H.D.
Founder/CEO
NAVH

* Thorndike Press encompasses the following imprints: Thorndike, Wheeler, Walker and Large Print Press.

◆ Part 1

1991

1

In a lower-class Chicago high-rise, Ricardo Alvarez jabbed the switchblade into his desktop, gouging out splintered chunks of pine and flicking them onto the floor. He hoped his mother would come into his room at any second, see what he was doing, and start yelling at him.

He gripped the switchblade tighter. Let her yell. It would give him an excuse to scream and curse right back at her.

She had just informed him that she was going to marry the crew-cut, nonsmiling Special Forces soldier she had been dating. At the thought of it, Ricardo plunged the knife again, prying loose a silver-dollar-sized piece of wood. She was nothing but a cheap barfly, Ricardo decided. He might as well be an orphan. She had never cared about his feelings. *Never.* She knew he couldn't stand the sight of the jarhead jerk she was dating — but did it matter? No! Not to her.

He snarled as he twisted the blade back and forth in the top of the desk.

He'd heard them talking through the thin wall that separated his bedroom from the living room. He'd heard Mitchum — that was the Green Beret's name — talk about the fact that he was being transferred to Germany. He'd heard the louse ask his mother if Germany was okay with her. "Sure," she'd said, with a drunken giggle.

Ricardo raised the knife high above his head. Did anybody think to ask what *he* thought about going to Germany? Did anybody care at all what a sixteen-year-old guy with friends of his own felt about being jerked halfway around the world with a mother who stayed drunk and a stepfather he couldn't stand?

He thrust the knife into the desk, wishing this time that the blade were striking something besides unfeeling wood.

At 11:30 p.m., Jordan Rau stood in the dark, staring out the living-room window of his family's fifth-floor Munich apartment at the empty, mist-shrouded streets below. It was late and he was tired, but the nagging frustrations in his mind kept him from going to bed.

For the first time in weeks, he was wondering if he had done the right thing. This particular evening, like many others during the last month and a half, had been a miserable one for his family, filled with arguments, shouts, and short tempers. His wife and children had finally marched off to their bedrooms to be left alone.

What's wrong with them? Jordan asked himself as he glimpsed the dark outlines of Grunwalder Stadium, four blocks away. *Why can't they be reasonable?*

Evidently he was the only one who could understand the logic of moving here from Chattanooga. After all, the financial incentives were too significant to pass up: The mission board was guaranteeing them a monthly salary that was a full 50 percent more than he had been paid by his church in Tennessee. Not to mention the generous medical benefits package — no small consideration, in light of their son's epilepsy.

Despite his annoyance, a tiny smile came to his lips as he thought about Chase. The seventeen-year-old had, against all odds, found his first girlfriend — here, in Germany. Her name was Heather Anne Moseley, and she was a classmate at the Department of Defense high school for American military dependents. This friendship alone was enough to justify the move, as far as Jordan was concerned. For the first time in many years, his son — his pride and joy — was taking an active interest in life, an interest that was perhaps strong enough to pull him beyond the reclusiveness and caution that the epilepsy had forced on him since childhood.

Then Jordan thought of Susan, his wife — and frowned again. She didn't share his enjoyment of Chase's budding romance, or of anything else related to the move. Since the day the letter came from the mission board announcing the opportunity for this overseas project, she had planted her heels in opposition. Again, Jordan replayed their conversation — the same conversation that had consistently surfaced, with minor variations, since he began talking about the possibility of making the move:

"Why do we have to move so far away?" she would demand. "Is it just the high salary? Is that the reason? If it is, I'll get a full-time job. We can use my paycheck to pay back the bank loan. We don't have to go all the way to Germany just to recover from our debt!"

At this point in the exchange, Jordan usually became annoyed. Susan insistently played up their financial difficulties, tacitly declaring that Jordan's only motivation was "money." True, the debt was bothersome, but that was hardly —

"And another thing," she would continue. "If it were just the two of us, maybe I could handle the move. But doesn't it matter to you that Chase is just now, after nine years, starting to feel comfortable with his peers in Chattanooga? Doesn't it matter to you that we have a thirteen-year-old daughter who needs her friends right now? And doesn't it matter to you that your church doesn't want to give you up as their pastor?"

Jordan sighed. On and on it went. Susan just couldn't seem to understand the opportunities opening up in this part of the world for their denomination. The emotional insecurities that she felt for herself and for the children were blinding her. She wasn't comprehending the importance that the denomination was attaching to their specially selected five-family team: a team set up, along with four other joint teams specializing in various Eastern European languages, to staff the new seminary their denomination was building in Leipzig, Germany.

She couldn't grasp anything of the vision, not even when he tried to describe it for her. Whenever he tried to be persuasive, she would badger him with her simplistic, timeworn phrases that were always shrouded in a cloak of religious respectability:

"Jordan, I just can't see that this move is God's will. I know it's something *you* want; but are you sure it's something *He* wants? Have you even prayed about it?"

Turning away from the window, he rubbed his face in irritation. Susan and her narrow-minded evangelical upbringing . . . She couldn't seem to outgrow it, not even after all these years. To Susan, God's will was a black-and-white immutable fact, unique for each individual, and something that could be unmistakably determined if a person only prayed hard enough for long enough. But if Jordan had learned anything during his time in seminary, it was that God's purposes for man were not so easily understood or defined. Of course, he knew Susan wasn't completely at fault for her lack of religious sophistication. She had only inherited the naive tenets that her parents had drummed into her since birth. For her, Christianity wasn't something to be critically analyzed and sifted. It was rather a whole list of beliefs that had to be

14

accepted in their entirety without serious or creative questioning. In a way, though, he knew that this was what had drawn him to Susan in the first place: She was like an easy-believing child, sweet and unpretentious. Yet, as he had learned through twenty years of marriage, her simple way of thinking could also lend itself to unreasonableness and stubbornness.

Jordan stretched his six-foot-four, 245-pound frame and turned toward the bedroom. He realized that people like Susan sometimes had to be pushed against their wills like children, until they saw the light. That's what he had to keep doing, he decided.

He knew this move was right. He'd just have to maintain his course until Susan was as convinced as he was.

Lying in bed alone, trying in vain to fall asleep, Susan Rau felt swallowed by an unshakable emptiness swirling around her. Like tireless animals of prey, the difficulties of her uprooted life continued to stalk her, denying her the rest she so badly needed.

Since the day her family stepped from the plane at the Munich airport, nothing had gone right for them.

It had taken an unexpected seven weeks to find a place to live. The large number of East Germans now moving freely into the West was creating a severe housing shortage. Their mission board had somehow missed this detail.

Jordan had not been allowed to collect their car or any of their household goods from customs until they had first acquired a permanent address and a residence permit. Before finding their apartment, they were forced to live out of their suitcases at a German *Gasthaus* twenty-three miles outside of Munich. Susan had felt isolated — trapped.

Chase was late in starting his senior year at the American Department of Defense high school in Munich. He was struggling to adjust and to catch up.

Their daughter, Donica, also starting late, was not adjusting to the German school she was attending. Chase was allowed to attend the American school simply because it was his senior year. Donica, however, was put in the German school system because she was younger, and because it was already costing $500 a month to send Chase to the DOD school. But trying to learn German by total immersion and trying to make new friends with the

16

German students was more of an emotional struggle for Donica than she could handle. Normally a bubbly optimist, she was becoming withdrawn and silent.

Susan found herself in a constant battle with loneliness and depression. Uprooted from her friends and relatives in the States, she longed to lean on Jordan for the emotional support that could perhaps help make a difference in her situation. But because of his responsibilities, he was less able now than at any time in their twenty years of marriage to give her the attention she needed.

Jordan's language classes at the Goethe Institute lasted three hours a day. Then there was homework, ongoing arrangements with the mission board, telephone conversations with other team members, planning sessions, and a host of other activities that seemed to constantly pull him away.

The four other families who were on the German-language mission team with the Raus had planned to join them in Munich for language training. But due to the severity of the housing shortage, the mission board chose at the last moment to settle the other families in Nürnberg, an hour and a half to the north. Thus, Susan was deprived of even the minimal companionship that could have been provided by another missionary wife.

The weather in Munich had been miserable. The Alps were normally in view to the south of the city, but the Raus had scarcely been able to see and enjoy them. The dense fog and clouds just wouldn't seem to go away.

Susan was sure that if the attractive salary weren't such a lure for him, Jordan — despite his never-say-die optimism — would have already packed it in.

"God," she moaned into her pillow, "is this really Your will?" She grabbed the bedspread in her fingers and squeezed. "I don't think I can . . ."

It was no use. Prayer didn't seem effective anymore. She should have been comforted by pouring out her soul to God, but everything seemed so confusing right now.

Jordan seemed to regard her faith as something primitive. She remembered quoting a verse to him from 1 Peter, about casting all your cares on God. "Honey," Jordan replied, "Peter was a fisherman, an uneducated man with limited resources. He was only speaking out of a desperate sense of his own need. But we can't expect God to be our beast of burden. Day-to-day pressures and pains are *our* responsibility, not God's. They're common to everyone. Have you ever known a Christian who didn't face any struggles? No, of course not. And that proves my point."

Rolling onto her side, she stared up at the ceiling. Maybe Jordan was right. He seemed so self-assured, so determined. So utterly confident that being in Germany was right for them.

Maybe she was the problem. Maybe she just needed to grit her teeth and keep going, like Jordan. It seemed to work for him, all right. But would it work for her?

She heard the bedroom door opening, followed by the sound of Jordan's bustling movements to get ready for bed. She closed her eyes and breathed deeply, feigning sleep. She didn't want to talk anymore tonight. She wouldn't know what to say, anyway.

2

"Anybody want a piece of gum?" Jordan asked as they left the Munich city limits, driving south on E-11 toward Bad Aibling.

"Sure . . . I'll take a piece," Donica said from the back seat.

"I'll take one," Chase added.

"Me, too," Susan said with a smile, reaching for the pack of gum to pass it around.

Jordan realized that the anticipation of the evening out had put them all in a good mood. It wasn't difficult to understand why. Their dinner engagement at the home of Ralph and Lynn Moseley — Heather Anne's parents — would be the first time since coming to Germany that they had been in anyone else's home. The contact with another American family in a casual atmosphere would be therapeutic for each of them. Besides, it was just good to get away from the fifth-floor apartment for a while. *God knows we need it,* Jordan thought.

During the remainder of the drive they played a car game, teased Chase about being in love, and talked about the highest peak overlooking Bad Aibling — Wendelstein mountain, supposedly picturesque but currently hidden from them in gray clouds growing darker with the evening.

They exited the autobahn, approaching Bad Aibling, a small township nearly forty miles southeast of Munich. Susan, with her hand-drawn map, helped Jordan navigate the last five miles of intersections, traffic lights, turns, and residential streets.

They made only one wrong turn. It cost them a few minutes and some consternation before Jordan realized their mistake and retraced his way back to the correct street, but they still arrived at the Moseley home on time.

Stopping the car at the end of the gravel driveway, they were greeted by the sudden illumination of a floodlight mounted on the side of the house. Before they could all get out of the car, the front door of the house opened and out stepped a pleasant looking man with a genuine smile.

"Welcome! Welcome! I'm Ralph Moseley," he said, extending his hand first to Jordan, then to Susan and the kids.

"We've been looking forward to your visit." Jordan felt himself warming to Ralph Moseley's genial nature.

As they stepped inside and went through more introductions, Jordan knew the evening would be a good one. The whole setting was inviting and refreshing — exactly what he and his family needed. He even thought he saw Susan's shoulders relaxing, and the sight made him more hopeful than he'd been in some time.

The two families shared a delicious steak dinner, then moved into the living room. The conversation moved easily among a variety of topics: the work which had brought each family to Munich, the ceaseless Bavarian rain, culture shock, the abundant possibilities for downhill skiing in the area, the high cost of phone calls in Germany, and German engineering — "the best in the world, along with their chocolates."

They also talked about church. Jordan listened with interest as Ralph told about his family's conservative Christian background. It was a detailed and rich history.

"When my company, Raytheon, transferred me here a little over a year ago," Ralph added, "we spent several months looking for a good English-speaking church. We visited the military chapel here at Bad Aibling, along with the ones at Bad Tölz and Munich, but they were a little too political for us. The only other alternative was St. Jude's International Church in downtown Munich. It's a little more liturgical than we prefer —"

"— and farther away than we prefer," Lynn Moseley added.

"That's true," Ralph acknowledged. "But, as a family, we feel that we need a solid church home while we're here. So we finally chose tradition over politics, even at the expense of convenience." Pausing just for a second, Ralph added, "So what about you, Jordan? Where do you all attend?"

"We've never heard of St. Jude's before," Jordan told the Moseleys. "But we do know about the military chapel in Munich." He, Susan, and the kids had attended there a few times. But they hadn't continued, because not a single person there had reached out to welcome or befriend them. "We thought the congregation at the chapel was a little . . . well, a little cold, if you want to know the truth," he finished.

"Yeah," piped Donica from the next room, "and majorly boring."

Amid the laughter, Lynn said, "I'm not sure that you'd find St. Jude's to be any less dull, but I do think you'd find it to be a little friendlier." She paused, then added, "Why don't you go with us on Sunday if you don't already have something else planned? We'd love for you to be our guests."

Jordan looked at Susan to get her opinion.

"What do you think, kids?" Susan questioned Donica and Chase across the room, allowing their preference in this situation to determine her own.

"Yeah, let's do it," said Donica.

"Sounds great to me," replied Chase.

Heather Anne, sitting next to Chase, smiled with excitement.

"Well," responded Jordan, turning to look at Ralph and Lynn, "it looks like a unanimous decision. I guess all we need to know now is how to get there."

"Actually, it would be easier to show you than tell you," Ralph said. "Why don't you just meet us at the American high school, say about ten-thirty Sunday morning? You can follow us to the church from there."

"Sounds good," agreed Jordan. "It's a date."

On the following Thursday morning, near lunchtime, Ricardo Alvarez drove into the parking lot of the Burger King located in the off-base American housing area of the McGraw *Konserne* in Munich.

The Burger King was next door to the American Department of Defense high school. It was the only American fast-food restaurant in the area where food was sold at American prices for American dollars. The restaurant was open to the public, but it was primarily for the families of American military personnel — including the Tenth Special Forces Group to the south in Bad Tölz, where Ricardo and his mother were now living with her new husband.

Being in Germany had done nothing to change Ricardo's opinion of the move forced upon him. He hated the German weather, hated the German people, hated the German language — hated everything about this gloomy, rain-drenched country.

Skipping school this morning, he had come to the Burger King to eat a late breakfast. He had already missed more than half of the school days since his arrival at the DOD high school. It was a foregone fact that he would fail the school year. But he had no intention of repeating the tenth grade — not next year, not ever. In fact, he had recently decided to phase out of school all together.

Mitchum had been away on field exercises for most of the eight weeks they had been in Germany, which suited Ricardo just fine. The less he saw of the man, the better.

His mother was spending most of her time at the bar just inside the Flint *Konserne*. Nothing different in her life. The street signs around her were now in a different language, but drunk was still drunk.

Fighting boredom, Ricardo spent the majority of his days lying around in his room listening to his heavy metal tapes and watching videos.

Occasionally, as he had today, he would sneak away in Mitchum's BMW while the soldier was out of town and his mother was over at the bar.

It was illegal in Germany for anyone under eighteen to drive on the open road — even for someone like Ricardo, who had an American driver's license. He had found that out from Mitchum, who read it to him from some military orientation papers. He had also been informed that a violation of that particular law by an American soldier's son or daughter could jeopardize that soldier's tour, rank, and career.

Eyeing an empty parking space, Ricardo reminded himself that he couldn't care less about his stepfather's career or reputation. Nevertheless, he wasn't eager to get caught violating the driving rule. For one thing, the German police were no more appealing to him than anything else in this country. For another thing, Mitchum would beat the daylights out of him — or try to. As much as he despised the Green Beret, Ricardo wasn't sure he wanted to try to take him on man-to-man.

Parking the 1979 silverish-gray BMW, he got out and slammed the door.

Before ordering his food, he strolled through the dining area and into the men's rest room, about halfway back along the inside wall.

After using the facilities and washing his hands, he turned to the exit door and gave it a hard shove. To his shock, the door stopped in midswing and came careening back at him. He barely managed to get his hands up in front of his face before the door hit him.

Knocked off balance, he stumbled back against a urinal. "You jerk!" he yelled, adding a profanity at the unknown person on the other side of the door. He started to shove the door back. But before he could regain his balance, three tall, lean, brown-skinned guys shoved their way into the room. The first one grabbed Ricardo by the collar and slammed him against the far wall of the rest room.

"What you call me, mon?" he demanded, his voice a dangerous whisper.

Ricardo found himself staring up into the scariest pair of eyes he had ever seen — dark eyes with a flat, empty stare like that of a shark. The man's oval, caramel-colored face was surrounded with shoulder-length reddish-brown dreadlocks. From their looks and their accent, Ricardo knew that the guys were Jamaican. The neighborhood adjacent to his high-rise in Chicago had been filled with them.

Too late, he realized he had taken too much time to answer the question. One of the other Jamaicans, signaled by a nod from the first, made a quick move and was suddenly holding a switchblade to Ricardo's throat.

"Ottey ask you a question, mon," said the knife-wielder, a wicked expression hardening on his face.

Ricardo felt the point of the blade dimpling the skin of his neck. His whole body tensed with fright.

"Uh . . . I . . . uh . . ." he stuttered, his

tongue tangled with a rush of fear. He felt a sting as the blade moved slowly across his neck, drawing blood. A dribble of the warm liquid ran down over his adam's apple.

"Okay, man, I'm sorry!" he panted. "I didn't mean it!" His voice strained with terror.

His tone apparently wasn't apologetic enough. Two of the Jamaicans grabbed him by the shoulders of his jacket and threw him headfirst into one of the toilet stalls.

Sprawled across an open toilet seat, Ricardo felt every muscle in his body stiffen. Fearing for his life, everything inside him shouted to fight back.

But before he could react, the Jamaican with the knife was on top of him again, once more with the knife to his throat.

Ricardo, motionless and breathing hard, knew he was trapped. His heart was hammering at his breastbone like a wild animal.

"You say you didn't mean it," said the Jamaican holding the knife. His voice was even and controlled. "Den how sorry are you, mon?"

"How sorry do you want me to be?" Ricardo asked, his voice breaking.

"You sorry enough to buy us our lunch?" asked Ottey from outside the stall.

Ricardo didn't know if the Jamaican was serious or not. He wasn't sure how to answer, and he was afraid of the consequences of saying the wrong thing.

"Well mon, what is your answer?" demanded Ottey.

"Sure, man. I can do that," he said in a tight whisper, thanking his good fortune that he'd lifted a twenty from his mother's purse before she left this morning.

The Jamaicans stepped back at the signal from the leader. Ricardo edged to the back of the stall, his widened eyes glued on the Jamaicans. He bent forward and pulled some toilet paper from the roll. He wiped away the blood from his neck. Then he tore off a small piece of tissue, doubled it over, got up, and cautiously walked over to the sink and mirror.

Trying as inconspicuously as possible to watch from the corner of his eye to see if the Jamaicans were going to make another sudden move, he looked in the mirror at the cut on his throat. It was much smaller than he expected. He placed the folded tissue on the cut and held it there until it absorbed enough of the oozing blood to be held in place by itself.

Ricardo straightened his clothes.

"What is your name?" the lead Jamaican asked.

"Ricardo . . . Ricardo Alvarez," he answered. He realized that his voice still trembled with fright.

"Believe yourself to be lucky today, mon," one of the other Jamaicans said to him. "Ottey has had people killed for less den what you call him."

Ricardo, his heart still pounding inside him, could feel the guy's seriousness. It was as cold and hard as the knife blade that had cut his throat.

"Like I said, man, I didn't mean it." Ricardo's voice tapered off to a whisper. He had been humiliated. But what could he do? Whoever these guys were, they were bad, mean, and fearless. All business. No play.

Ottey looked at Ricardo, once again penetrating him with a hard stare. "I'm still hungry, mon," he said, motioning with his head toward the rest room door.

"Okay," Ricardo said in a defeated voice. "It's on me."

At the table, which was spread with burgers, fries, and shakes, Ricardo sat in nervous silence as the Jamaicans ate, conversing among themselves. Intimidated by the three men and their unflinching hostility, Ricardo caught himself thinking, *I bet nobody ever forced these guys to do anything they didn't want to. Like make an international move. I bet they don't take crap from anybody.*

He wondered what it would be like to be part of a group like this — defiant, breeding terror, taking what you wanted, when you wanted . . .

His daydreaming was interrupted by the entry of a girl. He had seen her twice before in the halls of the American school. She was a senior. He didn't know her by name, and he had never talked to her. But she was one of the most beautiful girls he had ever seen. Long, thick, dark hair. Brown eyes. Sculpted features. Radiant smile.

His eyes followed her intently as she ordered her food and sat down with two other girls to eat lunch. Then he realized with a start that Ottey was speaking to him.

"You want her, don't you, mon?"

"Huh? What?" Ricardo answered, now embarrassed.

"Ottey ask do you want her?" interjected Martin, the third Jamaican.

At first Ricardo remained silent. He didn't know what to say. Why were they asking him such a question? Were they serious? Were they making fun of him? Sure, he'd like to have the girl. What red-blooded, living, breathing male wouldn't?

Before Ricardo could answer he heard Ottey say, "Martin, you and Tito follow her after school. Find out how she get home, who she go wid, where she live. Tomorrow we will take her. First us and den our little friend Ricardo." Ottey turned his menacing eyes on Ricardo. "She go to school wid you, mon?"

They were serious.

Ricardo nodded, hesitantly.

"Den you will show us when she leave de school."

Ricardo froze, his mind jarred by a dozen unspoken questions. Finally he nodded again.

It was then, for the first time, that he saw the three Jamaicans smile.

3
—

Heather Anne Moseley had no idea, later that afternoon, that her school bus was being followed at a distance by a silverish-gray BMW.

The school bus route from the high school to the Bad Aibling Station followed the autobahn for all but six of the thirty-seven miles. As the student-filled bus traveled south on the no-speed-limit expressway, the BMW followed at a discreet distance. The heavy afternoon traffic helped obscure the car from the notice of the bus's passengers. So did the usual activity and noise inside the bus.

Heather Anne wasn't paying attention to any of the expressway traffic anyway. As always, she was taking full advantage of the forty-five-minute ride. Between brief glimpses of the sunset and the passing German countryside, she was trying to make progress on her book report assignment. Holding her paperback copy of

Catcher in the Rye in her left hand, she made hasty notes with her right on a notebook cradled on her lap.

She was within two pages of finishing a chapter when the bus stopped to unload just outside the main security gate at Bad Aibling Station.

The local Bad Aibling school bus was, as usual, waiting in the parking area to transfer her and the other students to their final destinations in and around the small township.

About seventy-five meters down the road from the gate to Bad Aibling Station, the BMW moved into a small grocery store parking lot. Camouflaged in the colorless blanket of dusk, it waited.

Getting off the first bus, Heather Anne walked to the local bus and stepped inside. The silhouette of her thick, long hair was distinct.

Twenty minutes later, at 5:40, the bus reached Heather Anne's final stop. Heather gathered her books and reached for her bright orange, tasseled umbrella, which she had recently purchased to brighten up the rainy Bavarian autumn. Disembarking with two younger students who lived in the adjacent subdivision of German row houses, she waved good-bye to them for the evening. She followed her normal route to her family's two-story house on the back side of the subdivision.

In the evening quietness she walked about a hundred yards down the street, then turned left onto a worn grass pathway that led across an open field parallel to the housing complex. Beyond the field the path led her through a four-acre patch of tall Bavarian pines, through another, smaller field, and then to the gravel driveway of her house.

The tall dark figure, trailing her on foot, went unnoticed.

Heather Anne entered her house, shouting out a greeting to anyone within hearing range. Her mother was in the kitchen preparing dinner. "Chase wasn't at school today, Mom," she said. "Do you think maybe you should call his house and find out if they're still planning to come for dinner tonight?"

"I talked with Susan this afternoon," Lynn Moseley answered. "She mentioned that Chase stayed home today because he had a seizure this morning. But she was sure they would still be able to come."

"Should I call and find out how he's doing?"

Her mother stopped cutting celery to

give Heather her full attention. "I know you'd like to call. But because of the expense, why don't you wait? Susan said if Chase wasn't feeling better by three or four o'clock, she would call and let me know. She hasn't called. So that means they should be here in about an hour."

Pleased with the news, Heather agreed to wait.

Dinner that evening was a pleasant recap of the previous week's experiences. The two families enjoyed a delicious meal and the talk was relaxing and friendly. After the meal the adults moved into the living room, while Heather, Chase, and Donica cleared the kitchen table for a game of Monopoly.

"I really enjoyed the service last Sunday," Susan remarked as the others seated themselves. "The sermon was quite interesting." With a grin she added, "And despite the 'high-churchiness,' the congregation seemed really friendly." She glanced at Jordan and was pleased to see him smiling and nodding his agreement.

"Yeah, it was a good service," he said. "Maybe we'll just make St. Jude's our church home for a while," he added, expressing the thought aloud for the first time.

The grownups didn't see Heather squeeze Chase's forearm, nor did they see the broad smile on Chase's face.

"Well, that's great!" said Ralph Moseley, beaming. "I hoped you'd find something to like at St. Jude's. We sure have."

"So — now that you know the way, I guess we'll just meet you there," said Lynn. "By the way," she continued, "we were wondering if it would be all right for Chase to ride the bus home with Heather tomorrow? They've got a book report due on Monday, and I think they wanted to work on it together." She grinned at her daughter, but Heather had turned her head to hide the obvious blush of pleasure on her cheeks.

Donica smirked. "Yeah, right." Everyone chuckled.

"Anyway, we could bring Chase home sometime Saturday," finished Lynn.

"And stay for dinner Saturday evening!" suggested Susan, glancing at Jordan for confirmation.

"Why not?" said Jordan. "Of course, that's if Chase wants to."

"Dad!" puffed Chase, amused and exasperated at the same time.

Susan grinned. "I think that means yes."

On the way home that night, Jordan felt

pleased with the way things were turning out.

He was thankful for their new friend-ships. The Moseleys were the first real bright spot in their German experience. He could see Susan relaxing, responding to the enfolding charm of the other American family. This was the key, he decided. They had turned the corner. From now on, everything would be better.

With a smile, he glanced in the rearview mirror at Chase in the backseat. Even in the dark he could see the pleased look on his son's face. He knew Chase was already daydreaming about tomorrow evening.

At five-thirty the next evening, in the semidarkness of an overcast dusk, Ricardo — with Ottey, Tito, and Martin — entered the four-acre pine grove in Bad Aibling. In a few minutes, the girl would pass through here on her way home from the bus stop. And they would be waiting for her.

Ricardo tried not to show his nervous-ness. He had joined the Jamaicans one hour earlier outside Munich's central train station. As they drove down to Bad Aibling in his stepdad's BMW, he had grown pro-gressively more uncomfortable. The Jamai-cans had conversed among themselves in words he couldn't understand. They had brought out some white powder, and the three of them sniffed the drug with obvious enjoyment.

Ottey had seen Ricardo's nervous eyes flickering from the highway to the contraband. Grinning, he held the packet of cocaine toward Ricardo. "How about it, mon? You want some?"

Despite his nervousness, there was a part of Ricardo that envied his three passengers. Maybe it was their lawless attitude. Maybe it was their fearless composure, or their lack of consideration for normal limits. Or maybe it was just their intimidating looks. Whatever it was, he felt overpowered by their presence, and a little intoxicated by it. "Yeah, sure," he heard himself saying. "I'll take some. But later," he added hesitantly.

Ottey had laughed at him, then turned a steeled gaze on him. Without breaking eye contact with Ricardo, he said, "Tito, tell de little mon who we are."

Tito's stare at Ricardo was as penetrating as Ottey's. "Caribbean Parade," he had said. "Jamaican brudders takin over de drug turf in America. De three of us be masters of de Detroit posse — ruled by Ottey's older brudder."

If Tito meant to impress, he succeeded.

Ricardo had heard about Jamaican posses and the terror they bred. He knew of a senior at his Chicago high school, a member of a drug ring, who was killed by a Jamaican posse, his head reportedly shot off with an Uzi. Ricardo wondered if the silent and sudden envy showed on his face.

Now, standing in the grove, he saw Tito pull a switchblade from inside his jacket. With a wicked snap, the blade ejected. Tito tested its edge with his thumb, looked at Ricardo, and gave him an evil grin. Ricardo looked quickly away.

Just then, from their hiding place in the trees, they saw the bus. It moved slowly down the road toward its stop at the front entrance to the subdivision, then went out of sight behind some houses.

To Ricardo, the next minute seemed an hour long.

Finally the girl appeared at the other end of the field — but not alone. Some guy was walking with her.

Ricardo looked at Ottey to see if there would be a change of plans.

There wouldn't be.

Lynn Moseley, working in the kitchen, glanced at the clock. Five forty-five — Heather Anne should be here any time now, she thought.

Five fifty . . . five fifty-five . . .

She decided that Heather and Chase were probably lingering along the trail somewhere between the house and the bus stop, engaged in a pre-romantic conversation. She smiled. She was not too old to remember her teenage years and the magical feel of a youthful romance. As she continued preparing dinner, her mind started conjuring up old memories.

When she heard the living room clock strike six, she stopped letting her mind wander and concentrated on putting the last few touches on the evening meal and getting it on the table. Ralph would be home and ready to eat in about fifteen minutes.

When she had everything ready except for setting the table, she stepped outside into the cool dark evening to see if she could find Heather and Chase. From the front yard she looked down the driveway into the dark shadows and called Heather's name.

There was no response.

For the first time she started to wonder if something might be wrong. Perhaps the bus was running late. Maybe it had broken down somewhere.

Going back inside, she went to the telephone and called the main desk at Bad Aibling Station. Upon her request, she was rung through to the main security gate.

"Can you tell me if the high school bus has arrived from Munich yet?" she asked the guard who picked up the phone.

"About an hour ago," the man replied.

"What about the local bus? Has it already started dropping off the students?"

"It's already completed its run and returned to the station, ma'am. I saw it come through the gate less than five minutes ago."

Lynn hung up and called the Raus' number. Maybe, for some reason, Chase and Heather had gone to Chase's house, and Heather had not yet had a chance to call and notify her.

As she heard the first ring on the other end of the line she waited for Susan or Jordan to pick up the phone and tell her that the kids were there. Subconsciously, she slowed her breathing as she made ready to offer up a sigh of relief.

But no one answered.

After the phone rang twelve or thirteen times, she realized no one was at home. The relief she was hoping for eluded her. If the buses were on time and had not broken down, what had happened to Heather and

Chase? Why hadn't they shown up yet? Why hadn't they called? Where were they? Did they need help?

She tried to rationalize that everything was okay, but the more she questioned, the more she felt anxiety starting to control her thoughts.

She was straining to know what to do next when she heard Ralph's car door slam. She hurried out to meet him.

"Ralph . . . Heather and Chase aren't here yet," she announced with concern. "The security guard at B.A. just told me that the local bus has already delivered the kids. It's getting pretty late. What do you think?" Her voice was calm, but the vague anxiety was beginning to show in her face.

"There's probably nothing to worry about," Ralph responded as he gave her a reassuring hug. "They probably just missed the bus, that's all." He turned to lead her inside. "While I change clothes, why don't you call one of Heather's friends. They'll know if Heather and Chase were on the bus or not."

Before Ralph finished changing his clothes, Lynn appeared in the bedroom with confusion written on her face. "I just called Eve Johnson. She said Heather and Chase *were* on the bus today and she saw them get off out here at the stop. At the usual time."

"Then that means they're just outside walking around somewhere," Ralph answered.

"Ralph, Heather wouldn't just wander around and not let us know where she was. She knows we would be worrying about her. Besides, I went outside just a few minutes ago and called for her. And I didn't get an answer."

"I'll go outside and see if I can spot them," Ralph said. "But don't worry. I'm sure everything's all right."

As Lynn had done earlier, Ralph stepped outside and from the front yard called Heather's name. When he didn't get an answer, he walked to the back of the house and called from there. Still no response.

Standing alone in the cold and dark of the evening — the moon and stars were hidden by the omnipresent rain clouds — a voice of doubt began to whisper inside his head. He started to question his own logic. Would Heather and Chase really be just wandering around out here?

Probably not.

Then where were they? Had something wrong happened? His reasoning tried to persuade him that there still must be a logical explanation. Nevertheless, for the first time since Lynn expressed her concern, he began to worry.

He walked back to the front of the house and down the driveway. He then turned off onto the trail that led across the fields and through the woods to the bus stop.

Walking across the first field toward the pines, he scanned the flat open area with the sharpened eyes of a concerned father. He squinted and strained in vain, looking for human silhouettes.

"Heather!" he shouted. No answer.

"Chase!" He strained to hear a response. Nothing.

He walked on and entered the long stretch of tall pines. Here the shadows were darker, the silence thicker. He stepped slowly until his eyes adjusted. As the blackness divided into different shades, giving vague outline to the trees, bushes, and trail, he picked up his pace, scanning the path ahead.

Exiting the woods a few minutes later, he emerged onto the large field. With his eyes probing the night for his daughter, he crossed the field, walked down the side-walk, and came to the bus stop.

With no sign of Heather or Chase any-where, and no clue as to what had happened, he stood alone at the entrance to the housing complex, now praying earnestly that nothing was seriously wrong.

After standing there awhile and looking up and down the empty street and sidewalks, wondering what step of action to take next, he finally decided they should try calling the Raus again.

Still hopeful that the mystery would soon be solved, he headed back toward the house.

A cold drizzle started to fall, making him quicken his pace for the shelter of the pine grove.

He was midway through the woods, wondering if Lynn had heard anything yet, when he caught a glimpse of something lying on the ground at the base of a tree — something out of place. He walked the five or six steps to the tree, straining all the while to detect what the object might be.

He squatted down to get a close-up look. And suddenly he identified it.

Heather's orange umbrella.

It hadn't been there long; it was neither wet nor dirty.

Still he would not permit himself to think of anything more than the likelihood that Heather had unknowingly dropped it. But . . .

If Heather had gotten off the bus and had been heading home through the forest as the umbrella indicated, then why . . . ?

With his mind casting about for a calming answer, his eyes fell upon another object which didn't belong in the grove.

It was a school textbook, lying to the right of the tree in some weeds.

Picking it up, he trotted to the house and rushed inside. "Lynn, you'd better try the Raus again," he said, panting.

He showed her the textbook; showed her where Heather's name was written in it. "It was lying on the ground in the pine grove. I also found her umbrella. I left it there to mark the location. While you try to get through to the Raus, I'll get a flashlight and go back out there."

The blood drained from Lynn's face as she looked at him. Then she turned away, grabbed the phone from its hook, and dialed furiously.

"Honey," he cautioned, "try to stay calm." Struggling to control his own breathing, he said, "Let's not jump to any conclusions. Everything is probably okay."

Nevertheless, he couldn't keep himself from taking the stairs two at a time on the way to fetch his flashlight.

On his way back to the woods, Ralph tried

unsuccessfully to suppress a new and disturbing thought: Maybe Chase had somehow instigated whatever had happened. Could Chase be so unpredictable? Did he have a history of bizarre and psychological problems — related perhaps to his epilepsy — that could lead to such behavior?

Those thoughts remained with him, adding anger to his fear, all the way back to the wooded site.

Though he prayed and asked God to help him control his anger and to help him refrain from casting a wrong judgment, he still felt a spirit of stinging bitterness trying to sweep through his emotions.

Then, as he swept the flashlight beam across the ground near the umbrella, he saw another textbook lying open on the ground, its pages facing upward. He stepped closer. In a moment of horrible clarity, he realized that the pages were colored with large splotches of blood.

"Oh God, no!" he shouted.

Within a split second, dynamite feelings exploded inside him, forcing him to lean against a tree to catch his balance and gasp for air.

No longer attempting to restrain his panic, he fled back to the house to call the police.

4

In half an hour, four U.S. military policemen and six German policemen were on the scene — car lights flashing, radios crackling and buzzing — roping off the area and beginning an investigation.

Five additional textbooks were found in the same area, three of them marked with Heather's name, two with Chase's.

The textbook blotted with blood was Chase's. More blood was found puddled and splattered throughout the grass and weeds, leading from the books to the trail.

Two of the policemen, working together, put out an all-points bulletin, along with descriptions of Heather and Chase. Then they joined the others who were continuing to search the area.

The Raus, summoned by Lynn's phone call, arrived shortly after the police. In shock, they watched with blanched faces and listened in silence as the investigation swirled senselessly about them.

★ ★ ★

The police continued a detailed search of the area for the rest of the night, but no other signs of Heather and Chase were found anywhere.

A German chief detective from the district police station met with the two couples around ten o'clock the next morning at the Moseley's house. He first questioned each couple separately, asking for basic information, including detailed descriptions of the missing kids — their height, weight, hair color, eye color, the clothes they were wearing when last seen, and any special features visible on their bodies that might help identify them.

The couples were then asked to explain, based on normal routine, the general movements of Heather and Chase throughout Friday up to the moment of their departure from the evening bus. Also, what were their personal suspicions about the kids' mysterious disappearance?

Did either couple consider the other teenager to be a suspect? If so, why? How long had the kids known each other? Had they spent a lot of time alone together? What kind of relationship did they have with each other?

Did either of the kids have a known antagonist or enemy, someone who might be jealous of their relationship? Were there any reasons why some outsider might want to hurt them or kidnap them — possibly for a ransom? Had they ever been threatened by anyone? Had they ever reported being followed by a stranger? Were they or had they ever been involved in any way with illegal drugs?

The fifty-five-minute sessions were intense and filled with emotion. The fact that none of the parents had slept for twenty-eight hours did not make it any easier. Neither did the fact that every question and answer, according to German procedure, had to be written down and then read aloud by the stenographer for the parents' confirmation.

After the separate sessions, the chief then met with the two couples together. He asked two or three more questions for their mutual input, then told them, "Early this morning, samples of the blood found on the textbooks and in the grass and weeds were tested by our lab technicians. The results show that all the samples match Chase's blood type. None of them match Heather's.

"Of course, we do not know the nature of Chase's injury or the severity of it. Assuming that he was perhaps taken for medical treatment, we've already sent men to the local hospital and to the hospitals in Rosenheim. However, no one matching the photographs you gave us last night has been admitted to any of these hospitals during the last seventeen hours. Nevertheless, we will continue to stay in contact with them, in case the kids show up at one of them later. In the meantime, we'll make new inquiries at other hospitals in the surrounding cities.

"In addition, we'll question the students, along with the driver, that were on the Bad Aibling bus yesterday evening. And we'll extend our ground search to cover all the neighborhoods here in the Bad Aibling area." He paused, giving the four haggard faces before him a meaningful look. "I assure you that we'll do everything we can to find your children."

After a brief pause, he added, "Now, at this time I'll try my best to answer any questions."

Jordan heard Ralph Moseley's voice as he posed a question, but the words didn't penetrate his consciousness. He looked over at Susan. Tears were hanging on the crest of her cheeks. Her eyes reflected inner pain and desperation. *The results show that all the samples match Chase's blood type . . .*

God in heaven! What did it all mean?

Jordan could feel his lower neck muscles tensing. His exhausted mind was staggering in circles, trying to come up with answers. Where was their son? Was he okay? Was he in pain? Was he . . .

Jordan's thoughts shuddered, then plowed ahead — was he dying? Was there still time to help him?

The blank agony of uncertainty was paralyzing. *If something bad has happened to him . . . how can I go on living? How can I ever bear the pain? And the guilt? After all, I'm the one who forced my family to move here. If it hadn't been for my stubborn insistence, Chase would never have been in the middle of — of whatever has happened.* Jordan knew he would forever hold himself responsible for his son's fate.

"Mr. Rau . . . Mr. Rau . . ."

With an effort, Jordan brought his attention back into the room.

"Uh . . . I'm sorry," he said.

"Quite all right, sir," the chief replied. "Mrs. Moseley is wondering whether or not her daughter would be able to give sufficient aid to your son if he had a seizure. What is your opinion on that?"

54

"Well . . . uh," he half muttered, rubbing his hand up and down his jaw, "I've explained to Heather a couple of times in detail what she would need to do to help Chase through a seizure if no one else was around who knew what to do. But to my knowledge," he added, turning to look at Lynn, "she has never had to go through the actual procedure."

"But she *has* seen Chase's teacher assist him several times," Susan interjected.

"Yeah, that's . . . that's true," Jordan responded. "So I'm sure she would be able to manage just fine. I'm *sure* she would . . ." His voice fell silent.

After another ten minutes or so of questions, the chief brought the meeting to a close.

"I'll keep you updated as we gather new information," he finally told them, rising. With a final glance at the blank, drawn faces of the four parents, he excused himself and left.

Later that afternoon, the two couples were summoned to an hour-long interview with a team from the U.S. military's Criminal Investigation Division. Since Ralph's employer was working under contract to the Department of Defense, and since Ralph held a top security clearance inside the Bad Aibling Station, the U.S. military was taking an active part in the investigation. The CID team would collaborate with the German police, sharing any material evidence or clues.

Late that afternoon, Jordan, Susan, Ralph, and Lynn were left alone with the rest of the uncertain weekend before them. What were they to do now? Sit and wait? Pray and hope? Carry on in their regular routines? Contact all their friends and associates in the U.S. for moral support? Go for a long walk and think, try to process their thoughts and feelings, try to keep a tenuous grip on normalcy? Get some sleep?

Jordan realized, despite his fatigue, that he had to go searching. He had to keep his family's life under control. His son was out there somewhere. He had to look for him. He had to find him.

Leaving Susan at the Moseleys' to try to rest — Donica was staying with a neighbor in Munich — Jordan went cruising.

First, he drove to the bus stop where Heather and Chase were reportedly last seen.

He parked there for a few minutes and left the engine running. He stared out the rain-streaked windshield, lost in his thoughts, trying to visualize by what means and in which direction Heather and Chase had left the grove of pines. Did they leave on their own and by themselves? Or were they helped — or forced — by someone else? Were they being aided, with the intention of being brought home? Or . . .

The unanswered questions and their frightful implications sent a fresh surge of fear through him.

He drove his car into the row-house complex, steering slowly up and down every street, scanning each yard and unshaded window for any sign of the two lost teenagers.

Out of sheer desperation he stopped a German man who was walking a cocker spaniel. "Have you seen any unusual activity involving teenagers in this area in the last twenty-four hours?" he asked in his halting German. "Two teenagers — one of them my son — are missing. Did you hear anything suspicious out here last night? Anything at all?"

The man shrugged, shook his head, and walked on.

Jordan finished scouting the complex. Feeling more and more hopeless and scared, he drove to other nearby residential areas.

For two more hours, until it started to get dark, he combed the different streets, yearning to come across a clue of some kind.

By the time he returned to the Moseleys' to pick up Susan, he was irritable, depressed, and frustrated. As he entered the house, the three faces turned toward him. He shook his head in wordless answer to the unspoken question. He didn't want to talk. He just wanted to go home to rest a few hours — and then return to the grim search which at the moment was his sole reason for being.

Ralph told Jordan that he had contacted the pastor at St. Jude's about their crisis. "Tomorrow morning during the main Sunday service he's going to lead the congregation in a special prayer for Heather and Chase — and for us," he said, his lips trembling with emotion.

Jordan acknowledged the news with a half-hearted nod.

On the way back to Munich that night, Susan told Jordan she was planning to take Donica and attend the St. Jude's service the next morning. "You're going to come with us, aren't you?" she asked, laying a hand on his arm.

He shook his head curtly without

looking at her. "I'll be driving back to Bad Aibling early in the morning. At first light I'm gonna continue to look for Chase."

"But Jordan," she began, "don't you think —"

"You can pray," he interrupted in a tight voice. "I'm gonna look."

5

When Susan walked into St. Jude's with Donica, Ralph, and Lynn the following morning, she broke down and cried.

Since leaving America, she had tried every day to pray. She had tried hard to trust God with childlike faith. But her pains had been so strong and her faith so weak.

As she sat down in one of the old pews and stared tearfully at the communion table, the chalice, the hymnals, and then the seven-foot wooden cross mounted on the front wall overlooking the pulpit, she pleaded with God to help her, to give her a real faith, a faith that would raise her above her fears and anchor her in the storm.

I want to trust You like Job did, she told God. I want to trust You, even if You slay me.

By the time the pastor stood to lead the congregation in the special prayer for

Heather and Chase, Susan was emotionally and mentally spent.

For the thousandth time, Jordan felt despair rising in his throat. Heather and Chase had been missing for more than forty hours. Copies of their photos had been circulated to every police station in the country and to every border crossing station.

Still they had not been sighted. Neither had anyone been contacted by them, not any of the police departments, not any of the hospitals, not any of their parents, friends, schoolmates, or acquaintances.

The kids' silence, more than their absence, now convinced Jordan that they were victims of some kind of ruthless tragedy.

With each passing hour he felt the sickening knot in his stomach grow tighter. He was already beginning to taste the bitterness of feared news.

Nevertheless, as he continued to drive through the streets of Bad Aibling, he steeled himself to continue the search. He wouldn't give up. He couldn't.

They just have to be okay, he told himself. They just have to.

By midevening, with no new developments on his part or the part of the police, he called Susan from a pay phone.

"Why haven't you called me?" she demanded. "I've been waiting all afternoon to hear from you."

He was barely able to keep from shouting at her. "Susan, I have been combing Bad Aibling all day — searching for *our* son. I'm sorry if I haven't checked in with you every few minutes." The cutting bitterness came through.

There was silence on the other end.

"Look, honey," Jordan said, instantly regretting his caustic tone, "I'm sorry. I'm just tired, that's all. I've driven up and down every street in Bad Aibling at least three or four times. I've talked to people on the streets, at the gas stations. I've shown them photographs of the kids. Nobody has seen them; nobody knows anything. Not even the police have found any clues. I don't understand, Susan. How could two teenagers just disappear off the face of the earth? It doesn't make any sense —" His voice began to break.

"I know you're tired, Jordan. So why don't you come home now? You need the rest, and Donica and I need you here for a while. The police will continue to look."

"It's no use, Susan," he replied, sighing

deeply. "If I came home while there's still some daylight, I'd just pace the floor wishing that I were still out here searching . . . I feel like we're running out of time . . ." He caught his voice rising in panic. Sweat was beading on his brow.

Again, there was silence on the other end.

Why doesn't she understand? he asked himself.

"I went ahead and called Mom and Dad," she said in a lifeless voice. "I know you asked me to wait, but I needed someone to talk to . . . I —"

"Susan, I wish you hadn't done that," he interrupted. "I told you we should wait until we know . . . more." He paused. "Now they'll be worrying themselves sick . . . probably for no reason."

"I'm afraid, Jordan!" she half shouted. "I needed their prayers. I need the prayers for me *and* for Chase. I need to feel that God is somehow in control of what's happening. Don't you understand? I need that security."

"That's good, Susan," Jordan retorted, trying to keep the sarcasm out of his voice, "but you also need to understand that *I* need to know *I'm* doing all I can to find out what's happened. I have to *do* something, Susan, no matter how many people are praying. I won't just sit on my hands and pretend to toss everything in God's lap."

He could hear her sobbing.

Once again remorseful, Jordan realized that they were both too emotional at the moment to carry on any kind of reasonable conversation.

"Look," he told her, "you just keep praying, if that's what makes you feel good, all right? And get as many people as you can to join you. But as I told you yesterday, I intend to keep looking. So don't wait up for me."

He hung up, standing silently at the pay phone, hating the circumstances, hating himself.

Susan cried herself to sleep that night. Alone.

At five o'clock the next morning, Jordan lay wide awake in the bed next to Susan. On his back, he stared at the ceiling. For four and a half hours he had tossed and turned, trying to get some solid sleep.

But it was hopeless. His mind, running at a manic pace, would not shut down and allow him to relax.

Unable to lie there any longer without

losing his grip on sanity, he decided to get out of bed and call the Bad Aibling police station to find out any new information. As he lifted off the comforter and sat up, he heard Susan speak from the darkness.

"What if they're never found?"

Her words, hoarse and raspy, struck without mercy at the fear in his heart.

Without turning to face her, he gave his response, hard and resolute.

"Understand this, Susan." One of his fists clenched as he spoke. "They *will* be found. If the police don't find them, I will. I'll search for as long as it takes." He paused, then added, "Even if it takes the rest of my life."

Even as the words came from his lips, he knew he was showing major disregard for his responsibilities as a husband and father.

"Look," he told her, "I . . . I want to be strong for you and Donica. It's just that . . . at the moment I'm caught up in my own feelings."

He knew he was telling the truth. Yet he knew also that Susan was scared and needed reassuring. He realized he should somehow give that reassurance to her, a commitment of stable and supportive leadership. And he wanted to. But he was afraid. He was no longer sure he could honor such a commitment. He was, he realized, hopelessly obsessed with finding Chase.

"I'm sorry," he said, getting up from the bed. He wanted to say more, but the words wouldn't come.

"Where is Dad?" Donica asked two hours later as she came into the kitchen for breakfast. She was still in her nightgown, her hair not yet brushed.

"He drove back to Bad Aibling about an hour ago," Susan said, trying to sound matter-of-fact.

"I wanted to go with him!" Donica said, her voice whining to a high pitch.

"Maybe we all should have gone," Susan tried to explain, "but we thought it would be best if you went ahead and went back to school today. Since everything's —"

"That's not fair. If Dad's going to skip his classes at the Institute, then I should be able to skip mine . . . I want to help find Chase, too!"

"Donica! We all want to help find Chase. But I think it's best if you and I do what we can right now to maintain a stable home . . . especially to be praying. The police are doing everything else that can humanly be done. If there was anything we could do that would help them, they would have asked us to do it already. I'm trying —"

"Did they ask for Dad to help?" Donica interrupted.

Susan sniffed, feeling as if she was coming down with a cold. "They've told him there's officially nothing he can do, and that to work on his own like he's doing is a waste of time."

"Well, I still want to help him!" Donica blurted out.

"The best way you and I can help him right now is to pray," Susan said, her voice beginning to quiver. "There's nothing else we can do."

Donica was not convinced. "If Dad's out there helping, then I want to be out there helping, too! Chase needs us! You can stay here and pray if you want to, but I care more for him than that. I want to be out there with Dad. I want to be out there looking."

"Donica!" Susan rebuked. "If I thought . . ."

"I'm not going to school!" Donica interrupted her again, stomping out of the kitchen. "I'm going to get on the train, and I'm going to Bad Aibling! I'm going to find

Dad!" Her voice barely faded as she disappeared into her bedroom and slammed the door.

Susan felt the world pressing in on her. She collapsed onto one of the kitchen chairs and started sobbing.

"Dear God," she whispered from a tight throat, "We need Your help . . . We need You . . . We're . . ." Pain engulfed her as her words melted into speechless groans.

After a few minutes something stiffened within her. She stood up, sniffed, wiped the tears from her eyes, and headed for Donica's room, entering without knocking.

Donica had already changed out of her nightgown into some jeans and a sweater. She was now scurrying around the room collecting her purse, money, umbrella, and her monthly public-transportation pass. She ignored her mother's entry.

Susan stood just inside the doorway, watching, waiting for Donica to look her in the eye.

When Donica finished gathering her things, she headed for the door, attempting to walk around her mother without acknowledging her.

"Donica."

There was a moment of volatile silence as they stared at each other.

"Why don't we go to Bad Aibling together?" Susan finally suggested.

Donica paused, then nodded her agreement.

Within minutes they were descending the steps of the subway station three blocks from their apartment.

6

Susan and Donica arrived at the Bad Aibling train station at 9:45. They headed toward the police station, fifteen minutes away by foot.

Neither of them spoke more than a dozen words as they made their way along the downtown sidewalks.

The overcast sky, dark and wet, created an atmosphere of foreboding. Here in Bad Aibling, as in Munich, the gray sky seemed to steal the color from the store-window displays, from the automobiles, and from the top-grade clothing of the German shoppers, merchants, and business people. The inescapable grayness extracted vibrancy and replaced it with gloom.

The *Polizei* headquarters finally came into view. Susan wondered how long she and Donica would have to wait before the officers on duty would be able to help them locate Jordan.

The moment they climbed the six or

seven steps and entered the building, the bustling activity and worried glances of the on-duty officers told Susan that something out of the ordinary was happening.

The officer at the front desk, sitting behind a protective wall of bulletproof glass, glanced up at Susan and Donica, then did a double take and peered closely at them. Pushing his chair back from the desk, he moved quickly out into the reception foyer.

"Excuse me," he said in hurried and broken English. "You're Mrs. Rau, the American, aren't you?"

Susan nodded hesitantly. "Yes, I'm Susan Rau, and —"

His eyes widened. "Can you and your daughter follow me to the back office, please?" he asked, gesturing toward a nearby doorway.

Adrenaline rushed into Susan's system. What were they getting ready to tell her? What had happened?

Taking a deep breath, Susan looked at the officer and tried to nod.

The man led them through the door into a long hallway lined on both sides with offices.

As they quickly walked down the hallway, Susan's breathing became shallow and rapid. In her heart, she pleaded for

God to sustain her in whatever situation she was about to face. She reached behind her and took Donica's hand.

When they finally turned right through one of the open doors, Susan was confronted by the sight of Ralph and Lynn Moseley. They were sitting close to each other in a couple of side-by-side chairs, in front of a police superintendent who appeared to be taking down information. They were both weeping.

When Lynn saw Susan, she leaped from her seat and threw herself toward her. The superintendent left his seat to try to stop her.

Susan's stomach twisted into a painful knot.

Chase! Heather! There had been some news! And then the realization hit her. *No! No! It can't* . . .

But before she could react, Lynn fell sobbing at Susan's feet.

Disregarding the superintendent's attempt to stop her, Lynn looked up at Susan with agony-filled eyes. "Their bodies have been found, Susan . . . they're dead!"

For a moment the room was robbed of sound and motion, except for Lynn's helpless weeping.

The superintendent then motioned for an officer to escort Susan and Donica to another office.

While Susan was being led from the room, she glanced over her shoulder. Lynn was still shaking and sobbing as Ralph rushed to her side and squeezed his arms around her.

"There's been a mistake," Susan whispered to herself. "This can't be happening. Not to us . . . not Chase . . ."

Echoing her mother's words, Donica whimpered, "He *can't* be dead . . . No, he *can't* be dead . . ."

A giant wave of inner screams struck without mercy. Susan wanted to drop to her knees. It all had to be a dream. But deep within she knew she was trying to deny what was painful, horrible, unthinkable — and true.

Fighting with all her might to confront that truth and to control herself, she pulled her arm from the officer's light-handed grip and tried to console her daughter. But Donica fought her. As she tried to push Susan away, her whimpering turned into loud screams.

Susan managed to get a tight grip on the teenager's tear-covered face, and look directly into her red, weeping eyes.

"I love you, Donica!" Susan whispered to her, gently stroking her wet cheeks with her thumbs. "We're going to make it, honey." She tried to communicate without crying. "We're about to face the greatest challenge of our lives. But together, with God's help, we're going to be strong."

Hearing herself speak, Susan began to believe, even in the midst of the suffocating anguish, that she somehow meant what she was saying.

As Susan continued giving solace to her child — now her *only* child — the superintendent approached her and apologized for the abrupt way the news had been broken. "We've been trying to contact you at your apartment," he explained. "We planned to tell you in the privacy of your home."

"Have you notified my husband?" she wanted to know, wiping her eyes with the heel of her hand.

"You and the Moseleys are the only ones at this point who've been informed," he told her. "We reached the Moseleys more than an hour ago. They've just come from the morgue, where they confirmed the identity of the bodies."

"We've been getting needed information and signatures from them," the superintendent went on to explain, "in order to have their daughter's body released from German jurisdiction and readied for flying back to the U.S. You and your husband need to be prepared to do the same."

Susan battled furiously to keep from fainting and to hold back the nausea that she felt in her throat.

"If you can tell us where we can find your husband," the superintendent said, "we'll dispatch some men immediately to look for him."

"He's supposed to be here in Bad Aibling somewhere. He's still driving around looking for . . . Chase . . ." Overcome by a flood of emotions when saying her son's name, she went silent. Unable to deny any longer the untold agony ripping through her heart, she sank to the floor, pulled Donica to her chest, and gave way to her tears. From the pit of her soul, she screamed out to God, begging Him not to forsake her now.

Jordan was pumping gas into his car at a Texaco station between Bad Aibling and Rosenheim. A passing officer spotted the vehicle and license plate matching the description provided by Susan. He pulled into the gas station lot and approached Jordan at the car.

"Excuse me . . . Mr. Rau? I've been sent to find you and tell you that you need to come to the Bad Aibling police headquarters immediately."

"Is it about my son?"

"Yes, sir. It's about your son."

"He's been found?" Jordan asked, his heart crowding into his throat.

With a solemn nod, the officer replied, "He's been found, sir . . . He was . . ."

In the second of time before the officer completed his statement, Jordan felt the momentous strain of uncertainty. He wanted to picture Chase sitting at the police station with a smile on his face and an adventurous story to tell. He wanted . . .

"He was found earlier this morning. He's dead, sir."

Jordan's chin fell to the top of his massive chest as he buried his face in his big hands. "No! That can't be!" he yelled.

The officer reached out to place a hand on Jordan's shoulder. "I'm sorry, Mr. Rau . . . I . . ."

"No! Not my son!" Jordan yelled louder. His pain-filled wail shattered the air of the gas station. He lifted his clenched fist into the sky and drove it into the windshield of his car. There was a sickening crunch as the top corner of the glass caved into a

massive spiderweb of cracks.

Ignoring the officer, Jordan rushed blindly to get behind the wheel of his car, his knuckles bleeding all over his shirt, pants, and car seat.

The police station was only about four and a half miles away.

I've got to get to those who know . . . to those who know . . . to those who know, he told himself. Cranking the car as fast as he could, he slammed it into first gear. He then smashed the accelerator pedal into the carpet. Launching the car toward the road, with the rubber of his tires screaming on the concrete pad of the gas station, he nearly collided with a Mercedes that was making a turn into the lot.

Yanking the wheel to avoid an accident, he recovered and sped out into the road.

Tears flooded down his cheeks, and his breathing was shallow and rapid. "Hang on, Chase," he groaned. "Dad's coming to help you, son! Don't die on me . . . Do you hear me? *Don't die on me!*"

He sped through a red light, going forty miles an hour over the speed limit, barely registering the blue rotating strobe light of the German police car behind him.

As he approached the downtown area of Bad Aibling, the patrol car swerved in front of him and forcefully reduced his speed.

"Don't do this to me, you idiot!" he bellowed inside his car. "I've got to get to my son, don't you understand?"

Just as he was about to plow his bleeding fist into the dashboard, he heard the police car's siren bleep on and saw the car speed up, acting as an escort.

He accelerated to follow the officer through the downtown traffic and crowded intersections.

When he drove into the police station's parking area a few minutes later, he barely let his car come to a full stop before he was out and running.

Leaving the accompanying police officer behind him, he could feel the pounding of his heart as he raced across the asphalt lot and into the building.

I've got to get to those who know, he kept telling himself.

Entering the building, half tripping up the concrete steps, he saw Susan standing in the reception foyer waiting for him. Standing behind her were Donica, the superintendent of the station, and another policeman.

They had been awaiting his arrival. He didn't know how Susan and Donica had gotten here, but when he saw them standing across the room from him, their eyes red with grief, he knew the truth.

"He's dead, Jordan," Susan confirmed, her lips trembling.

Jordan watched in a daze as Susan rushed into his arms, burying her face in his chest. He raised his hands to her back. He strained to keep his vision in focus as he looked over Susan's shoulder at the superintendent.

Over Susan's sobbing and his own raspy breathing, he managed to direct his one-word question to the man who knew.

"Dead?" he whispered, hoping he had somehow misheard.

"I'm sorry, Mr. Rau," the superintendent said. "Both the teenagers were found around six o'clock this morning." He paused. "They are both dead . . . It appears they were murdered."

Again Jordan felt the earth tilt beneath his feet. The superintendent's words began to echo in his brain. *Both dead . . . they were murdered . . . both dead . . . murdered . . . dead . . . murdered . . .* The echo swallowed him — mind, body, and soul. It took him deeper and deeper into uncertain darkness. He pushed Susan away and squeezed his head between his hands. He tried to stop the pulsating madness.

He burst into tears. *NOOOO!* he cried to himself.

When Susan started to embrace him again, he pushed her away. He lifted his chin. "How did it happen? Who did it?" he demanded of the superintendent. He was tensing his fist. Blood started flowing again from his cut knuckles.

The superintendent knew that the reception foyer was not the place to be discussing this type of information, but the situation had become too messy and too emotional to try to move everybody to a back room. He gave a quick command to an officer, who moved to lock the front door and guard it against any intrusion. He sent another officer to get a rag for Jordan's bleeding hand, then walked across the small room to stand within three feet of Jordan.

"Mr. Rau," he began, "your son, Chase, and his girlfriend were found about twenty kilometers from here in a wooded area at the foot of a mountain. A farmer's son stumbled onto their bodies at about six o'clock this morning. They were lying among some boulders in a dry creek bed.

"The young man returned home and called the Rosenheim police. The medical examiners collected the bodies forty minutes later and transported them to the Rosenheim hospital, where they were pronounced dead. The bodies are now in the morgue."

Jordan, in his state of shock and unbelief, started to insist that there was a mistake about the identity of the bodies when the superintendent's next words cut him short.

"Mr. and Mrs. Moseley have just returned from the morgue . . . and have made a positive identification of the bodies."

Images of Chase, alive and smiling, burst into Jordan's mind with heartbreaking clarity. Only three days ago, on Friday morning, he had eaten breakfast with his son. They had talked and laughed together. They had hugged each other. Chase had been filled with breath and with life. He had been dreaming about the future . . . about the weekend with Heather and her family. He —

"Mr. Rau?" he heard the superintendent say, snapping him out of his inner world. "Would you like to sit —"

"*How* was he murdered?" Jordan asked.

The superintendent sighed, then answered slowly, "His throat was cut."

"What . . . ?" Jordan tried to digest what

he had just heard. My son's throat? His throat was cut? Who in God's name would . . . ?

He felt someone tug on his arm. The tug was accompanied by a sound that brought him out of his vacuum.

"Daddy?"

He shook his head to clear his vision. It was Donica. She was standing there in front of him, her teary eyes begging him to comfort and protect her.

"My baby!" He pulled her into his arms. As his chest heaved with sobs, his parental instincts rushed to the surface with more emotion than he had ever felt in his life. He swung his arm over Donica's head and smashed the stucco wall with his bleeding fist.

Holding Donica and feeling his world spinning out of control, Jordan realized that one thing within him was as clear and hard as a cut diamond: He would find out who had killed his son. And he would make absolutely certain that person paid with his life.

◆ Part 2

♦ Part 2

7

To conduct Chase's funeral, Paul Krueger, the president of the mission board, flew down to Chattanooga from the mission headquarters in Chesapeake, Virginia.

"Remember," he told Jordan at the funeral home prior to the memorial service, "things like this don't always have a reason; they just happen. So don't blame yourself. Don't think God did this to punish or to teach you. He didn't. It's no one's fault. Not yours. Not Susan's. It just happened."

To Jordan it made no difference. God's actions, plans, or schemes were too abstract to understand or blame or rely on. God and His reasons — or lack of them — were the last things on his mind.

But Jordan was blaming himself. Miserably so. How in the name of life could he do otherwise? Wasn't he supposed to be his son's protector?

Sitting in the funeral home chapel, surrounded by Susan and Donica and extended family members, Jordan was sweating heavily. He could feel the sweat penetrating his suit. Again, his tortured imagination saw the haunting vision of Chase lying in the German morgue.

It had been a week since he walked into that unforgettably cold room and saw his son's stiff body lying dead — gray and naked on the medical examiner's metal gurney.

Against the expressed wishes of the police authorities, he had insisted that he and Susan see the corpse.

The medical examiner had also tried to dissuade him. The man explained to him that the body had been lying out on the open ground, in the elements, for two and a half days. "It will not be a very pleasant sight," the man had emphasized.

But Jordan had been adamant.

And now he was wondering if he had made a mistake. The sight, he now knew, would haunt him for the rest of his life.

How could he ever forget the travesty — Chase's eyes frozen wide with horror, the gaping mouth, the slit throat — which was all that remained of his son? How could he forget the depravity that had cut down his child, that had marked and forever ruined his family's future?

He fidgeted in his seat.

The guilt, the anger, the intolerable grief, the lust for vengeance — all of it was too much. It was changing him, gnawing at him. Perhaps destroying him.

He was neither eating nor sleeping — he had already lost several pounds. And the tension within his family was at an all-time high.

He stared at the closed coffin in the front of the small chapel, wondering how the Moseleys were coping in California, where they had gone to bury Heather. Heather's body had sustained three stab wounds in the chest. They had found out from the medical examiner's report that she had been raped, possibly by more than one man, prior to her death.

Were the Moseleys going insane like he was, or were they trying to escape the pain by leaning hard on their faith?

He glanced at Susan, seated beside him. He knew she was praying constantly, begging God to help her make some sense of this tragedy. Time and again in the last days, he had seen her with her Bible open on her lap — usually to the Psalms. Despite the magnitude of her pain, she seemed determined that God would show her a path through the indescribable agony.

In the final analysis, he concluded, one's

coping tactic really didn't matter. Unimaginable pain was unimaginable pain. It was a feeling that taunted and devastated, and couldn't be vanquished — no matter what.

Believing this, Jordan clung to the promise he had made to himself in the Bad Aibling police station: Somebody would *pay* for putting two innocent families through this type of hell.

He had heard that the German police force was one of the toughest and most efficient in the world. He didn't doubt their reputation, but he was determined to push and hound until they found the criminals and prosecuted them.

In the middle of his thoughts, Jordan suddenly realized the service had begun. He struggled to listen as the soloist sang her two songs.

He had never been shy or uncomfortable in crowds. But in this setting, and in this overflow crowd of nearly three hundred people — many of them standing — he felt nervously suppressed. He wanted to scream out loud and vent some of his tension, but couldn't. He wanted to throw a hymnal across the room and stand up and curse, but couldn't. He wanted to kneel beside the coffin and cry uncontrollably, but couldn't.

When Paul Krueger stood to deliver the eulogy, Jordan found himself hoping it would be eloquent, memorable — and short.

"The fatality rate of every generation is 100 percent," Paul said to introduce his thoughts. "Even though some of us will live longer than others, like Chase Rau, we will all die.

"Some of us will die suddenly and unexpectedly. Others of us will die a slow death over a period of weeks and months, maybe even years. Some of us will die peacefully; others will be taken in much pain and misery. Some will die old; others will die young.

"Death is no respecter of persons. It is an absolute part of life. We come into the world through the miracle of birth. We exit the world through death. Knowing this, of course, doesn't chase away the grief, the sorrow, the bereavement, the loneliness, the anger and the fear we feel when one of our loved ones goes before us. But it's permissible to be overwhelmed by these feelings. They're a part of life, too.

"Perhaps these feelings are even helpful. After all, they grab our attention and make us focus on the value of life, on the importance of active involvement in the world around us . . ."

Jordan's mind began to wander. He fidgeted with the handkerchief in his pocket.

He noticed out of the corner of his eye that Susan appeared to be growing restless as well. No doubt she was upset that Paul wasn't quoting from the Bible.

He felt obligated to help her by trying vicariously to cater to her faith somehow, but at the moment, it was all he could do to battle his own anguish.

He did manage to put his arm around her. For a moment, his feeble attempt to show support took away his thoughts of revenge. But as Paul Krueger rambled on in a vain attempt to bring comfort and healing, Jordan's mind envisioned again the bringing of swift justice to the killers. He started planning his next phone call to Germany to get the latest report on the investigation.

When all the friends and relatives had left Susan's parents' home that evening, and all the donated food had been dealt with, Jordan broke the news to Susan. "We're going back," he said.

"But you said —"

"I know what I said. But I've changed my mind. I can't stay here in Chattanooga."

"But the church has already offered you

90

your job back, and you've told the mission board —"

"I'll talk to Paul first thing tomorrow morning. I'll let him know we'll be staying in the States for one more week, and then going back."

A look of stark unbelief came over Susan's face. "Jordan, after all that's happened you can't really mean —"

"One more week. Gear your mind up for it. I'll tell Donica tomorrow at breakfast."

Ricardo slowly entered the living room, where his mother was alone watching television. He had to talk to her. Since that night in the woods, he had lived every waking hour with the feeling that he was being followed by someone who knew.

The German police.

The MPs.

The girl's dad.

The boy's dad.

A vigilante who spent his time fighting evil.

Even now, alone in the apartment with his mom, he felt that the imagined follower, whoever it was, would come bursting through the front door at any moment and take him away.

He felt that his involvement in the cold-blooded murder and rape was somehow written all over him — in his eyes, in his voice, even in his movements — and that it was just a matter of time before he was caught. Maybe a few days. Maybe a few hours. Maybe a few minutes.

There was a part of him that wanted to be callous, even proud of what he had done. After all, hadn't he proven to himself that he was as bad as the baddest? But the biggest part of him was living with a fear that wouldn't go away.

Even at night, recurring nightmares of the forest, the blood, and the awful screams stole sleep from him. He would wake in a cold sweat, his heart hammering.

He couldn't keep his feelings bottled up anymore; he had to tell someone.

But he didn't know anyone he could trust. Except . . . maybe his mom. Maybe she would listen. And maybe, just maybe, she would try to understand. After all — she was his mother. That meant something, didn't it?

"Mom," he said to her nervously.

She ignored him, so he spoke a little louder, to make sure he was heard above the noise of the TV.

"Mom, I need to talk with you for a second."

"What?" she snapped, her eyes still glued to the television set.

"Do you mind if I turn the TV off for a second?" he asked, starting to feel frustrated.

"Get me another beer, will you?" she said, ignoring his question.

His chest began to heave as he tried to keep himself under control.

"Mom, I need to talk to you."

"I said get me another beer! *And then get outta my face!*" she shouted.

He almost tried once more, then stopped and wheeled about in anger. "Get your own lousy beer," he growled. Cursing between clenched teeth, he marched out, slamming the front door behind him.

8

For Donica Rau, the day of the return flight to Munich was one of the most depressing of her life. It was November 11, her fourteenth birthday.

As she stared out the small passenger window into the night, thirty-seven thousand feet above the Atlantic, she felt lonely and scared.

Never before had she seen her mom and her dad so short-tempered with one another.

It was mostly her dad's fault, she had decided. He was the one being confrontational. Since Chase's death, he had been out of control. He was always brooding, always angry. It disturbed her, deep inside. Daddy had always been her idol, the one she looked up to and tried to imitate. But now . . .

Mom was at least trying to be strong. And sensitive. But Dad was being totally selfish. Completely absorbed in his own secluded world, his own grief.

"*I need* to be near the investigation," he had said over and over again. That was it; it seemed to be his only reason for rushing them back to Germany.

It didn't make sense.

Why was he making such a stupid move? Couldn't he see that everybody else in the family was hurting just as much as he was, that they all had needs right now?

Couldn't he understand that Mom needed to stay in Chattanooga for a while, just to be near the family and friends who could give her support — to be near Chase's grave?

And what about her? Couldn't Dad understand that she desperately needed help to struggle through this trauma? Was Chase the only person he cared about? What about the people who were still here with him?

Until now, Donica had never believed that anybody in her family was loved less than anybody else. But now she wondered. When she now needed her dad the most — needed to hear his comforting reassurances and to feel his strong arms around her — he was totally neglecting her, and had been for weeks. He had not even wished her a happy birthday.

Still staring out into the darkness, and feeling more depressed and lonely by the minute, Donica just hoped her dad knew what he was doing. Right now, she couldn't see any evidence that he did.

Jordan sat at his desk in the corner of the master bedroom, staring out the window at the snow-covered city. In his frustration, he snapped in two the pencil he held in his hands.

For the three weeks since returning to Germany, he had waited.

It was true that he had been impatient — calling the U.S. military and German police headquarters twice a day to get an up-to-the-minute report. But he had waited.

He thought that surely by now the combined investigations of the two police forces would have made some substantial progress toward the capture of his son's killer.

But neither of the police organizations knew any more now than they did five weeks ago — that Chase had been murdered in the pine thicket near the Moseley's house, that Heather had been raped and murdered at the site where the bodies were found, and that at least one of the two or three assailants involved had reddish brown hair — Heather's right hand

96

had six such hairs clutched in her fingers.

In the weeks since the murder, those working the case had uncovered no witnesses and no clues as to the identity of the perpetrators.

Jordan couldn't decide if the police departments were incompetent or just not interested.

As he stood up from his desk, he realized that he could no longer just sit around inside the apartment and waste his time on hope and patience.

It was time now to do something.

Susan was just getting ready to put lunch on the table when she saw Jordan go to the front door, take his heavy winter coat from the rack, and slip it on.

What was he doing? She had just told him five minutes ago that lunch was almost ready.

"Where are you — ?" She stopped herself. Why bother asking? He wouldn't communicate with her, anyway. If he was leaving, he was leaving. She didn't have the emotional strength to try to question or oppose him anymore.

He glanced at her, then at the food on the table. "I'm not hungry," he grunted.

As she watched him walk out the door,

she realized that what was left of their family was quickly falling apart, like a house being dismantled piece by piece in hurricane-force winds.

During the last month she had watched Jordan gradually cease to function as a husband and father. It had been unnerving for Donica, but it had been worse for her. She and Jordan had bickered continually, until Jordan finally refused to communicate with her anymore.

For the last four days, he had shut himself away in the bedroom, sitting like a recluse at his desk and staring out the window. He had not bathed or shaved. He had come out of the room only to eat, and barely that. The only time she heard him speak was when he made his calls to the police station, or when he made a statement of intent, like the one at the door. Otherwise, he just sat like a wooden Indian, being eaten from within by bitterness and hate.

So where was he going now? Why was he going?

She was certain he wasn't heading for the Institute. Even though he had assured the mission board directors that he could recover from his grief and resume his commitment to the seminary project, he had stopped attending his German classes three days after returning to Munich — without the mission board's knowledge or permission.

Susan picked up one of the sandwiches and took a bite, chewing without tasting. She desperately needed someone to talk with. Otherwise, she was sure she would go insane.

Donica was in school — forced there by German law. Susan had wanted to keep her home for a while and homeschool her, but the government stated emphatically that homeschooling was not allowed in any fashion, under any circumstance, for any reason.

Even though Susan and Donica had attended the Sunday services at St. Jude's a few more times, she didn't feel close enough to anyone there to lean on, now that Ralph and Lynn Moseley had decided to remain in the U.S.

Susan wondered if anyone at the home mission board knew or cared that she was dying on the inside. Judging from the tone of his remarks at Chase's funeral, Paul Krueger would probably give her a lecture on the importance of thinking positively and staying involved with life and with the world around her.

"Well, I can't!" she shouted aloud in the empty apartment.

Though she wanted to believe that God cared about her and was somehow in control of what was happening, she now felt hopeless. Devastated. Abandoned.

She leaned over the kitchen table and laid her head on her arms. "Why, God? Why are we here?" she spoke through tears. "I can't go on like this!"

9

For three cold and snowy days, Jordan knocked on doors at the row-house complex near the pine grove where Chase had been murdered.

Trying to find a witness who saw anything that could be a clue, he questioned everybody he could — kids, housewives . . . even some construction workers who were remodeling a bathroom in one of the homes. In his weak German, with frequent references to the English-German pocket dictionary he carried, he asked, over and over, the same questions: *"Haben sie mein Sohn gesehen? Er ist verloren?"* ("Have you seen my son? He is missing.") He showed them a photograph.

He had decided not to reveal Chase's murder, fearing that if anyone knew the situation was so serious, they would go straight to the police, cutting him off from the information he needed. He was anxious to avoid that.

He found out that most people in the neighborhood had already been questioned by the police, but none of them — neither those whom the police had visited, nor those he alone had interviewed — had seen anything questionable, suspicious, or memorable on the Friday evening of the murder.

Tired and discouraged, he had just gotten back into his car and kicked the snow off his shoes — ready to call it quits for the day — when he spotted a medium-sized man a half-block away, unloading suitcases from a small Russian-made automobile.

The car was parked on the street in front of an apartment where Jordan had not previously found anyone at home. Judging by the man's olive-toned skin and the car he was driving, Jordan knew that the man was not German.

Jordan cranked his car and began to drive away. He assumed that the man, whoever he was and for whatever reason he was here, would be the last person who would be able to provide him with any information.

As he watched the man grow smaller in the rearview mirror, Jordan felt a gnawing uncertainty. What if the man *did* know something? Jordan was sure he didn't. He was an outsider who had probably been in another country, hundreds of miles away, on the evening of the killing.

Nevertheless, Jordan decided, for his own peace of mind, to go back and talk with the man. He knew he would never rest if he consciously left a stone unturned. He'd make it quick, satisfy his doubts, then go to a *Gasthaus* and get something warm to eat before heading back to Munich.

As he drove up to park behind the Russian car, he saw for the first time a woman and two teenage girls accompanying the man out of the house. They were all heading toward the street to help finish unloading the luggage roped to the top of the vehicle.

Jordan got out of his car and met them on the snow-covered sidewalk.

"Entschuldigen sie, bitte," he said, directing his attention to the man, *"sprechen sie Englische?"* ("Excuse me, please. Do you speak English?") It was a vain hope, Jordan realized, but his mind was so fatigued by a day of trying to communicate in German, he had to at least ask.

To Jordan's delight, the man said in a slow and hesitant voice, "I speak a few English, yes."

Jordan looked the man in the face and spoke slowly and clearly. "My name is Jordan Rau. I live here in Germany, but I'm from America." Jordan waited until the man nodded his understanding, then continued. "I was just wondering if you visit here very often?"

"This country, you mean?" the man answered.

"No, no, I mean this house. Do you come here and stay in this house very often?"

A look of suspicion and uncertainty spread across the man's face to his dark brown eyes. "Why you need to know that?" he asked. At the same time, the man looked to his side and said something to the woman and the teenage girls in a language Jordan didn't recognize. The woman, with the help of the two girls, started tending to the ropes and suitcases atop the car.

"I'm trying to find someone who was at home, here on this street, on a certain day a few weeks ago — on Friday night, October the twenty-fifth," Jordan explained. "I'm trying to find someone who saw something."

Jordan paused to give the man a chance to respond. But it was apparent by the man's sudden silence that he was not going to offer up any kind of reply until he heard more details. So Jordan proceeded.

"On October twenty-fifth my teenage son was walking through the field behind these houses." Jordan gestured toward the field with his hand. "It was on a Friday evening after school. He was with a friend, a teenage girl living in the big house just on the other side of the woods back there. They were walking to the girl's house when somebody attacked them with a knife over there in the woods, in the dark.

"I'm helping the police search this area for any possible eyewitnesses. The identity of the attacker, or attackers, is unknown, and they haven't yet been caught. So, we're trying to find someone who might have seen something that night that could be a possible clue to help us track them down."

After hearing all that Jordan had said, the man just stood there, his breath visible in the cold air around him, exhibiting a blank expression. Still he remained silent.

Just as I expected, Jordan thought to himself. The man doesn't know anything. It's a waste of time trying to talk to him. He probably didn't understand half of what I said.

He was about to turn away when the

man spoke. "This is strange," he said slowly, with a look of recollection in his eyes. "This night I do see something. I remember, because on same night I leave Germany to go and get my family."

Now Jordan was silent. Had this man really seen something? His mind exploded with hope. He waited, listening carefully to the man's thick accent, trying to hear and understand what he was saying.

"I am Muslim from Bosnia, in Yugoslavia," the man said as a preface. "Because my country fall apart and kill Muslims, I go to find safe country for family."

Jordan nodded, indicating that he was following him.

"Two month ago, I come to Germany where many Muslim brothers have come away from killing. I first go to get visa, because I only one in family who have passport. When I come here, German government give visa to be refugee. They help find this house so family can live safe here. I —"

He stopped when one of his daughters interrupted him, speaking in their native language. Jordan willed himself to be patient while the man turned away and gave his attention to the teenager.

After about five minutes, the man turned back to Jordan while the girls started folding up a tarpaulin and carrying the remaining suitcases into the house.

"Anyway, as I say to you," he resumed, "I leave Germany to go get family on Friday, twenty-five October. I lock house and am leave when I hear strange noise. Someone — how you say it? — crying. Behind house in field. I go back garden to see. It was dark. I try to see, then I see five, six, or seven young people walk fast to road. One —"

"How do you know they were young people?" Jordan interrupted.

"Young people move not same as old. This I am see . . . even in dark."

Jordan nodded for the man to continue his story.

"One is carry something over . . . uh . . . over back. Something look like another person."

Jordan interrupted again. "You mean it looked like one of the people in the group was carrying a person across his shoulder?"

"Yes," the man confirmed. "And crying sound like girl. I think maybe the one on back, or the . . . uh . . . shoulder, as you say, is maybe sick. I think maybe they go doctor."

"Did you say anything to them, or try to help them?" Jordan asked.

"No, they are go too fast. Then I think what can Yugoslavian help five or six Germans, anyway."

"Are you just assuming they were German, or do you know that for certain?"

"No, no, not German. At first I think so. But no. I see they are American."

"You saw they were Americans?" Jordan nearly shouted. "How . . . ?" He suddenly lost his words. His mind started reeling faster than he could logically think.

The Bosnian continued. "When I go my car to leave, I drive to end of street. There I nearly hit car come too quick from dark. I think driver is maybe crazy. In headlights, I see little inside. I see same many young people from field."

"But how do you know they were American?" Jordan pressed.

"That is easy," the man said matter-of-factly. "Car is have USA — how you say? Regis . . . regis . . ."

"Registration plate? The number plate on the back of the car?" Jordan jumped in, trying to help him.

"Yes, number plate."

Jordan was momentarily stunned. This unlikely witness had just handed him a critical piece of information.

Like everyone who lived in Germany for any length of time, Jordan knew that every automobile registered to any American military personnel — a soldier, a department of defense employee, or a contractor like Ralph Moseley had been — bore a special plate. The plate was easily distinguishable. The letters *USA* were stamped across its middle. And unlike its German counterpart, which was narrow and nearly two feet long, the USA plate was shorter and deeper, the same shape as license plates in America.

Jordan's mind was now racing. "Do you remember any of the other numbers or letters?"

"Only USA," the man answered.

"Do you remember what kind of car it was?" Jordan asked him.

The man paused for thought. "Big gray car. Mercedes. BMW maybe."

"Do you think you could identify it if you saw it again?"

"Maybe yes. I see big dent over back wheel."

Gotcha! Jordan shouted in his mind. "What is your work schedule?" he asked.

"Government not yet giving work permit." The man grunted. "They give some money all month, but give no work." Then he added, "They no let foreigners have jobs to take away from Germans."

"Well, then . . . since you have a flexible schedule, I'll pay you to help me find that car."

"You pay me?" the man replied with a tinge of surprise in his voice.

Jordan struggled not to appear too eager. "You're the first eyewitness we've found who saw something that night. And I think what you've just shared with me might prove to be the clue we've been searching for."

"These people must hurt your son real bad," the man stated.

"Yes," Jordan told him, massaging his aching temples, "they hurt him bad. Real bad."

Jordan looked at the man and said, "If you'll help me, I'll give you a hundred German marks a day. Or if you prefer, I'll give you American dollars — sixty a day."

An uncertain smile formed on the man's thin lips. "I can no help you today," he responded. "Or tomorrow. As you see, I have just come from Bosnia with family. I must take to *Rathaus* tomorrow to sign papers."

Jordan understood the man's legal responsibility to register his family with the

German officials. "Then what about Friday?" he asked.

The man shrugged. "I guess okay."

Before the man had time to change his mind, Jordan said, "Fine. I'll be here to pick you up at eight o'clock Friday morning. And I'll have the money with me."

The man nodded and extended his hand. "I am call Gagic."

After shaking the man's hand and thanking him, Jordan repeated to him the time of the rendezvous, then got in his car and drove away.

Then the mental struggle began. Should he inform the police?

It was clear to him that the only reason the criminal investigators had not yet come across Gagic as an eyewitness was because he had not been home when the police canvassed the neighborhood. If he did not tell them about the Bosnian, they would eventually find him, Jordan realized — just as he had done.

So should he tell them? Or should he take advantage of what he alone now knew?

He debated the question intensely as he devoured a couple of bratwurst sausages at a Bad Aibling *Gasthaus*.

But in the end, Jordan realized that he

had already made up his mind while listening to Gagic share his revelation. He would keep the information to himself.

Before the police discovered Gagic on their own, maybe he — with Gagic's help — could locate the killers, do what had to be done, then take Susan and Donica out of the country.

After all, even if the killers were apprehended and brought to trial, the chances of justice being served by the law were not guaranteed.

But if he could track them down first, apart from the police department's knowledge, justice would be certain.

Oh yes, he told himself, if he found them first, they would pay.

They would die in the same painful fashion that they had killed his son. At the end of a knife. His knife.

As he sped toward Munich on the autobahn, he didn't notice the mountains to the west, their majestic snowcapped peaks clearly visible in the early evening twilight. His knuckles showing white on the steering wheel, he was contemplating his mission of vengeance.

10

Jordan left Munich bright and early Friday morning. The day was clear for a change, the air crisp and invigorating. As he raced southward toward Bad Aibling, he reviewed his strategy for the next couple of days. He had not told Susan about Gagic. He didn't want to risk her carrying the information to the police.

Arriving at Gagic's house shortly before eight, Jordan had to wait less than a minute before the Bosnian came out to meet him at the car.

When Gagic crawled into the heated automobile, Jordan asked him, "Do you prefer marks or dollars?"

"Marks," Gagic answered with a smile. "American dollar getting weaker every day. I lose money before I get to bank."

Jordan pulled a hundred-mark note from his shirt pocket, handed it to him, and said, "We're going to the American high school in Munich this morning. Every

American teenager from Bad Aibling, Bad Tölz, Garmisch, and Munich goes to school there. If the young people you saw are American teenagers from any of those communities, then we'll find them at the high school. All I need for you to do is identify their car. I'll take it from there."

As they drove the thirty-five minutes back into Munich, Jordan turned on the car radio to the American Forces Network station. Some of America's top-twenty country songs played in the background. As the music droned on, Jordan again reviewed his strategy. He knew that the driver of the car had to be at least eighteen, the minimum age for legal driving in Germany. So if the murderer was a high school student, he would have to be a senior, or possibly a junior if he had failed a few grades. If the person was in his early twenties, then either he was a student at the University of Maryland's Munich campus or he was a soldier. If he was a soldier, he would be more difficult to find; he could be stationed at any of the more than three dozen bases scattered throughout the country.

But as long as Gagic would be willing to help him, he would search all the American communities for the getaway car. He only hoped they spotted the car before Gagic's daily hundred-mark retainer bankrupted him.

When they arrived at the McGraw *Konserne* housing area, Jordan drove to the outer edge of the complex, where the American high school facility was located.

Turning to Gagic, he said, "This is the school. I'm going to cruise the entire area. The parking lots. The streets. Point out every car that in the slightest way resembles the car you saw that night. Keep in mind that the damaged fender could have been repaired by now."

Gagic nodded.

Like an eagle looking for his prey, Jordan began his search.

First, he drove up and down every row in the high school parking lot until Gagic had a chance to view every car.

Gagic shook his head. The car wasn't there.

Next, Jordan canvassed the PX and Burger King parking lots, next door to the high school. At one point, Gagic pointed to a silver Mercedes and said, "I think that is the one!" But a closer look revealed that the car carried a German license plate.

Jordan next surveyed the streets of the large housing area. There were no garages provided for the soldiers, so all of their cars were parked out in the open, on the curbs.

But Gagic didn't spot the car.

Skipping lunch, Jordan drove to the commissary parking lot, then to the University of Maryland parking lot.

When the search of those parking areas also proved to be fruitless, Jordan returned to the high school and repeated his passes through all the parking zones. By midafternoon he was once again back at the University of Maryland.

Still nothing.

Jordan then backtracked to the Burger King and bought Gagic a meal. He asked Gagic to eat in the car. Gagic was eager to oblige, but before he could get his hamburger out of its wrapper, Jordan cranked the car and drove around to the front of the high school.

"We'll wait here and watch while the students come out of school," Jordan told him. "Especially watch the cars driven by parents who come to pick up their kids."

While slowly eating his burger and fries, Gagic scrutinized every vehicle that moved in and out of the area.

Jordan waited until four-thirty. By that time, all the students had left the premises.

Gagic still had not sighted the car.

"One more time," Jordan insisted. "We'll drive through all the parking lots one more time, then I'll take you home."

Jordan returned to his apartment in Munich at seven forty-five. When he walked in, Donica was sitting in the living room doing her homework. She didn't even try to talk to him as he passed through.

Susan, sitting at the kitchen table writing a letter to her parents, put the pen down as he entered.

"Are you hungry?" she asked. "There are some fresh sausages in the fridge."

"No, thanks," he said without breaking his stride. "Maybe later."

He went to the bathroom — locking the door behind him — to take a long hot bath.

He just wanted to be alone.

With Donica at her side, Susan walked into the St. Jude's church building at eleven o'clock Sunday morning to attend the worship service.

In the midst of her own unrelenting grief, she was plagued with worry for her daughter.

Donica was becoming more and more

withdrawn. Yet she also seemed to have an aversion to being by herself, constantly lingering near her mom during off-school hours. But the sparkle, the tireless optimism of the old Donica was gone. She now wore the tired and lethargic look of a cancer patient.

Susan had tried to get her to talk about her feelings, but Donica would usually respond with silence.

Last night, though, Donica had looked her in the eye and in a dead voice announced, "It's Dad. He doesn't care about us anymore."

Choking back her despair, Susan had tried to tell Donica that her father did love her, but that he was hurting, too, and in his own way was trying to cope. But Donica appeared unconvinced.

Despite her attempts to reassure her daughter, Susan was forced to admit doubts of her own. Did Jordan truly love them? If he cared about them, how could he be so inconsiderate? Why had he insisted on bringing them back to Germany? And now that they were here, why did he seem so insistent on avoiding them — staying gone from the house until all hours of the day and night?

They found a seat near the back of the

auditorium just as the organist began the prelude. "God, please help us," Susan prayed silently.

Feeling a desperate need for some sort of anchor, Susan had begun praying with Donica every day. For two weeks now, they had been praying each morning before Donica left for school and each evening before she went to bed. Actually, Susan had done most of the praying. Donica's lethargy prevented her from taking an active part, but at least she didn't seem to mind listening to her mother's entreaties to God.

"Even if Dad's love is hard to see right now," Susan had told Donica three or four days ago, "we need to keep reminding ourselves that God loves us, that He cares." As the first hymn began, Susan fervently hoped that she was telling the truth.

At the front of the sanctuary, a small choir of sixteen people was opening the worship service with a special rendition of the *Gloria Patri*.

As had happened the last three times she had attended a service here at St. Jude's, she felt quiet tears coursing down her cheeks. Somehow, she keenly sensed the presence of God and the vastness of her need for Him.

After the songs, the liturgy, and the communion, the pastor stood and introduced a guest speaker for the morning — a Scottish missionary who had lived and worked with the Muslims of North Africa for twenty-three years.

"My text this morning will be Hebrews chapter eleven, verse six," the nearly bald Scotsman said in his thick accent when he walked up to the lectern. " 'Without faith it is impossible to please Him,' " he began to read as he held his small Bible up close to his glasses, " 'for he who comes to God must believe that He is, and that He is a rewarder of those who diligently seek Him.' "

He laid his Bible down on the podium and said, "As a preface to my sermon this morning, I want to share with you a story so fascinating that it borders on the unbelievable."

Susan found herself, despite the many troubling thoughts within her mind, entering into the missionary's narrative.

"It occurred twenty years ago in the North African country of Algeria when I was serving my first term as a novice missionary. I had been on the field for three years, and was just becoming proficient in the Arabic language. As you can probably imagine, my ministry at that point was only in its infancy stage.

"There were just three people attending a Sunday morning Bible study that I was conducting in my home in the capital city of Algiers. All three of them had been meeting with me on a regular basis for about seven months. They were middle-aged men who worked as merchants, men I had met through my cover as an importer of textile machinery from Scotland.

"One of those men, at great expense to his business and family, opened his heart to the gospel. He publicly renounced Islam, trusting the Lord Jesus Christ to take away his sins, acknowledging Him as God and Savior incarnate. The man's name was Ahmed.

"Shortly after his conversion to Christianity, he became so burdened for his family that he began a crusade of evangelism among his Muslim relatives. 'We as Muslims have believed a lie about Jesus,' he would tell them. 'The truth is, He is more than just a supreme prophet equal to Moses and Muhammad. He is the Creator God who became a man to die for the sins of His creation. He is the Savior. We must trust Him for salvation.'

"Except for one of his cousins, all of

Ahmed's relatives disclaimed him as their kin. That one cousin, however, Ahmed was able to lead to a saving knowledge of Christ. The cousin's name was Chadli; he was a teacher. He lived beyond the Saharan Atlas Mountain range in a desert-oasis town called Touggourt.

"Following Chadli's conversion, he and Ahmed started corresponding with each other by letter, encouraging one another to be strong in the faith.

"They had been writing to each other for about two months when Chadli shared a story with Ahmed that left us all speechless.

"According to Chadli's account, he left his town of Touggourt one morning and rode his camel forty miles into the desert to a small oasis where eighty to a hundred people were living. One of those people was Chadli's oldest brother, a devout Muslim. Chadli made the journey for the express purpose of sharing the gospel with his brother. He went with the intention of staying at the oasis for three or four days. He wanted to make sure that he had enough time to discuss the matter thoroughly. He knew his brother would not be easily persuaded.

"Now remember," the Scotsman emphasized while gesturing with his hands to the audience, "Chadli had been a Christian for only about eight weeks. From his lifetime background as a Muslim, he knew how Muslims viewed converts to Christianity. He knew there was an inherent risk involved for a Christian, especially a Muslim convert, to publicly proclaim the Christ of the Scriptures. Nevertheless, his newfound relationship with the Savior moved him to take the risk and approach his brother. As he stated in his letter to Ahmed, he was more concerned about the safety of his brother's soul than he was about the safety of his own body.

"Well, as the story goes, Chadli had been at the oasis for about five hours when the situation became very tense. He had been awake most of the night zealously trying to persuade his brother that the teaching of Islam concerning Jesus Christ is untrue and eternally misleading.

"At some point early in the morning, the brother became so upset that he went to other tents and awakened several of the leading men in the *wadi*. Together they formed a tribunal and sentenced Chadli to die, because of his repudiation of the teachings of Islam.

"As the sun was rising, they stripped him

of all his clothes except for his undergarments, and walked him to the edge of the oasis. Keeping his camel, food, and water, they expelled him into the desert to die."

That's me, Susan thought. *In the middle of a desert of the soul — without shelter or water.*

"Now, this is where the story ceases to be ordinary and becomes, as you will agree, quite unnatural," the Scotsman continued.

"Chadli had been walking for five hours, heading hopelessly back toward Touggourt, using the sun as his compass, when a vicious sandstorm blew up.

"Let me just emphasize here, folks, that a Sahara sandstorm can be paralyzing. The strength of the wind shoots the grains of sand like bullets in all directions. And of course, when that happens, the sand, like fine mist, penetrates everything in it path. And when you add the deafening roar of the wind, you can well imagine the disorientation and the danger it can cause, especially to a lone and unsheltered man who is almost naked.

"When the storm finally passed, Chadli had survived. But barely. He had no idea how long the storm had beat down upon him, but at that point he knew he was going to die. His exposed skin was so raw, he could hardly move. And the sand was irritating the inside of his parched throat. He did get up and start walking, but his progress became unbearably slow. As the midafternoon temperature soared above forty-three degrees Celsius — that's one hundred and ten degrees Fahrenheit — he finally gave up and lay down to die in the sweltering sun.

"In his letter to Ahmed, he said that at that point he was not afraid of death, only of the probability that his brother and his other relatives would never again hear the truth about Jesus and would die in their sins.

"Lying helplessly on the desert floor, this was his prayer . . ."

Susan felt herself edge forward on the pew.

" 'Jesus,' he prayed, 'will you consider sparing my life somehow, so that I might continue to be a messenger of truth to my family?'

"Almost immediately after finishing that prayer, he saw another sandstorm moving toward him from the south. He positioned himself so that he was seated snug in the sand, his back to the approaching wind, and his face buried between his hands and knees.

"According to Chadli's account, when the storm reached him, he braced himself. With his head buried between his knees, he heard the storm all around him — but he didn't feel it. When he lifted his head and opened his eyes, he saw a miracle. All around him, the wind was blowing loud enough to drown out the rest of the world. The sand was being spun and thrown in every conceivable direction, fast enough to put out a man's eyes. And yet, in the circle where he was sitting, the air was still and the sand was motionless.

"For over one hour, he sat in the very heart of that Sahara sandstorm and was untouched by either the wind or the flying sand.

"When the storm subsided, Chadli found himself staring at an oasis just beneath the horizon. It was there at that oasis where, an hour or so later, he was given clothing, water, food, and ointment. He was burned badly from the first sandstorm and the sun, but he survived.

"The miraculous protection from the storm, however, had elevated his spirits far beyond any physical pain he might have been feeling. And so did the knowledge, at the end of that day, that the oasis where he found his physical salvation was located only ten miles from his hometown of Touggourt, a full *thirty* miles north of the oasis where he had been banished. That, too, was a miracle, since he could not possibly have covered that distance by foot in a day's time, especially in his condition.

"When he wrote and told Ahmed this story, he said, 'I have not yet told anyone else about this experience. I have shared it with you, because you are the only one I know who will believe me.'

"He ended the letter by saying, 'During all the years that I practiced the teachings of Islam, I prayed faithfully five times every day. And never once do I remember a prayer being answered. Thank you, Ahmed, for risking your career, your reputation, and your life to introduce me to the salvation of God and to the resurrected Savior who hears the cry of a helpless man in the desert, and cares.' "

Susan felt a window opening in her soul. Could it be? Could hope conquer the devastation she carried inside?

"Now, why did I tell you this story?" asked the missionary. "I told it to make this point: During my twenty-three years as a missionary to the Muslims of North Africa, I've observed that God is more liberal in working miracles with these poor people who convert to Christianity out of Islam than He is with the affluent Christians in the West.

"Years ago, out of curiosity, I consulted western missionaries working with the Hindus of India and the Buddhists of Asia to find out if they were making the same observation. 'Yes!' was their constant reply.

"I reasoned with myself that God needed to reaffirm to these converts that He indeed is the one true God, and that in choosing Him over false gods, the people were making a right decision.

"I held to that view for years, until 1985 when I met an American missionary who for thirty-two years had worked with tribal people in the jungle of New Guinea. He had made the same observation about miracles that I and the other missionaries had made. But he had come to a different conclusion about the reason. And when he shared it with me, I knew that he was right. And in sharing his thoughts with you, I have now come to the crux of what I wanted to say this morning."

The missionary raised a finger and punctuated the air with his next words.

" 'God is not a respecter of persons,' he told me, 'but *He is a respecter of faith.*' The reason God is more liberal in working miracles among converts in the third world, my friends, is not because those people have greater needs. It's because they have greater faith.

"The American went on to observe that in our western cultures we have become so high-tech and have developed so many human resources for meeting our needs and desires, that in a practical sense we don't need God anymore.

"Oh yes, we call on God in times of crisis, but our lack of faith in God is manifested by the fact that we immediately start gathering together all available resources and start assembling Plan A, Plan B, and Plan C, just in case God doesn't come through."

Susan gave a soft gasp of agreement.

"What you and I must learn, my brethren, is that God alone can truly meet our needs. All our technology, all our resources, all our planning and evaluation are an illusion! They are empty distractions from the central requirements of human life — to love and to trust the Lord God with all our hearts, souls, minds, and strength.

"With that in mind, listen once again to the strong words of Hebrews chapter eleven, verse six: 'Without *faith* it is *impos-*

sible to please Him. He that cometh to God must *believe* that He is, and that He is a rewarder of those who diligently seek *Him*'."

The words of the text rang in the sanctuary as the Scotsman challenged them all with his eyes.

A few minutes later, when the benediction was offered and the congregation dismissed, Susan sat amazed. Not since she was a child had she heard such a clear and strong sermon on the subject of faith. She knew that the contents of her heart had just been weighed — and found wanting.

The sermon's profound effect on her soul was a vivid indication to her of the distance she had strayed from this simple yet fundamental teaching of the Christian life: "You must believe that He is."

As this fact became plain to her, the challenge she felt was mixed with shame. She realized that for years now she had allowed her faith to be undermined by the persuasive liberalism of Jordan and their denominational leaders.

At that point, she didn't know whether to stand up and walk out of the building with a new and determined hope, or fall prostrate on the concrete floor and weep with guilt. "Lord, I want to learn to trust

You again," she prayed as the congregation filed past her on the way to the doors. "Teach me how . . . please, Lord!"

When she rose from the wooden pew and walked with Donica out to the street, she felt a renewal of strength and hope. She didn't know how long it would last, but for now, her load was bearable. *That's all I can ask,* she thought.

And for this moment, it was enough.

11

Every shade was pulled and every room light turned off. The only visible light inside the apartment was the shifting, bluish illumination of the television, its sound muted. The only noise was the grinding, crashing sound of heavy metal music, the lead singer shouting unintelligible lyrics from the stereo speakers.

Scattered around the coffee table — some on the table, some on the floor — were twelve empty beer cans. Six full cans, unopened in their six-pack, were sitting on the rug next to the couch.

The pressure in Ricardo's bladder forced him to open his eyes and attempt another trip to the bathroom. He tried to sit up, but the pounding in his brain threw the room into a dizzying spin. He thought he might throw up.

He knew he was going to have to get to the toilet somehow, but the pounding in his head continued to defeat him. Out of desperation, he rolled over onto the floor and crawled to the bathroom, first on all fours, then on his belly.

Once seated on the toilet, he tried to remember, against the swirling going on in his head, what was happening. *Where am I? What day is it? Where is everybody?*

It didn't take him long to remember the answers.

He was alone, in the Bad Tölz apartment. His mother and Mitchum had taken a long weekend drive to Paris. Naturally, he hadn't been invited. Not that he'd have cared much for a weekend spent in the company of either of them. Still, they could have at least asked.

So he had taken a little "trip" of his own this weekend, helping himself to the generous stock of household booze. He had now been drinking for three days. It *was* Monday, wasn't it? He grinned sickly to himself. He had another eighteen hours to stay bombed before they returned to Bad Tölz around noon tomorrow.

When he managed to reach the sofa again, he opened another beer can. Setting it on the table, he remembered that Mitchum would be leaving again on Wednesday morning for a two-week field exercise. He belched in satisfaction. He'd been afoot while Mitchum was home. He didn't dare violate the under-eighteen driving ban while the Green Beret was around to catch him. But with the man gone, he'd have wheels again.

Another wave of nausea overtook him, and he lay back on the couch and closed his eyes.

Jordan and Gagic had been sitting at the Burger King in the Munich housing area for about twenty minutes. They had spent most of the Wednesday morning and afternoon scouting the large military community in Augsburg, forty miles northwest of Munich.

Jordan's frustration was mounting. Bad Aibling, Bad Tölz, Garmisch, Oberammergau . . . For the last three days they had cruised every town within a sixty-mile radius with an American military presence, but so far they had not sighted the gray car with the damaged rear fender.

Today, at Jordan's insistence, they had worked right through lunch again. So, before taking Gagic back to Bad Aibling, he had stopped at the Burger King to get them a late afternoon meal, and to again survey the cars going to and from the high school. From where they were seated, they had a clear view of the side of the school and the entrance to the parking area for the PX.

Jordan was just finishing his second hamburger when he saw Gagic set down his Coke, stand up, and stare out the window, his eyes widening with recognition. The Bosnian pointed toward the parking lot and said, "There it is!"

Jordan swung around in his seat and looked in the direction Gagic was pointing.

Slowly entering the PX parking lot was a silverish-gray BMW — with a large crumple over the left rear fender. With his eyes riveted to the vehicle, Jordan broke toward the restaurant exit. Gagic followed on his heels. Jordan sprinted across the Burger King lot, up a two-foot terrace, and into the PX lot. With the BMW captured in his vision, he watched as it drove near the front entry to the PX, then made a left turn into one of the parking rows.

With Gagic at his side, Jordan watched breathlessly as the driver emerged from the BMW — a woman! *Of course,* Jordan thought to himself. *Gagic mentioned hearing a female voice crying that night.* Jordan had assumed that voice belonged to Heather, but maybe . . .

Jordan watched the slight figure with

bleached-blond hair till she disappeared through the front doors of the PX.

Then, without a word, he turned and led Gagic back to his car. He drove out of the Burger King parking lot and into the PX lot, finding a parking space near enough to the BMW to allow them to observe it without being conspicuous.

Jordan scrabbled through the glove compartment of his car, locating a pen and a scrap of paper. As he wrote down the license plate number, he heard Gagic say, "What you are do now?"

Instead of answering, Jordan pointed at the car and queried the Bosnian, "Are you absolutely sure this is the car?"

Gagic paused, studying the car and its U.S. license plate.

"Yes," he said finally, "I am sure is car I see."

Jordan went through his billfold to see what money he had left. There was a one-hundred-mark bill and two fifties. He grabbed the hundred and one of the fifties and placed them in Gagic's hand.

"Here's your hundred for today, and an extra fifty. I want you to be responsible for getting yourself the rest of the way home today. Now that we've found the car, I'll have to stay here. I've got to make a quick call to the police," he lied. "And then start the surveillance work. You've been a tremendous help, Gagic. Thanks."

He held out his hand, anxious to terminate Gagic's involvement and free himself to pursue his plan of vengeance, alone and unobserved. The Bosnian looked from Jordan's hand to his face. After a lengthy silence, he slowly reached out and accepted Jordan's handshake. With a final dubious glance at the American, he exited the car and walked away toward the nearest train station.

Jordan settled in to wait for the driver to reappear. In a few moments, she emerged from the store. She appeared to be in her early- to mid-thirties, and about five feet five. She had a worn, tired, cheap look about her. *Sleaze,* Jordan thought to himself.

The woman placed a couple of small shopping bags on the BMW's backseat, then seated herself behind the wheel and closed the door. Jordan watched as the engine started with a small puff of exhaust and she backed out of her parking place. He waited until she had almost reached one of the parking lot exits. Then, when he thought he would not be observed by her, he pulled forward, watching to see which way she would turn.

He trailed the car through the housing area and out to one of the main city streets, maintaining a discreet distance. However, when the BMW turned onto a two-lane street filled with rush-hour traffic, Jordan nearly let the car get out of his visual range. In his panic to keep it in sight, he accelerated out into the traffic in front of an oncoming taxi, forcing the cab driver to hit his brakes. Jordan ignored the taxi driver's shaking fist and cursing lips.

He could feel his eyes and the muscles in his neck burning with the strain of his intensity. His whole universe, at this moment, consisted of the taillights of the silverish-gray BMW.

Who is she? he wondered. She surely wasn't Chase's murderer . . . was she? She didn't fit in with Gagic's description of "young people." Had she been an accomplice? If not, what was her relationship to the killer? Whatever she knew or didn't know, she *was* driving the car. And no matter who she was or what role she played in the story, she would lead him to the one who was guilty. She had to.

The BMW veered out of the main flow of traffic and went up an exit ramp to the right.

138

He put on his blinker and changed lanes, following her a few miles through the outskirts of town to autobahn E11, heading south.

When she turned south onto the expressway, Jordan reasoned she was going to either Bad Aibling or Bad Tölz, the only two American communities in that direction.

A headache, spawned by the tension in his neck, had slowly crawled up the back of his skull and was now pounding behind his eyes. He was almost wincing with the pain, but he dared not take his eyes off his quarry. Driving along the busy autobahn in the gathering darkness, he kept two or three other vehicles between himself and the BMW, carefully maintaining an anonymous distance.

After about eleven miles, he watched her turn signal blink on. She was moving toward the Holzkirchen exit.

"Bad Tölz," Jordan whispered to himself. "She's going to Bad Tölz."

On the narrow and twisting road from Holzkirchen to Bad Tölz, Jordan had to stay close in order to keep her within his range. Being so close, he feared that she might become suspicious of his actions, so he fell back a few times, allowing the distance between them to grow, but never to the point that he would lose her if she made a sudden turn.

As they approached the Flint *Konserne* housing area at the edge of Bad Tölz, her blinker and brake lights flashed on. She was going into the housing area. If this was indeed where she lived, he wondered how he and Gagic had failed to spot the car during their earlier sweeps through the area.

He slowed behind her as she turned into the housing complex, then drove on. He didn't want to pull into the housing area behind her, knowing such a maneuver would make her more likely to notice him and become suspicious. Instead, he drove down the road, watching his rearview mirror. As soon as the BMW's taillights disappeared behind a row of trees lining the entrance to the main housing area, he hurriedly made a U-turn.

He then drove through the entrance just in time to see the BMW making a right turn into a dead-end parking area between two of the five-story apartment buildings.

He drew a deep breath and tried to quiet the jangling of his nerves and the pounding in his head. The initial search was over. But just to make sure, he drove up to the next parking area behind another apartment building, parked in a visitor's slot, and got out of the car.

After giving the blonde enough time to unload her shopping bags, Jordan walked back to the section where he had seen her turn. In a minute or two, he found the gray car, parked in front of stairwell A, next to a building marked number 131.

He wrote down those numbers on the same scrap of paper that bore the BMW's license plate number.

He rubbed his eyes and massaged his temples. He was exhausted. It was time to go home.

But he'd be back here — tomorrow.

12

The next morning before driving back out to Bad Tölz, Jordan went into Munich to do some shopping — for a hunting knife and some rope.

The rope he bought was 8-mm nylon, fifteen feet of it. The knife he finally selected was a German-made Hoffritz with a steel blade, eighteen and a half centimeters long. *When the time comes,* he thought, thumbing the keen edge of the blade, *this will do the job.*

His nostrils flared as he imagined what he would do to his son's killer, once he had him in his power. Because of some lawless animal, he thought, he would never have the opportunity to teach his son to ski . . . never get to support him in a career . . . never know the joy of watching him fall in love and marry . . .

His one and only son was now gone — and the murderer was going to suffer.

When he returned to his car, he tossed

the rope and knife into the trunk of his car and headed for Bad Tölz.

It was around noon when he reached the housing area. The BMW was gone from the parking slot where the blonde had parked it the night before.

He would wait, but not here in front of the apartment. To keep from arousing any suspicion, he drove out of the housing area and located a side street that intersected the main road leading to the housing area's main entrance. He selected a spot about a hundred and seventy meters from the entry street and pulled off the road onto the snow-covered shoulder, angling his car away from the street. Turning off the engine, he got out of the vehicle and lifted the hood, pretending to be a stranded motorist. Sitting in the front seat, he would have a clear view of any cars entering or leaving the housing complex.

He flipped up his coat collar, got a cap from the back seat, then settled in to wait for the silver, dented BMW to appear.

His mind started sifting through the possibilities he might encounter. Could the blond lady be married to a soldier considerably younger than she was? The minimum driving age in Germany was eighteen; could the woman have a younger brother or sister

143

living with her? As young as she looked, could she have a son or daughter who was already eighteen? Or had she herself been there on the night of the murder, and been mistaken at a distance for a teenager? Whoever in the family was involved, he would find them. He would work his way to them, one step at a time.

After waiting an hour or two, he started to feel cold. It was minus one degree Celsius outside — about thirty degrees Fahrenheit. The cold air was seeping into him, chilling him.

A tap came at the window. He looked up to see the face of an older man, who was motioning toward the lifted hood and saying something. Jordan rolled down the window.

"Haben sie Autokummer?" ("Having car trouble?") the stranger was asking.

Jordan shook his head and smiled. *"Mein Freund kommen,"* ("My friend is coming") he lied.

Hearing Jordan's American accent, the older man switched easily into English. "Are you sure? I will be glad to give you a ride somewhere."

"Thank you, no. He'll be here any moment, really."

The man shrugged, smiled, and

crunched away in the snow.

Jordan realized that the stranded motorist ploy wouldn't work indefinitely — at least not in the same location. Tomorrow he would have to figure out another way to maintain his surveillance or find another place to strand himself.

Shivering, he pulled his coat collar tighter around his neck.

Then the BMW came into view. It approached on the main road, slowing as it neared the entrance to the housing area. As the BMW turned in, Jordan jumped out of his car, slammed down the hood, and got back in.

He drove into the compound and made the right turn leading to the front of building 131. He saw the blond lady, alone, as she began climbing the three or four outside steps to the small front porch of stairwell A.

He parked in a visitor's slot about four cars from the BMW, trying to decide what to do. One part of him wanted to stay on the premises to see if he could come up with more information about others who had access to the BMW. The other part of him was tired and cold and welcomed the idea of returning home to a hot bath.

While he tried to decide what he should

do, he pulled out a road map of Munich from his glove compartment, opened it up, and feigned busyness. He let the engine idle, glad of the warm air starting to come from the heater. He looked at his watch. It was 2:55. Daring to take the risk of creating suspicion, he decided that he would stay put for one hour, to see if anyone else might use the BMW.

Ten minutes. He turned the car engine off. A few kids dressed in snowsuits were starting to walk home from the on-location elementary school.

Thirty minutes. He started to get cold again.

Forty-five minutes. He put the map away. For the first time he noticed Christmas decorations on some of the apartment windows — Santa Claus, reindeer, nativity scenes. Christmas seasons with Chase flashed in his mind. Tears came to his eyes.

Fifty minutes. A few cars had pulled into the street. A few adults had moved in and out of the apartments. But no one had approached the BMW.

He cranked his car and backed out.

Maybe tomorrow.

Susan watched as Jordan swallowed the

last of his morning coffee and reached for his coat. He glanced up at her and started buttoning his coat.

"You aren't going to the Institute, are you?" she asked.

He turned to stare at her. In silence.

She motioned toward the German texts lying on the counter. "You haven't even glanced at those books in weeks, other than to carry them out the door with you every morning. You aren't studying German, Jordan. So what are you doing every day? Where are you going?" She tried to keep her voice calm, but the edges of her control were beginning to unravel. Jordan's alienation from her and Donica had become unbearable. She and Jordan hadn't made love — hadn't even touched one another with affection — in weeks. She was frightened.

Jordan turned away. His voice was flat, uninflected — the voice of a machine. "I have to go now, Susan."

"Jordan! Wait! I know you're hurting. Can't you let me help carry some of the load? Why can't we all fight this thing to-gether?"

He turned back to look at her. For a fleeting instant, Susan thought she saw a flicker of . . . something. She started to throw herself into his arms when he wheeled about and walked out the door.

"Then why can't we just pack our belongings and go home?" she cried aloud toward the empty doorway.

With her insides collapsing in despair, she turned and saw Donica standing in the hallway, watching and listening.

Before getting on the autobahn for Bad Tölz, Jordan stopped at a public phone. He dialed the number for the Institute. When the receptionist answered the phone, he imitated a congested, weak voice. "Hello, Heidi, this is Jordan Rau," he husked. "I'm sorry, but this flu bug has still got me confined to the house. It's going to be a few more days before I can make it back to class. Can you please pass the word to Dr. Honecker?"

"Certainly, Herr Rau," she responded in slightly accented English. "I will tell him. I'm so sorry you're still sick."

"Thanks," he said, with a cough. "Goodbye." He hung up and stepped out of the phone cubicle, striding briskly toward his car.

Driving toward Bad Tölz, he planned his strategy for the day. Instead of posing as a stranded motorist, he decided that once he got to the apartments he would enter into stairwell C of building 133, facing directly across the street from stairwell A of building 131.

He would start at the fifth floor and knock on the two apartment doors on that landing. If someone came to the door, he would pretend that he was out visiting on behalf of St. Jude's Church in Munich. However, if no one came to either of the doors on that landing, he would remain there — assuming that no one was at home in either of the two apartments — and use that landing and its outside window as an observation deck to monitor the BMW and the people going in and out of stairwell A of 131.

He had five floors — five chances — in stairwell C to find a private observation point. The same in stairwell B. If that didn't work, he would make his final move over to stairwell A. He had three stairwells, each with five floors. Fifteen chances to find a vacated and secure landing.

When he exited the autobahn at Holzkirchen, he stopped at a travel agency. He spent about forty minutes talking with one of the agents, getting a list of all the airline carriers that flew from Munich to New York and Atlanta. He also wrote down a list of their best prices. He wanted to begin to prepare for his family's quick departure from the country.

By the time he arrived at the housing area in Bad Tölz it was around nine forty-five.

As he turned onto the parking street between buildings 131 and 133, he decided to park at the head of the street, away from the other end of the apartment buildings where he would be waiting. He didn't want to make it easy for anyone to link him with his car and license plate number.

He took a quick glance across the way and saw that the gray BMW was in its parking place.

When he entered into the stairwell C foyer, he took a deep breath, slowed down, and headed upward to the fifth floor. As he climbed the steps, he went over in his mind what he was going to say when people came to the doors.

He stopped at the third-floor landing to assess the view of the entryway to stairwell A across the parking area. Excellent.

He had just started turning away toward the fourth floor stairway to finish his climb when a glimpse of something moving on the outside caught his eye.

The entry door to stairwell A had been flung open, hard. Even through the stairwell window where he was standing, he heard the big metal door across the street bang against its doorstop at the top level of the outside steps.

Through the door burst an angry-looking, dark-haired teenager. Clenching his fists, the boy turned and started shouting at someone who was following him down the stairwell.

The person pursuing the teenage boy was the blond driver of the BMW.

Jordan watched the woman rush up to the boy, yell at him face-to-face, then slap him.

Jordan's mind was churning. Could this be the young person he was looking for? Maybe the boy was a neighbor. Or maybe he was the younger of two or three brothers — he didn't look old enough to drive. Maybe he knew nothing about Chase's death.

But when Jordan saw the boy shove the woman out of the way — nearly throwing her to the ground — then run to the BMW and jump in, his limbs flooded with adrenaline.

He was down to the second-floor landing and moving fast when he saw the smoky exhaust spew from the tailpipe of the BMW.

Taking three steps at a time, he reached the ground-level landing in seconds. Before pushing his way through the outside door, he jerked his coat collar up around his face. And then he was outside.

The BMW was already spinning its tires backing out of its designated space.

Not wanting the woman to get a good look at his face, he avoided looking in her direction. Instead, he focused on his own car at the end of the street and broke into a jog.

The BMW shot past him before he covered half the distance.

No! he shouted to himself. *I can't let him get away!*

By the time he reached his car, he saw the BMW gunning its engine at the exit/entryway stop sign, waiting for traffic to pass so that it could pull out onto the main road.

"Can't let him get away!" Jordan repeated, this time out loud.

Looking into the rearview mirror as he started his car, he saw the BMW turn right out of the housing area.

At least the boy was taking the direction leading out of town, away from the maze of city streets.

As Jordan launched his car in reverse, trying with difficulty not to spin his wheels, he took a quick glance in the mirror to see if the blonde's attention had been attracted by him. The mirror was at the wrong angle. He couldn't see if she was watching him or not.

Not taking the time to turn around and look over his shoulder, he moved away as quickly as he could.

When he turned right on the main road, he tried to drive normally for the first two hundred or so yards, until the apartments were no longer in view.

Once he was out of the apartment's range of vision, he quickly accelerated to around seventy miles per hour. As far as he knew, there were no other cars between him and the BMW. Now it was a simple matter of driving as fast as he could.

He started slinging his automobile through tight curves as the road wound its way through a heavily forested area. He tried not to slow his speed. He knew he was risking an accident, but he had to catch up. Fortunately the Germans were punctilious about salting and clearing their roadways in winter.

After three or four minutes, he still had not spotted the BMW. What was wrong? What had happened? Had the boy turned off onto one of the several side roads he had passed?

He was just about to slap his steering wheel in frustration when he swung out of a curve and saw the BMW up ahead, disappearing over the crest of a hill. He gunned the engine, and the car lanced forward.

Jordan's mind went into overdrive. Should he strike now? Or should he continue to trail the boy and pick up more information? Maybe he could plan his attack for a later, more ideal time. But . . . would this be his last chance? Could it be that the blond woman saw him leaving the apartments just now, recognized his car as the same car that followed her from Munich two days earlier? Would she be suspicious? Would she alert the authorities?

Then the image of Chase's body flashed into his mind. The stiff, decaying corpse of his son, lying on the gurney in the cold morgue.

With renewed rage and blood lust, his jaw clenched and his hands tightened around the steering wheel.

He would not wait for another chance.

He would strike now.

And he would make it work.

He stomped the accelerator. He whispered as the car sped forward: "This is for you, son . . ."

13

Ricardo swore as he drove, calling his mother every foul name he could think of, when the honking of a car horn jolted him out of his inner world.

What the — !

There was a car on the wrong side of the road, running side by side with him.

Was this guy an idiot? What was he trying to — ?

Then Ricardo saw the big man in the other car hold up some kind of official identification card and motion for him to pull over.

Ricardo's nerves jolted with panic.

Before he had a chance to react, he saw the man speed around to the front of him and start flashing his brake lights.

Who was this man? What did he want?

Ricardo's breath was coming in quick, shallow gasps. He started to go around the man. He looked at the license plate now staring him in the face. It was German.

It didn't make sense. Was this guy an undercover German cop in an unmarked car who had clocked him speeding?

That's what it is, he thought. Great. He was deep in it now, for sure. He evaluated his chances of losing the guy, and decided against it. The cop was certainly more familiar with the roads than he was. Ricardo followed the car over onto the side of the road and turned off his engine.

Unless . . . unless this was someone else — someone who knew something about what happened in the woods that night. Feeling trapped and panicked, Ricardo reached for the ignition switch.

But it was too late.

His driver's-side door was yanked open with so much force that it nearly came off the hinges.

Stuffing his German bank card into his back pocket, Jordan stood there breathing hard, face-to-face with the dark-haired kid in the BMW.

"Do you speak English?" Jordan shouted at him in a feigned German accent.

Fear, strain, and uncertainty spread across the teenager's face. He didn't respond to Jordan's question. His eyes darted back and forth, from Jordan's face to the road.

Jordan looked up and down the highway. There were no cars in sight, in either direction.

He grabbed the boy by the wrist, squeezed until he saw pain in the boy's eyes and said, "Follow me to my car."

"Who are you? What is this —" the boy gasped.

With one quick swoop, Jordan's free hand was around the back of the boy's neck. "I'll tell you one more time," he said with fire in his eyes. "Get out of your car. Now!"

The boy slowly began getting out.

Jordan grabbed the front of his shirt and hauled him out of the BMW.

The boy grunted in fear and pain. "What do you think you're —"

Jordan kicked the BMW's front door closed with his foot and shoved the boy through the snow to his waiting car, its engine still running.

Holding the boy's collar with one hand, Jordan opened the driver's-side door and forced the teenager's head down and through the opening. "Crawl through," he growled.

"You can't do this!" the boy objected.

Ignoring him, Jordan gave him a forceful shove. With the electric panel on the armrest of the driver's door, he locked all four doors and crawled in behind the wheel.

Jordan yanked the car into gear and pulled out onto the road, his tires spinning on the wet, salty asphalt.

The boy was approaching hysteria. He was trying to maintain an attitude of defiance, but he was starting to tremble. His eyes were wide with fear.

Once Jordan had shifted through the gears, he put out his hand and said, "Let me have your driver's license."

"Who are you? Where are you taking me? Why do you want my license?" The boy's shrill words erupted from a quavering throat.

"Your license!" Jordan snapped, thumping him in the chest with his fist.

The boy was now sweating. He removed his billfold, pulled out his license, and with obvious confusion and hesitancy handed over the plastic-sealed card.

Jordan took it, scanning its vital information.

"Ricardo Alvarez," Jordan said out loud as he slipped the license into his coat pocket. He pronounced the name as if it tasted like sour spit. He looked over at Ricardo and grated, "You're in big trouble, boy."

"What are you talking about, man! I wasn't going that fast!"

Without even looking at him, Jordan said, "We're going for a ride, Ricardo. A little ride — just you and me." By now, he no longer bothered to maintain the false German accent. The game was over.

Ricardo was scooted over against the passenger door, staring with panic at the man who had grabbed him from the BMW. He was scared witless, but it was a new kind of fear. Ricardo thought the man must be crazy or something. He was driving about seventy miles an hour, daring the car to spin out of control on the sharp curves. A sneer was on his face as he glanced back and forth from the winding road to his unwilling passenger. This guy didn't act like any cop he had ever encountered. Ricardo was more afraid than he had ever been in his life.

Forty minutes later, Jordan parked the car on a desolate side road at the foot of one of the baby Alps south of Schliersee, near the Austrian border.

When they stopped — not at an official building or office, but in a wooded area in the middle of nowhere — the fear in Ricardo's eyes leaped into horror. What was the guy going to do to him?

Grabbing Ricardo by the nape of the neck, Jordan pulled him out of the car through the driver's side, then around to the back of the car.

"Bon voyage, punk," Jordan said as he opened the trunk and pulled out an old rag.

"You're not the police, are you?" Ricardo could barely make his voice work.

"Who I am is not important, Ricardo. What's important is that we both know who you are — don't we?"

Ricardo gulped. "I don't know what you're —"

Before Ricardo saw it coming, the big man clamped his hand over Ricardo's mouth and nose, cutting off his words and his breath.

"Shut up!" Jordan barked at him. Then he shoved the rag through Ricardo's clenched jaws, tying it in a painfully tight knot on the back of his head. He could hear the gagging sounds the boy made as he tried to get his tongue clear of the obstruction.

When the boy tried to break free and run, Jordan tripped him up with his foot.

Lifting him off the snow-covered ground as if he were a pound of flour, Jordan slung him hard against the car — so hard that

160

the boy collapsed to his knees. He was whimpering hysterically through the gag as Jordan went back to the trunk of his car and removed the fifteen feet of rope and the hunting knife.

He then patted snow on his front and back license plates to conceal his car's registration number. Just in case someone with a keen eye for detail passed through the area.

"All right, let's go," Jordan told the boy while motioning into the woods. "You can walk, or I'll drag you; it's your choice."

Ricardo stumbled to his feet.

For forty minutes Jordan led him by the arm deep into the woods, then about two hundred yards up the side of a mountain. A few times along the way, he had to haul the boy roughly over fallen trees and up steep, snow-covered grades.

Finally Jordan halted in front of a tree on the side of the mountain, and shoved Ricardo against the trunk. He began unwinding the rope that had been draped around his shoulder.

At that moment the terror in Ricardo's heart made him fall to the ground and weep for mercy. He tried desperately to accompany those tears with words, but the rag running through his mouth turned his speaking attempts into muffled high-pitched grunts and groans.

Once again Jordan lifted him from the ground.

As he began tying Ricardo to the tree, the youth started shaking. His young face became wet with tears and sweat; his eyes were squinting so badly he could hardly hold them open.

By the time Jordan finished securing the boy to the tree, he had used all fifteen feet of rope. The boy's feet, legs, arms, and torso were pulled so tightly against the tree trunk that they were incapable of any movement. Only the boy's head was free to shift from side to side. But the gag was still in place, forbidding him to speak.

Jordan stepped back and looked at his prey. He didn't see a terrified boy who was close in age to his son. Ricardo Alvarez was not a person to him, he was a perpetrator. A "subject," as the police termed it, who matched a description and who drove a vehicle that was involved in the death of his son. The question that mattered now was whether or not the bound and gagged figure had taken part in the killings, or possessed information that would lead Jordan to those who had.

It was now time for justice.

Staring at Ricardo with crazed eyes, Jordan slowly removed the hunting knife from his coat pocket.

"Look like a familiar weapon, boy?" Jordan hissed, holding the knife in front of Ricardo's face.

Ricardo's eyes closed tightly. His teeth clamped down on the rag.

Now breathing in a smooth and controlled rhythm — like a personified machine — Jordan drew back his arm and waited for Ricardo to open his eyes. His mind was now empty of every other thought. He was ready.

The moment Ricardo opened his eyes, Jordan plunged the knife deep into the tree about three inches above Ricardo's head. He watched as every muscle in Ricardo's body went rigid.

"Fun, isn't it?" Jordan remarked with an evil grin.

As he pulled the knife out of the wood and cocked his arm again, he said, "And the fun is just getting started."

As Ricardo clenched his eyes, Jordan plunged the knife again, this time a few inches from the right side of Ricardo's face.

"Now then, Mr. Alvarez, I want you to hold your head real still," Jordan said as he worked the knife loose from the tree. "I want to see how good my aim really is."

Replaying in his mind the imagined scenario of Chase and Heather's death, Jordan then slowly shifted on his feet until his back was toward Ricardo.

With a yell of fresh agony, he spun around and drove the knife into the tree so close to Ricardo's face that the blade grazed Ricardo's jaw.

Ricardo screamed through the saliva-soaked rag, his body convulsed with terror.

Jordan heard a trickling sound in the snow at Ricardo's feet. The teenager was urinating in his pants.

"Like I said, it's a whole lot of fun, isn't it, boy?"

When Ricardo's shock started to subside, Jordan spoke to him again. This time he held the knife between Ricardo's legs. "In just a moment, I'm going to let you talk. I'll give you one chance to tell me everything you know about the murder of Chase Rau and Heather Anne Moseley. You remember them, don't you, son? Two nice kids who got jumped in some woods near Bad Aibling? You're going to tell me everything you know about what happened. And you better make it good, because if you're not convincing —" He stabbed the tree close to Ricardo's groin three quick times, as the boy yelped in fear. "Do I make myself clear?" he finished.

The muscles in Ricardo's neck were almost too rigid for him to nod his cooperation, but he finally managed a quick, spasmodic assent.

Knowing that Ricardo had now been sufficiently traumatized, Jordan used the knife to cut away the gag from Ricardo's mouth.

"Now talk to me, Ricardo," Jordan prompted when the rag fell free.

"I didn't do it! I didn't do it!" He wailed and wept, alternating with bouts of hard coughing and panting. "It was the Jamaicans! They did the killing! It wasn't me, man! It was the three Jamaicans!" The boy's words came out in a garbled rush, driven by his blinding terror. "I wasn't even a part of their group! I didn't know there was going to be any killing, or I wouldn't have gone, I swear! You gotta believe me, man, I'm telling the truth! I didn't do it! It was the Jamaicans . . . the three Jamaicans . . ." Ricardo's words melted into tears of desperation. His head bobbed up and down on his shoulders as he gasped for breath.

Jordan mentally recorded everything he

was hearing, waiting in silence for the boy to speak again.

When Ricardo caught his breath, he repeated his effort to make Jordan believe him. "The Jamaicans were just visiting from the States. I met them at the Burger King in Munich. We were only going to —" Realizing that he was on the verge of demolishing his own innocence, he stopped his confession in mid-sentence.

Jordan saw turmoil appear on the boy's face. "You were only going to what?" Jordan asked fiercely.

"I had just met the Jamaicans," Ricardo panicked. "It was their idea. I didn't want to go along, but they didn't give me a choice. They —"

"You were only going to *what?*" Jordan demanded again, grabbing Ricardo's face in a clawlike grip.

"I was just looking at a girl, that's all," he blubbered. "They asked me if I wanted her, and the next thing I know, we're following her to see where she lives. They made me go with them, man! They wanted to . . ." Ricardo's head twisted to one side. "They wanted to . . . to . . ."

"To *rape* her, Ricardo?"

"It was their decision, man!" Ricardo blurted.

166

Jordan knew the autopsy revealed that Heather had been raped prior to her death, but to hear one of the assailants confessing it was like watching a videocassette recording of the most tragic moment in his life. Seeing it, hearing it, and feeling it all over again. Before he knew what he was doing, Jordan's fist had tensed around the grip of his knife, the tendons of his arms tightening, ready to thrust the blade one final time . . .

No! he tried to convince himself. *Not yet. Not until I know everything . . .*

Jordan rubbed his face with his free hand, hard and slow. He had to be patient.

A few seconds later, he said, "All right, we're going to start from the beginning. I'll ask the questions, you answer them."

Ricardo gulped and nodded.

"First, I want you to tell me about the Jamaicans."

"All I know about them is that they're from Detroit. They're a part of a Jamaican drug posse, and their names are Ottey, Tito, and Martin. That's all I know, I swear."

"How did you meet them?"

"I had gone to the Burger King to eat lunch that day. I was in the restroom and was coming out when the Jamaicans came in and nearly knocked me down with the door. I didn't know who they were or anything. Before I could see them I yelled at them for banging me around. Then Ottey came in and threw me into one of the toilet stalls and threatened to cut my throat. They did cut me a little and made me bleed, and then made me apologize for yelling at them. Then they made me buy them lunch. I'd never seen them before until that day."

"Then how did you know they're from Detroit?"

"They were bragging about their drug posse . . . the Caribbean Parade or something like that. They said they live in Detroit, that that's where their turf is. That's all they said about themselves, except that they've killed people before."

"How do you know they don't live here in Germany?" Jordan pressed.

Ricardo paused and tried to think. "I don't know . . . I just . . . I do remember seeing a plane ticket. Ottey, the leader, said something to one of the others. I think it was the one called Martin. He pulled out a plane ticket from his jacket, held it up for Ottey to see, and then put it away again."

"You're sure it was a plane ticket?"

"Yeah, I'm sure!"

"All right, back to the Burger King," said Jordan. "What happened after you bought their lunch?"

"When we were eating, the girl came in. I guess I got caught up in looking at her. The Jamaicans asked me if I wanted her. Before I even knew if they were serious, they had made plans to follow her home to see where she lived. They said we'd take her the next day. I —"

"So you all followed her home?" Jordan interrupted as loathing boiled up inside him again.

"Only two of the Jamaicans."

"And you?" Jordan demanded to know, his voice growing louder.

"I . . . I . . . I didn't think I had a choice!" Ricardo cried out. "They made me drive. I thought they'd kill me if I didn't go with them!"

Jordan paused, breathing deeply. "So you took the BMW?"

Ricardo grunted an affirmation. "We followed her to her house in Bad Aibling . . . The Jamaican who followed her from the bus stop to her house decided that the woods would be a good place to . . . to, uh . . . he said it . . . it would, uh . . ." Ricardo started to stutter.

"What day of the week was that, Ricardo?"

"It was, uh . . . a . . . Thursday."

"So you were waiting for her the next day?"

"Yeah . . . we waited for her there in the . . . in the woods." Ricardo's head dropped in shame.

"Then what happened?"

"We weren't, uh . . . expecting a guy to be with her. I thought we would call it off, but the Jamaicans said . . . said the guy would make it more fun . . . That we would . . . uh . . ." The boy fell silent, his eyes averted.

" 'That you would' what, Ricardo?" Jordan said, grabbing the boy's face again and bumping his head forcefully into the tree trunk.

"Make him . . . make him watch. I never thought . . ."

"Make him *watch?*" Jordan exhaled the words like a maddened bull breathing hot air.

Ricardo's chest heaved with renewed fear. "Yeah, that's what they said. These guys were crazy, man! But things, uh . . . kinda got out of hand . . ." The boy began blubbering again as he approached the moment of ultimate confession.

"Yeah, things got out of hand," Jordan growled, then cursed beneath his breath.

"Just *how* out of hand did things get, Ricardo?"

Ricardo panted, not wanting to go any further.

Jordan slapped him. "I asked you a question, punk!"

The boy began gibbering. "When, uh . . . Martin and Tito jumped . . . jumped the girl, Ottey grabbed the guy and held a knife to his throat. When the guy saw what Martin and Tito were going to do to the girl, he, uh . . . he tried to break loose and fight for her. He started fighting so hard that he, uh . . . he . . . cut his own throat . . . nearly all the way through."

"He cut his *own* throat? You mean they *murdered* him, don't you? Isn't that what you're trying to say?"

"There was nothing I could do, don't you understand?" Ricardo wailed. "Ottey would have killed me, too!"

"Did he murder him, Ricardo?" Jordan yelled.

"Yes! He murdered him, okay?" Ricardo yelled, his voice breaking.

But Jordan wasn't finished.

"Tell me about the girl — Heather," he said.

Ricardo gulped several times, struggling to begin speaking again. "Ottey, uh . . . decided that since the girl had witnessed the killing . . . that she would . . . have to die, too. So they loaded them both in the car . . ."

Jordan recalled Gagic's original sighting. He had seen a person being carried on someone's shoulder across the field — Chase. He had added that there was someone walking with the group who was crying, and that it sounded like a female — Heather.

"Was the girl still alive when they took her to the car?" Jordan asked.

"Yes. We drove out of Bad Aibling —" Ricardo drew a deep breath — "to a wooded area we found several miles away. And then Martin and Tito . . . they, uh . . . they . . ."

Jordan grabbed Ricardo around the neck and squeezed while holding the boy's head straight up. "They *what*, Ricardo?"

Putting his face inches away from Ricardo's, Jordan continued to squeeze. "What did they do, Ricardo?"

"They . . . ahhhh . . . ahhh . . . raped her . . ." Ricardo managed to answer in a choked whisper. Jordan slowly released him. Ricardo gasped, his head surging upward for air.

Jordan stepped back, flexing his fingers.

The things he had just heard twisted in an obscene tangle inside his brain. "Two more things, Ricardo. Then we're finished. I want you to think clearly. First, I want to know which one of the Jamaicans knifed her to death. And then I want to know — and God knows I'll find out if you lie to me — if you took part in either the rape or the murders."

"It was —" the boy gasped for air again — "the one they call Martin . . . He's the one who knifed her . . . All I did was . . . drive the stupid car."

Jordan's blade flashed toward Ricardo's throat.

Ricardo stiffened, and his eyes flew open with terror. But instead of feeling his throat being cut, Ricardo heard the knife sawing through the nylon rope. Within two minutes he was free, sitting in the snow at the foot of the tree. He looked up and saw the big man walking away.

Jordan walked about six yards, then stopped. He turned, lifted his arm, and pointed at Ricardo. "If you've lied to me, I'll be back," he said. "I know where you live, Ricardo, and I know who your mother is. I'll be watching your every move. And in case you decide to run," he added, "I'll reveal your identity to the military police, the German police, the girl's father, and the boy's father. After that, you'll either be dead or in prison for the rest of your life. Think about it."

With his mind now focused on the Jamaicans, Jordan turned and walked out of the woods, leaving the boy to get back to the stranded BMW on his own.

14

Jordan walked into the apartment in the middle of the afternoon, and found Susan asleep on the couch. Looking down at her, he heard a small voice in the back of his skull asking, *What are you doing, Rau? What are you doing to your wife, your daughter? Chase is gone and you can't bring him back. What about the people who are left?*

Sternly he resisted such thinking. The worst is over now, he told himself. I've got the information I need. When I get back from Detroit, I can move Susan and Donica out of Germany, back home — back to Chattanooga, if that's what they want.

Again he glanced down at Susan. Her eyes were now open, studying him with a mixture of desperation and sadness. He collected his thoughts. His next words needed to be convincing. He sat down beside her, taking one of her hands in his.

"I've considered what you told me," he

said to her. "Maybe . . . maybe you're right. Maybe I do need help."

She roused slightly, her eyes taking on a new, more hopeful expression.

"Why don't I fly back to the States? I'll meet with the personnel committee in Chesapeake to discuss our situation. If they recommend that we move back to the States, then I'll fly down to Chattanooga, secure a rental house, and then come back to get you and Donica. I should be back in about two or three weeks."

Her eyes were wide, her mouth hanging open in surprise. "Jordan, are you . . . I can't believe what you're saying, after the way you've —"

"I know, I know," he interrupted. "Things have been pretty bad around here. I haven't been . . . I haven't been myself. I know that."

Her hand was on his arm, gently touching, encouraging. He knew she was responding to the sincerity he was putting in his voice. Again, that annoying voice spoke to him: *You're lying to her, Rau! You know it! You're setting her up for another cruel disappointment!* He shut the ears of his conscience against it. Perhaps when his mission was all over — when he had secured justice for his son . . . and for himself —

perhaps then he would be able to deal with other considerations, other people's needs.

Susan sensed his hesitation. "What's wrong, Jordan? There's something else you want to say, isn't there?"

He looked away, unable to admit it, unwilling to tell the truth.

"Jordan! Don't do this! There's something else, isn't there?" Her voice was rising as she sat bolt upright on the couch. "Why are you really going back? It has something to do with the way you've been spending your days here, doesn't it? Something about the murders? What do you know that you're not telling us?"

I don't need this, Jordan thought. He got up to leave the room.

Before he reached the door, he heard Susan jump up off the couch.

"Jordan, you can't keep going on like this. You're poisoning your family, can't you see that? Whatever's going on, Jordan, you're not helping Chase — or yourself, or us. You're killing Donica . . . you're killing me . . . just as surely as those people killed Chase! Don't you understand that?"

Her last words froze him in place. For a moment, he teetered on the brink of decision. But his hatred and his lust for revenge were too strong.

"Look," he said, turning on her, "if you'll just leave me alone, everything will be over in a few weeks!"

"I'm going to the police, Jordan," she said in a low voice. "I can't let you do this to yourself, or to us!"

Before he realized what he was doing, Jordan leaped across the room, grabbed Susan's shoulders, and started squeezing. "You're not going to the police, Susan!" he threatened, as he pushed her up against a wall.

Never before in their twenty years of marriage had he touched her in an abusive or angry manner. Shock replaced the anger in his expression. He released her with the motion of someone who has grabbed a hot pan.

"Susan, I . . . I'm sorry. I know that was out of line. But . . . you've got to understand; I've got to be left alone. Just for a while longer. I can't explain right now, but . . . in a few weeks, everything will be okay. I promise."

Her eyes were wide and scared, her face ashen as she stared at him. In a voice that was barely above a whisper, she said, "When, Jordan? When will it be okay? After you've destroyed us all? Is that when it's going to be okay?"

He turned away again and started to walk out, but not before being arrested by her next words.

"Why do you call yourself a Christian, Jordan?" she asked through tears. "You're not a follower of Christ; you're a follower of Jordan Rau." She continued staring at him. "You believe only in yourself, you listen only to yourself. That's why you never hear God's voice. Isn't that right, Jordan?"

Still standing against the wall where he had shoved her, she added, "I'm praying for you, Jordan, and I won't ever stop."

Jordan's shoulders stiffened with resistance. Realizing he could no longer reason with her, he turned and headed for the door. "I'll be flying out of Munich tomorrow," he said, slamming the door behind him.

Staring at the closed door, Susan whispered, "No, I'll never stop praying for you . . . but I don't know if it will do any good."

◆ Part 3

15

Jordan's TWA flight landed at Detroit Metropolitan Airport at 7:04 p.m. He eased his carry-on bag to the floor of the concourse and stretched. The flight, including a two-hour layover and aircraft change at JFK in New York, had taken thirteen hours. He was tired.

He claimed his luggage, rented a nondescript car at the Budget counter, bought a city map, then made his way to the courtesy shuttle that would take him to the rented car. When he stepped outside to board the shuttle, a cold, wet wind shoved him to one side. *Trading Munich weather for Detroit weather,* he thought. *Not a profitable exchange . . .*

Not unless he could somehow find the three Jamaicans.

Riding on the shuttle, he stared ahead as thoughts chased one another inside his mind. Susan had refused to tell him goodbye this morning. Seeing him prepare to leave, she had looked the other way. Donica managed to give him a half-hearted hug before he walked out the door.

It had now become clear to him that Susan and Donica were both hurting because of his neglect. With a few pangs of guilt, he leaned his forehead against the window of the bus. Maybe he should call home and try to talk to Susan again. Maybe he . . .

No! He was here now. He couldn't allow himself to be deflected. Susan and Donica would just have to give him more time. One day they would understand. One day they would . . .

The shuttle stopped with a jerk, and the passengers got up. Jordan rose with them, his face a blank mask, and shuffled out of the bus to claim his rental car. He was here. He would go forward with his quest.

As he drove down the expressway, he consulted his city map. He was approaching the inner-city district, where he wanted to target the initial phase of his search. Exiting the expressway, he began looking for a place to stay overnight. After driving several blocks, he spotted a sign that directed him to a slightly seedy, inexpensive-looking motel. He hoped it would help give him a low profile.

He checked in and tossed his bags on the velour-covered bed in his room. He was hungry. Bundling his coat about him, he walked out into the chilly night toward a twenty-four-hour grill he had spotted nearby.

He ate a cheeseburger and fries while he thought about different ways to begin his search. He was sitting in a smoky hangout in the middle of a city with over a million people. He did not know a single person who lived here. No relatives. No friends. No acquaintances. It wasn't as if he could just go to the police station and ask for information about Jamaican drug gangs in the area. He would then be spotlighted as a suspect after Ottey, Martin, and Tito were found dead. He wanted no official involvement of any sort, so he had to stay away from the welfare office, the city hall, the local school board, and any other public office that might otherwise be the source of a helpful lead.

Somehow, on his own, he would have to come up with a way to find the Jamaican community. But without help, he wasn't even sure he would recognize such a community if he stumbled onto it.

With no concrete ideas, but with his brain still churning, he finally left the grill and returned to the motel room.

Alone in the shabby room, he switched on the television set while he unpacked the suitcases and put away his clothes.

When the picture finally appeared, it was not worth watching. The image was fuzzy, the faces were purplish, and the sound was mixed with static. He twisted the control knobs in every conceivable combination, but the picture got no better. He switched off the set.

He decided he should try to get some sleep, after unpacking his clothes and taking a bath. He hadn't been able to sleep much on the plane. But the quietness around him made the room feel hostile. Jordan turned on the clock radio on the nightstand next to the bed. *That's better,* he thought as he started undressing. The nondescript music and talk made him feel less alone as he went into the tiled bathroom and turned on the water to fill the tub.

After bathing himself, he lay back and soaked in the hot water, trying to relax his body as well as his mind. A slow, melodic instrumental tune came on the radio which at first he found soothing. But as the meditative rhythm and melody progressed, he found himself lulled once again into thoughts of Susan and Donica.

Was he really so close to destroying his

family? *You're killing Donica and me,* Susan had said. *You're poisoning your family . . . You believe only in yourself, listen only to yourself . . .*

Not wanting to deal right now with those disturbing thoughts, he got out of the tub to change the radio station. What he needed to hear was a football game, he decided. That would get his mind out of this rut of melancholy.

Wrapped in a towel, he started scanning the different channels looking for a sports broadcast. He struck a strong signal, and paused to listen.

Then the phone rang.

Startled, Jordan reached beside the radio and lifted the receiver. "Hello."

"This is the front desk, Mr. Rau," a male voice said. "I'm sorry, but what time did you say you wanted that wake-up call?"

Jordan lifted his eyebrows. "Seven-thirty," he said.

After hanging up, then reaching again for the radio knob to continue his search, he started hearing the voice on the tuned-in station:

". . . retired Jamaican doctor who is now giving his free time to work with the inner-city Jamaican youth here in our city of Detroit . . ."

Jordan removed his hand from the knob and left the dial in place.

"Again," the voice continued, "you are cordially invited to attend this first annual missions conference being hosted by the All People's Church of Detroit, located in midtown on the corner of Warren Avenue and East Grand. The services begin nightly at six-thirty . . ."

Jordan opened the bedside table's single drawer, seeking a piece of motel stationery and a pencil, as he repeated to himself the facts he needed to remember — "All People's Church, corner of Warren and, uh . . . Grand . . . no, East Grand. Six-thirty."

Finding a pen but no stationery, he wrote down the information on his hand, then transferred it a few seconds later to the back of his airplane ticket envelope.

He wasn't a believer in miracles, but this was an odd and opportune coincidence. Now — was there a way he could use this information to help him in his search?

For nearly a half-hour, he tossed the question around in his head. Attending a missions meeting at a church seemed an unlikely way to track down a drug gang. On the other hand, this retired doctor was involved with Jamaicans in the inner city. Where else would a Jamaican drug ring operate, other than among Jamaicans in the inner city?

Jordan knew he couldn't just approach the doctor with all his questions. But he could perhaps go to the church service, identify the doctor when he spoke, then covertly follow him to his home after the meeting. If the man worked with Jamaican young people in the inner city, then maybe he lived in an inner-city Jamaican community. If he didn't, then he could always be followed later to the places where he conducted his ministry.

It wasn't an ideal plan. But at least it was a beginning.

Later, lying in the dark, his restless mind couldn't stop thinking about Susan and Donica. He wondered if Susan had already called the mission headquarters in Virginia to confirm what she no doubt suspected — that he had indeed been lying about his destination and purpose for returning to the States.

You're killing us . . . He flopped over onto his stomach and fluffed the lumpy pillow for the fifth time. He was fatigued, but sleep evaded him. The combination of the strangeness of the place and the troublesome thoughts in his head were conspiring to keep him awake. He tried to focus on the information that might lead him closer to his objective: retired Jamaican doctor . . . tomorrow night, at the corner of Warren and East Grand . . . All People's Church . . . tomorrow night . . .

Biding his time until the evening missions service, Jordan spent the late morning and early afternoon hours walking some of the city streets, questioning alcoholics and street people about their knowledge of Jamaican districts. The tiring effort, both to his legs and to his patience, produced nothing more than a few shameless pleas for his pocket change.

On the way to the church service that evening, Jordan spotted another potential source for information — street prostitutes. They were drug users, weren't they? If the missions meeting led him to a dead end, he could start questioning the street walkers.

By the time Jordan located the church building, the time was 6:27, three minutes before the church service was supposed to begin.

He parked on the street as close to the building as he could. He waited in the car until 6:35, then went into the building, hoping to find a seat near the back so he could make a quick exit.

Inside the auditorium, about fifty people were present in a sanctuary that could easily seat three hundred or more. They were all sitting up near the front. A quick exit, he realized, would not be a problem.

Good, Jordan thought. *The fewer people to see my face, the better.* He took a seat behind the last row of people.

One of the men in front of him turned around, said "Welcome" with a handshake and a smile, and handed him a program for the evening.

Scanning the two-page sheet while an elderly white lady sang a special solo, Jordan noticed that three men were scheduled to speak. The first was a Raymond Stewart, listed on the program as "Acting Director, Detroit's Inner-City Gospel Mission." He was scheduled for a fifteen-minute presentation. The next speaker was given a full hour — Jason Faircloth, a pastor from a church in New York City. Last on the program, with a scheduled allotment of only ten minutes, was a Dr. Percival Blake, listed as "Retired Physician from Jamaica."

Jordan was chagrined to realize that he had to sit through a one-and-a-half-hour program. He could think of better ways to spend a Saturday evening. He just hoped

191

that the long and unpleasant wait would pay off.

As the soloist began a second song, Jordan's eyes and mind started to wander.

A slow and careful gaze about the room confirmed what he had guessed when he approached the building from the outside. The facility was at least fifty years old, maybe older. And in recent years, very little money had been spent to maintain it. The tiny three-sided balcony, so constructed because of the narrowness of the sanctuary, looked as if it had sagged in several places through the years. The paint on the ceiling was cracked, and the carpet was so worn and threadbare that it looked as if it might be the original carpeting. Overall, the building looked . . . like an inner-city church.

Except . . .

Except that the people sitting in the pews were not all lower-class people. Many were, or appeared to be. But there were just as many others who appeared to be middle-class. Both black and white, as well as a few who were foreign-looking. The unexpected mixture of race and class made the congregation look a little strange, especially if this was the regular crowd.

Once the soloist finished her second

song, Jordan saw a young man — twentyish-looking — stand up from the first row of pews and go to the front.

"Thank you, Mrs. Parks, for the beautiful songs," he said, smiling at the older woman. "And thanks, everyone, for being here tonight. We've had good representation all three nights of the conference so far, and tonight is no exception. I want to be sure and encourage you to be here tomorrow morning at ten o'clock for the final session."

From the young man's relaxed presentation and articulate style, Jordan assumed he was part of the church leadership — probably the minister of music or assistant pastor, or maybe even the senior pastor.

"Now please give your attention to Raymond Stewart from the Inner-City Gospel Mission," the young man said. "He's a very special man with a very special ministry." He went on to say a few more things about Stewart and his work at the downtown mission.

But Jordan wasn't listening to much of the introduction. His only desire was to see and identify Dr. Percival Blake so he could trail him at the conclusion of the service.

When Raymond Stewart, a middle-aged African American, took the floor and started speaking, Jordan grew even more impatient. The man might be a saint, Jordan admitted to himself, but whoever or whatever else he was, he was not a public speaker. The guy sounds like a high school dropout, he thought to himself. Jordan kept looking at his watch. The fifteen-minute presentation seemed like forty. Jordan was relieved when the man finally sat down.

The young church leader stood again, earnestly thanking Stewart for his report and for the work he was doing. He then began to introduce the next speaker, Jason Faircloth.

"For the few of you who didn't make it to the three previous services, let me repeat that Jason Faircloth has had more of a positive influence in my life and ministry than anyone else on the face of the earth.

"Seven months ago, with the help of my home church in New York City, I rented this church building — which had been standing empty for over a year — and started the All People's Church. I made that move, and I stand here today as your pastor, mainly because of the influence of this man.

"If you haven't had the opportunity yet, make the effort tonight or tomorrow to sit down and talk with him. He's got a life story so incredible that, if he wanted to, he could hold you on the edge of your seat for hours telling you about it.

"I'm not going to waste his time trying to tell you that story. But before he stands up here, I do want to say that for ten years, from 1977 to 1987, he pastored the International Community Church of Oslo in the country of Norway. It's an incredible church with a rich history. And with the lessons he learned there, he was able to return to the States during the Christmas season of 1987 and help expand the ministry of the Liberty International City Church of New York City. Under his guidance, that church grew from one congregation to over twenty congregations, now spread throughout that entire city. He has now ministered there for four years.

"It was through the ministry of that church in New York that I became a believer and follower of Jesus Christ. It was also through that ministry that I surrendered to being a pastor. I'm grateful to God for Jason Faircloth, a man powerfully used by God to lead me to those life-changing decisions.

"I want to thank him publicly for his willingness to come here this week and be our featured speaker. His participation has been more than just a blessing.

"I've asked him to address a particular subject tonight, a subject I heard him speak on about a year ago at the church in New York." He nodded for Jason Faircloth to come to the front.

Almost against his will, Jordan's interest in Faircloth was piqued by the young pastor's introduction. The man he saw walking toward the podium was of medium height, trim, and a little earthy-looking for a minister. Maybe in his later fifties — it was hard to tell — he had white hair that was thin on top and longish in the back. He wore a closely cropped beard, the same naturally white color as his hair. He was wearing a crumpled pair of khaki pants and a leathery-looking button-up sweater over a tan shirt. *A maverick,* Jordan thought to himself. *Looks more like a radical university professor than a pastor.*

"As an American who has pastored overseas in Europe," Faircloth began, "I've been asked by Kerry to share with you a burdensome observation that I've made concerning the American church. It's the observation of an outsider, or of a missionary, if you will. It's an observation that recently became even more disturbing to me when my granddaughter and I returned a few months ago from Norway, where we spent the summer working with the International Community Church of Oslo, a church that is refreshingly unusual in its openness.

"The observation is this: The American church, generally speaking, possesses very little openness, honesty, and realism."

Jordan noticed that everyone was listening with intensity. The big room was heavy with quietness, except for Faircloth's gentle, captivating voice.

"All across America," Faircloth continued, "people enter the doors of their church behind a smiling mask and a locked-up heart. They sit front-to-back. Allowed by American tradition to be only spectators, they listen to one-man sermons. And then they go home. Very seldom, if ever, do they touch hearts with one another in a below-the-surface, meaningful, serious, edifying, and productive manner.

"On any given Sunday, when millions of believers meet throughout this country, there is a very large percentage of those people who are struggling so intensely in their lives that they feel as if they're dying on the inside. They're struggling with their

197

marriages, they're struggling with faith, they're struggling with addictions, they're struggling with unhealthy fears — the list goes on and on. These people look around in church, see everybody else smiling, and conclude that everybody else is healthy — emotionally, socially, and spiritually.

"And because there is virtually no forum or atmosphere for openness and honesty, nearly all of these hurting people, like individual islands detached from the rest of the body of Christ, sit in their pews month after month, year after year, and struggle alone and in secret until they become so pained, disillusioned, depressed, and hopeless that they break. At that point, many of them leave the church. Many of them leave their places of ministry. Many of them leave their marriages. Some of them even commit suicide.

"Now before I address this subject any further, I want to make it clear that I'm not advocating that people come together and always share with one another the intimate details of their struggles. Sometimes that would be acceptable, but at other times, of course, it would not be wise. Sometimes, just to stand up and be able to say, 'I'm hurting . . . I feel like I'm going under,' and to *know* that in your weakness you'll be accepted, loved, and rallied around, is enough.

"Unfortunately, this type of realistic sharing is unknown in most of our American churches, and I believe there are two primary reasons for this.

"Number one: Pastors do not breed honesty. As much or more so than anybody else, they hide behind their smiling masks, trying to always project an image of invincibility and impregnability, trying to play the role of perpetual conqueror and victor. They've been trained, both directly and indirectly, to do that. Bible colleges and seminaries teach them to keep a distance from their flock, to not let anyone get close enough to see their humanness, lest their people lose respect for them."

Jordan felt himself leaning forward. Despite his original intentions for coming here, he was being drawn in by Faircloth's straight talk.

"Our society compounds that directive by putting these men high on a pedestal and refusing to let them be human. The expectations and pressures placed on them by the general public drive them to hide their weaknesses.

"But the truth is, everyone in ministry — every pastor, every missionary, every evangelist, every theology professor, every high-profile leader, every low-profile leader — struggles in life just like every other believer. These people struggle with their marriages, they struggle with their tempers, they struggle with financial temptations, they struggle with lust, they struggle with addictions, they struggle with faith. Some struggle more intensely than others, and some struggle more frequently than others. But they all struggle.

"I know, my friends — I am one of them.

"If ministers will start taking off their masks . . . in a discretionary way . . . and being honest with people, then they will start breeding honesty. They will start breathing realism into the church.

"If they will dare to lead by example, the church will follow."

Even though Jordan was focused on Faircloth, he saw out of his peripheral vision a variety of heads wholeheartedly nodding their agreement.

"The second reason why there is so little openness and honesty," Faircloth proceeded, "is because our Christian communities in America have become masters at condemning and abandoning those whose major weaknesses and struggles are revealed. Instead of creating an environment of honesty in which these people can find it easy to get help at the beginning of their struggles, we force them to hide their weaknesses — right up until the very moment they break or fall. At that point, we feel lied to, betrayed, and deceived. We then broadcast their sins over the radio, print articles about them in the Christian periodicals, and spread the bad news through the gossip grapevines. We treat them as if they were impudent Satanists, usually driving them to complete estrangement from the organized church."

Jordan saw a lady on the pew in front of him start to cry softly.

"Before honesty becomes a significant element in our churches," Faircloth concluded, "we'll have to establish a new atmosphere of openness, with pastors and church leaders taking the lead. By their example, they can help turn the church into a place of needed intimacy, where hurting people can share their struggles while those struggles are still manageable. Then we must learn to rally around those hurting people with love, support, encouragement, prayers, and heart-to-heart friendship — and fight *for* them, not against them."

When Faircloth paused, Jordan saw a

guy stand near the front. He was bearded, with long hair tied back in a ponytail, and was wearing the attire of a motorcycle gang member. With tears streaming down his face, he started applauding. Within seconds, the rest of the audience was standing and following suit.

To keep from drawing attention to himself, Jordan stood, too.

He had to admit that he was touched by the man's words. Indeed, Faircloth's spoken observation had almost made him forget why he was here.

Faircloth soon motioned for everyone to be seated, and continued speaking.

"Naturally, you are relating to what I'm saying. That's because we are all familiar with trying to hide our weaknesses so that our brothers and sisters will not reject us, and yet at the same time secretly wanting to be accepted and helped by friends who know us as we really are.

"As a matter of fact, I don't know your faces and I don't know your names, but I know — simply because this is a group of human beings — that some of you here tonight are right in the middle of battles so intense that your very faith and sanity are being tested. And most of you in that situation are battling alone.

"My heart goes out to you. I know your loneliness. I've been there.

"And because I care for you, I want the rest of my time this evening to be spent encouraging you and giving you hope.

"Therefore, with Kerry's permission, I'm going to ask us to deviate from tradition and do something a little different.

"I want four or five of you who have survived lonely battles — battles that nearly destroyed you — to stand up one at a time and tell us your stories. Use discretion about the details you share. What I want to do is to help those who think they are alone in their battles tonight. Hearing honest testimonies will help them realize they are not alone, that battles are common to us all, and that there is hope.

"Now, to help make it easier for some of you to share, I'm first going to be open and honest with you. I'm going to tell you a small portion of my personal story."

16

For the next five or six minutes, Jordan listened with avid attention as Jason Faircloth gave a glimpse into his past. He told how, twenty years ago, as a high-profile Atlanta pastor, he had driven his teenage daughter and his wife to their deaths with his authoritarian, legalistic, know-it-all attitude. He told about his daughter's death during childbirth, after having run away from home a year and a half earlier at the age of sixteen. He told how his wife died after suffering long-term emotional abuse at his hands; and how such abuse, combined with her shock over their daughter's death, robbed her of the will to live. He spoke about his own grief, guilt, and disillusionment, his unsuccessful attempt to commit suicide, his abandonment of his ministry, and his search for the surviving granddaughter who was being abused and hidden from him by his son-in-law.

He told about his five-year odyssey,

trailing his granddaughter across America, to England, Cyprus, and Norway. About the reconstruction of his Christian life under the leadership of a wise old Burmese pastor at the International Community Church in Oslo. About miraculously finding his granddaughter in a New York City hospital eighteen years later — just two years ago, after she had tried to throw herself in front of a taxi, hoping to end her life as a prostitute, heroin junkie, and alcoholic.

In spite of Jordan's own looming pain, he could actually feel Faircloth's past hurt as the man recounted his dramatic journey. Jordan could empathize with Faircloth's story — more than he ever would have dreamed.

Suddenly a new voice was speaking in the auditorium. Jordan looked around and saw a lady standing near the end of the second row, weeping as she spoke.

"Nobody knew it," she was saying, "but for twelve years I was addicted to prescription drugs. Inside the walls of our home I created a living hell for my husband and my two daughters. My children still hate me because of the way I abused them during those years. My husband nearly walked out on me a dozen or more times . . ."

The lady went on to explain through tears that during that twelve-year period she and her husband were active leaders in their church, and were looked upon as a model Christian family. "For twelve long years I hid behind a mask. Nobody outside of my immediate family knew. Because of the pressure to always hide what was going on in my life, I grew to hate church . . ." The lady concluded by saying that she eventually found help outside the church, withdrew from the drugs, and that due to God's forgiveness and mercy she and her husband were now trying to rebuild all that she had been guilty of destroying. Before she sat down, she looked at Faircloth and added, "I'm fifty-two years old, I've been a Christian for over thirty years, and I've never heard a preacher talk as openly and truthfully as you're talking now. Where were you," she sobbed, before taking her seat, "when I needed a spiritual leader like you?"

Throughout the audience Jordan noticed several people, men and women alike, wiping their eyes.

Then another lady stood to her feet. She started to speak, then choked up. A feeling of touching hearts was now present in the room.

The lady began again, speaking through tears. "This is the first time . . . I've ever tried to talk about this in church . . . I grew up in a home with a brother six years older than me. He was very athletic, starring on all the high school ball teams. He was the first-chair trombone player in the school band. He made honor-roll grades. He was good-looking. I remember my mom and dad showering him with praise and affection. They bragged on him in public to all their friends . . . But not one time when I was growing up do I remember them hugging me or telling me they loved me. I always thought it was because I was fat and ugly. So I grew up hating myself.

"At the age of fourteen, when I became a Christian, I thought my new friends in the church would love me, despite my size and unattractiveness. But their joking remarks were more cruel and more constant than those of my non-Christian friends. I was already withdrawn and a loner. And because of the way my new Christian friends treated me, I quickly became that way in the church, too. I stayed that way all through my teens and my twenties. No one in any of the churches I attended ever reached out to me. I was the girl people whispered about behind my back. They thought I didn't notice."

The lady went on to say that four years ago she underwent an intestinal bypass and lost sixty pounds and had since that time made many receptive friends, but still struggled with forgiving those Christians from the past who had made her feel worthless. She then sat back down.

Jordan saw an older woman lean forward, reach over the pew, and hug the lady who had just spoken. Both of them had tears on their cheeks.

Another person, this time a black man, had already stood up and attracted the people's attention.

"I want everyone here to pray for me," the man told the group. "A lot of times I think I'm doing good. But every now and then I go back to my old feelings. As most of you know, my sister was held up and shot about a year ago when she was working across town at a convenience store. She died two weeks later."

Jordan lurched forward, as if jerked there by the man's last sentence.

"When she died in the hospital," the man went on to explain, "I got angry with God. I told Him that He could keep His Christianity if He couldn't do better than that. Instead of trying to trust Him in that dark hour and go on with my life, I turned on Him. I stopped going to church. I even started missing work. All I did was lay around all the time and stay eaten up with hate. I wanted to kill the man who took away from me my only family member. If I could have found him, I probably would have. I stayed that way for nearly two months. That's when I first met Pastor Kerry down at the Y. One night a couple of weeks later, after a basketball game, he tried to tell the gospel to me. I told him I was already a Christian, but that God had let me down.

"After he heard my story, he reminded me that 'the just shall live by faith.' He told me that I had two choices in my life: I could keep asking 'Why?' and continue to live in the darkness of hate and confusion, or I could start to grow out of my grief by believing that God is almighty, the Master of life and death, and by trusting His judgment calls — whether I felt like it or not. I knew Pastor Kerry was right. Because of his help, I decided to try to stop blaming God and start trusting Him."

The man went on to emphasize that such a change of attitudes, including the exchange of vengeance for forgiveness, was difficult to execute. "But with Pastor

Kerry's encouragement, and now with the help of all of you here at All People's Church, I'm slowly starting to think differently and feel differently.

"Sometimes I still have flashbacks," he concluded, "and find myself giving in to my old feelings, but the peace of mind that I feel when I trust the Lord and let Him carry the load makes me want to keep growing. So, please pray for me."

The man's testimonial stirred up Jordan's feelings like a giant whirlwind. Memories of Susan's words about faith and dependence on God swept through his mind, churning together with the man's words about forgiveness, and with his own drive for vengeance. The swirling thoughts came with such intensity that he momentarily forgot where he was.

He grew frustrated. How could this man just lie down, in the name of something as abstract as "faith," and willingly die to his feelings of hate and vengeance? In reality, wasn't he just weak? How could he love his sister and just walk away from her death, leaving the killer's fate solely to time and chance? Wasn't this the same fairy-tale faith being advocated by his wife, and now by this man? Wasn't it just a self-deceptive way of coping with one's weakness and fear? Wasn't it a fallacy of the church, taught to weak people by other weak people?

Or . . . was it a realistic and legitimate option for an intelligent and self-sufficient human being? Was there something real to it that he couldn't see?

The next fifteen to twenty minutes of the meeting passed Jordan by as he tried to re-group. The words that finally managed to reclaim his attention were the words *Percival Blake.*

Blake, a tall, slim man with coffee-colored skin and rust-red hair, walked to the front. He paused, wiped his eyes, and told the congregation in his distinguished Jamaican accent that he, like Jason Faircloth, was going to deviate from protocol. "Even though it is now my allotted time to tell you about my ministry among the Jamaican youth, I want to ask Brother Faircloth to return to the front. I believe that the heart-stirring momentum of what has taken place during the last sixty minutes isn't yet ready to be extinguished. Nor should it be. Therefore, I want to yield my part of the program to Brother Faircloth, and ask him to please return to the podium and continue leading us." He then sat down.

Faircloth returned to the front as the people in the pews nodded their heads in agreement and appreciation.

Now that Jordan had identified the doctor, he let his thoughts return for the next few minutes to his own mission. Whether he would hear the Jamaican give his presentation was no longer relevant. He now knew what the brown-skinned man looked like, and would be able to follow him after the service, to his car and then to his home.

Throughout the remainder of the meeting, Jordan's mind swayed back and forth from what was happening in the church to his strategy for finding Ottey, Tito, and Martin.

He heard Faircloth remind the congregation that they had just spent an hour trying to encourage those who were secretly hurting. Since everyone had responded so affirmatively, he suggested, perhaps they should now spend the next few minutes attempting to administer *direct* encouragement.

Faircloth's voice was sensitive and burdened. He invited those who felt they were "dying alone, behind a smiling mask" to raise their hands. He explained that no one who raised a hand would be asked to say anything.

After several seconds of silently waiting, a hand was slowly raised. Faircloth looked at the middle-aged man and almost cried. "Thank you for being honest," he whispered.

Faircloth then asked those who knew the man to raise their hands.

At least 70 percent of the people in the room lifted their hands.

"All right, I want two or three of you to stand up," Faircloth directed. "Remain in your place, and speak a word of encouragement to this brother, one at a time and in the best way you know how. Maybe you know the details of his struggle, maybe you don't. But right now, that's irrelevant. I just want you to let him know that there is hope, that it's too early for him to give up, and that you will pledge your unconditional support and friendship to him during this battle in his life. Remind him of how God has used him here in this church, and in your life. Don't let him struggle alone."

Mrs. Parks, the soloist, stood to her feet and spoke words of hope to the man. The verbal encouragement didn't stop with her. It didn't stop until nearly forty minutes later, after nine different individuals, several with tears in their eyes, had rallied around the brother with words of exhortation and promises of extended help, and the whole group had encircled him and prayed for him.

Then Jason Faircloth, with the light of compassion shining in his moist eyes, interrupted to explain that he would not prolong the meeting any longer. "Just remember what's happened here tonight. Let it be the beginning of a new church-wide friendship. Continue to build on this openness. Whatever else you do, in God's name keep interacting heart-to-heart with one another.

"For the church to function as a spiritual support group as God intended," Faircloth emphasized, "it has got to be more than just an information center where we gather together passively week after week and sing repetitious songs and hear repetitious sermons from only one person. We've got to get into each other's lives. When that starts taking place, our churches will naturally be better able to reach out in evangelism to nonbelievers. If we never learn to love and interact with our own brethren in a practical, beneath-the-surface, and scriptural sense, how can we learn to reach out to the world with the gospel?"

Faircloth nodded to Pastor Kerry and

started to sit down, when he suddenly stopped and looked out into the eyes of the congregation once more. "Remember this little formula," he told them. *"Relationships versus programs.* Programs ordinarily presuppose that the people in the pews are simply an audience. On the other hand, building relationships in the church — through scripturally teaching one another, encouraging one another, listening to one another, confessing to one another, forgiving one another, and interacting with one another in a host of other ways — will transform the church from a passive audience to a living family." Faircloth then took a seat.

During Kerry's closing words and prayer of benediction, Jordan could feel the contagiousness of Faircloth's insights, actions, and leadership style. It seemed evident that everyone in the auditorium was touched and was desiring more. Even Jordan, in the midst of his pulsating distraction, had been moved.

But in his case, was it simply emotion stacked on top of emotion that made him want to cry? He wasn't sure, but for a moment he wondered if he should attempt an open and honest discussion with Faircloth — to address the *question* of faith and its supposed validity.

Almost instantly, he decided against such a move. It could cause him to lose the Jamaican doctor, and that was out of the question. Faith or no faith, he would stick to his plan.

To keep from being distracted by having to shake hands and talk to people face-to-face, he turned and walked briskly toward the foyer when the final "amen" was spoken.

On his way out, he reached down and grabbed a church bulletin with Pastor Kerry's address and telephone number printed on the back. He then went to his car and waited.

Twenty-five minutes later, he was following the Jamaican doctor through the downtown Saturday evening traffic.

To an unknown destination.

17

Climbing the stairs to the fifth-floor landing, Susan heard the phone ringing in their apartment. She hurried to climb the last few steps and get the apartment door open.

It was half past noon in Munich — 6:30 a.m. Detroit time — and she and Donica were just returning from the St. Jude's Sunday morning worship service.

Could it be Jordan? She had not heard from him in over forty-eight hours. All she knew was that he had not reported to the Chesapeake headquarters. She had contacted the office yesterday afternoon. As far as she could tell, he had not made an appearance in Chattanooga either; at least her parents had not heard from him or seen him.

She had spent a sleepless night worrying about him and becoming more and more angry. It was clear to her that he had discovered something he was trying to keep a secret. And she was sure it was somehow related to the murder of Chase and Heather. But neither the German nor the American police authorities had a clue as to what it might be. She had called them yesterday as well, telling them about Jordan's deceptive behavior and her mounting suspicion. Despite her husband's threats, she could not stand by and watch him continue on a course that might destroy what was left of their family.

The German police superintendent told her he would check with the airline personnel at the Munich airport and find out what Jordan's flight destination had been. Maybe this was him calling back with that information now.

She tossed her purse onto the couch and grabbed the phone from its hook. "Hello, this is Susan," she panted, trying to catch her breath.

"Hello, I'm calling to speak with Mrs. Rau, the wife of Mr. Jordan B. Rau of Raintaler Strasse 37 in Munich, Germany," a female voice responded.

The call was long-distance. Susan could tell by the sound of the connection. Her heart started pounding.

"I'm Jordan's wife," Susan answered, hearing the tension in her voice.

"Mrs. Rau, my name is Shanda Jenkins.

I'm the head of the Patient Relations Department at Grace Hospital in Detroit, Michigan. I hate to be the bearer of bad news, but your husband, Jordan, has been involved in an automobile accident."

"Jordan — in Detroit?" Susan said, interrupting with as much confusion as panic. "Is he —"

"Mrs. Rau," the lady interjected, "you need to make plans to get here as quickly as possible. Your husband has suffered a severe head injury. He is lying in a coma in intensive care. The doctors are doing everything they can to save his life. But the situation doesn't look good."

Susan felt herself shaking uncontrollably. "Not my husband! Not Jordan!" she cried out. "How . . . I mean, he can't . . . Not my husband!" Susan felt her throat constricting with emotion.

"Mrs. Rau, the doctors are doing everything they can to keep him alive, but it's a serious situation. Please make plans to get here as quickly as you can."

Fighting to fend off hysteria, Susan copied down the name of the hospital, its address, and the telephone number as the caller dictated them to her.

Out of the corner of her eye, Susan saw Donica drop her purse and Bible onto the floor and step closer. When Donica saw what Susan had written down, she ran off to her room, covering her mouth with her hand.

With her mind buzzing with pain and confusion, Susan called the airport and made two seat reservations for the next direct flight from Munich to New York. The flight would leave in two hours, at 2:40.

During the several minutes of frenzied and chaotic activity that followed, Susan called and relayed the awful news to the missions office in Chesapeake, then to her parents.

By 1:45, Susan and Donica had put the house in order and thrown together three suitcases for their trip.

Locking the apartment door behind them moments later, they rushed down the stairs with their luggage in tow to the taxi awaiting them on the street.

Delroy, Ottey's oldest brother and the don of the Detroit drug posse, slammed his fist on the table as he looked across the back room of the nightclub into the hard faces of his nineteen Jamaican posse members.

"Dem Latinos be fools," he growled, his dark brown eyes looking as if they could pierce the metal door that divided the room from the hallway. "If it take two days, or two years, I want der leader — Mario. I want to hold Mario's head in my hands. I want de Latinos to know who be de true masters of destruction."

Delroy slowly scanned the room, locking eyes with each person present. The major portion of the inner city was his drug turf now. He had been engulfing the territory through two years of merciless killings. He had instilled fear into the hearts of his competition — the Hispanics, the Italians, the blacks — by killing dozens of their street pushers, pimps, and wholesalers. On the streets. In warehouses. In nightclubs. And in cars.

Among those who knew him, he had cultivated a reputation of possessing the black heart of a demon. Some even believed that he had the power of life and death over his enemies.

But under a newly arisen leader named Mario, the Hispanics were now fighting back, trying to reclaim former territory from him, and attempting to undermine Delroy's leadership and respect among the Jamaicans by planning to kill someone in his family.

The Jamaicans, however, had learned of

this plan, and the Hispanics had underestimated Delroy's capacity for evil. He would now have to give them a visual-aid lesson.

"We start from de bottom and we destroy der clan one by one. Der pushers, der guards, der drivers. Everybody. Including der families. We can use dis crusade to break in de new guns." All the posse members knew he was referring to the Heckler and Koch 9 mm machine guns that Ottey, Tito, and Martin had purchased in Germany. An underground German source had been dumping the weapons at a bargain price.

Delroy continued. "We slowly work our way to de top, to Mario himself, and watch him beg for mercy as we lay down de guns and cut his head off." He paused, then added, "Mario — him already be dead and him don't even know it."

He spat on the table.

All the men around him, including Ottey, Martin, and Tito, clenched their jaws with the spirit of brotherhood and eyed him with united hearts and minds.

Together they would breed their terror.

Nick Baldwin — nicknamed "Stinger" — the special agent in charge at the Drug Enforcement Agency's district office in

Detroit, stood before his new special agents — twelve men and three women. They had several weeks earlier completed their training in Quantico, Virginia, at the DEA's national training facility, and in the last three days had completed their orientation here in Detroit. They were now ready for their first undercover assignments.

Having finished reading an eight-minute opening statement to them, Baldwin stepped from behind the podium and spoke candidly from his thirteen years of law enforcement experience.

"The underworld of narcotics — the gangs, the turfs, the wholesaling, the retailing, the prostitution, the pimping, the killings, and the thievery — is a war zone. Fortunately, about 90 percent of the people in Detroit never see or experience this world. Only because of the media coverage are they even aware of its existence. However, this small and infamous world of violence is expanding a little more every month, engulfing more lives and claiming more victims, many of them innocent kids. It's the responsibility of those of us in this room to fight that war, to do damage to the gang structures, and to push back the tide of drug-related crimes in this city.

"To accomplish this mission, we will follow the eight-point procedure that has been drilled into you throughout the course of your training — to isolate, associate, infiltrate, captivate, interrogate, litigate, castigate, and eliminate.

"As special agents, you will be operating at great risks to yourselves, both physically and emotionally, to help achieve these goals and to win this battle."

Baldwin paused, put on his glasses that were lying on the podium, then picked up a sheet of paper with classified information.

"We now come to the moment you've been waiting for — your official team assignments."

He quickly read the assignments, which grouped the agents in teams of two or three. When he came to the last assignment, he glanced up from the sheet of paper to two brown-skinned men seated just in front of the podium. "You two will be operating with the Alpha three team under Senior Agent Seaga's command. Being Jamaican, you're aware of the vicious tactics of the Caribbean Parade. Be careful."

18

Susan and Donica's flight arrived late in the evening in Detroit. When they entered the terminal at Metropolitan Airport, Paul Krueger, the president of the mission board, was standing there to meet them.

Fearful of the answer, Susan asked, "Are we too late? Is he still — ?"

"He's alive, Susan, but barely. He's still in the coma."

As Paul helped them collect their luggage, Susan asked him if he knew anything about the accident.

Paul hesitated, then spoke softly. "According to the police report, Jordan's car was broadsided in the middle of an intersection by a drunk driver who ran through a red light and hit him on the driver's side. Both cars were totaled. The other driver didn't make it; he died in the ambulance on the way to the hospital."

Paul hesitated again, then continued, sounding even more solemn. "The doctors don't think Jordan is going to make it either, Susan. He's suffered a severe brain concussion. His brain is swelling. They're —"

Upon hearing those words, Susan groaned, as if someone had slammed a fist into her back.

Donica grabbed her mother's arm and started weeping.

Paul struggled to console them, then escorted them outside the building to hail a taxi. He had booked a hotel room for them about six blocks from the hospital.

"I know this is going to be an almost impossible time for you," Paul said, "but I promise you I'll use my position to help you get anything you need."

When they were all inside the taxi, Susan wept for several minutes. When she could speak again, she asked in anguish, "What was he doing here in Detroit, Paul?"

"I don't know, Susan. Several of us in Chesapeake asked the same question when we got your call, but none of us has the slightest idea why he came here. I suspect Jordan is the only one who knows that answer."

"The police? The doctors? What did he say to them?"

"He wasn't able to say anything, Susan. The policemen who responded to the 911 call said Jordan was unconscious when they arrived on the scene of the accident." Paul sighed. "And he's been unconscious ever since."

Susan wiped her eyes again. "What other injuries does he have?" she asked, with fear mounting in her voice.

Paul didn't answer. He just looked at her, the gears of his mind turning.

"What else do I need to know, Paul?"

"We'll be at the hospital soon," he finally answered in a near whisper. "When we get there, Dr. Pennington, the hospital's chief neurologist, will give you a complete diagnosis of Jordan's condition. He'll be ready to answer any of your questions." Paul paused, reached out and grasped Susan's hands in his, and said, "It's not good, Susan."

For the third time since getting into the taxi, Susan had to use Paul's handkerchief.

God, are You there? she prayed. Please don't be silent — not now! Please let me know You're listening. I want to believe in You, I'm fighting to believe. But You've got to help me. Please, God!

Dr. Pennington, a neurologist and neurosurgeon, was a tall lean man with reddish hair and distinctive brown eyes. He appeared to be in his middle or late forties. The look on his face was grave.

As they stood in the hallway outside the intensive care unit, Susan tried to brace herself for what she was about to hear. Donica, looking scared and uncertain, stood close to her mother's side.

"I'm sorry you've had to come here under these particular circumstances," Pennington began, looking primarily at Susan. "I know you're extremely tired. I wish I had some good news that would help you get some rest. But I'm afraid that what I'm about to share with you isn't very good.

"Your husband's in a coma. He has suffered a severe brain concussion," the doctor explained. "Whenever there's an impact on the head that's hard enough to bruise the brain, as is the case with Jordan, the brain often swells. That's what's happening inside Jordan's head right now. We're monitoring him closely. But due to the swelling that has taken place in the last eight or nine hours, there's already a lot of pressure on his brain. We're administering some medication to try to keep it from swelling more. Sometimes medication is effective in these cases; sometimes it isn't. If the brain continues to swell and starts to hemorrhage, then we'll have to drill a series of small holes in his skull — in order to relieve some of the pressure — and maybe even do surgery. The next three or four days will be an extremely critical period. All we can do is watch and wait."

Susan took several deep breaths and struggled to control her voice. "Does this mean he's never . . . going to be normal again?" She was starting to shake.

"I will not give you any false hope, Mrs. Rau. It is certainly possible that your husband could be normal again, but at this point it's too early to say."

"And if he doesn't return to being normal . . . ?" Susan asked in a stronger tone.

The doctor could see that she wanted a truthful answer. He tried to breathe evenly. "Paralysis is a possibility. Loss of brain function. Possibly even death."

Donica went limp at Susan's side, as if life's energy had leaked out of her. Susan reached out and held her daughter tightly. When she turned to face the doctor again, she focused her eyes and exhaled. "What other injuries are there besides the brain concussion?"

"He sustained a broken left shoulder, a broken left knee, and a broken back. The back injury will possibly be just as detrimental to your husband's quality of life as the brain concussion, assuming he comes out of the coma and survives."

Susan didn't need to respond with words. Her eyes alone were pleading for understanding.

"The last three vertebrae in the lower part of his spine have been fractured and twisted," Pennington explained. "The nerves going from the spinal cord to the legs have been smashed at the root area by those broken bones. How severely the nerves have been damaged, we're not yet sure. His legs are showing no reflex responses, so the damage could be major. If he survives the next three days, and if the swelling of his brain starts to recede, we'll open his back and do reconstructive surgery. If the damage is minor, he should be able in time to walk again, with therapeutic help. If it's major, he could be confined to a wheelchair for the rest of his life."

Susan swallowed hard.

"I'm sorry, Mrs. Rau," Pennington said.

At a loss for words, Susan now wanted to see Jordan, to stand by his side, and to touch him.

Pennington summoned a nurse from inside the ICU ward to take Susan and

Donica to Jordan's room. Holding hands, they followed the nurse into the ward.

Before they entered Jordan's room, Susan saw her husband through the opened partition. Her initial response was to deny the reality of what she was seeing.

She stopped at the door and whispered his name in anguish. Then, letting go of Donica's hand, she hurried to the bedside.

"Be careful, Mrs. Rau," the nurse instructed her. "Only touch him lightly."

Several seconds before Susan reached down to touch his hand, she stared longingly into his damaged, traumatized face.

His head and his face were swollen grotesquely. His eyes were nearly invisible behind the bruised mass of black-and-blue flesh.

A clear plastic tube extended up into Jordan's nose. Another tube, from what looked like a breathing machine, led into his mouth between closed and swollen lips. Susan noticed a third tube — no, a cable or a cord of some kind — running to the back part of the crown of his head. She squinted as new tears leaked from her eyes. The back of his head had been shaved clean. A bolt of some kind, attached to the cord, had been inserted into a drilled hole in his skull. She assumed it was the monitoring device used to measure the pressure on his brain.

She wanted to run.

Swallowing hard, Susan closed her eyes. No matter how hard she tried, the anguish in her heart wouldn't turn her prayer into words — only groans.

She reached down and placed her right hand on the back of Jordan's left hand. Rubbing his hand, she saw that it was tied down at the wrist. She looked across the bed. His right hand was also tied. She then saw the IV tube in his right arm, and another cord of some kind clipped to one of his fingers.

This can't be, she thought. Jordan . . . always so strong. So much in control. And now . . .

She felt the hand of the nurse patting her shoulder.

"We're going to do everything that can possibly be done to help him," she heard the nurse whisper. "Dr. Pennington is the best. If there's anything to be done, he'll do it."

Donica was standing beside her, looking down into Jordan's face. "Daddy?" she whimpered. "Daddy?"

Susan took Donica in her arms.

The nurse, without speaking, reached out and held them both.

19

At 9 a.m. on Wednesday, three days later, Susan, Donica, and Paul Krueger were standing in the hallway listening to Dr. Pennington give the latest report. With them was Susan's mother, who had flown in on Monday afternoon.

"As you know, the swelling in his brain halted about forty-eight hours ago. It's now starting to recede," the doctor told them.

Susan allowed a sigh to escape. The first good news they'd received.

Dr. Pennington told them he was optimistic. It looked as if Jordan would at least survive. The medication was working. "And so are your prayers," he said, looking significantly at Susan, Donica, and her mother. Paul Krueger, after a pause, nodded agreement.

Susan felt her mother gripping her hand. "Thank You, Lord," she heard her mom whisper. She knew that her dad, even though he could not be here, had been praying around the clock back in Chattanooga.

When she heard Pennington explain what his next step was going to be, she knew that God would soon have another opportunity to respond to their heartfelt pleas.

"If the swelling continues to recede," Pennington said, "we'll do the spinal surgery on Friday afternoon. I'll be able to give you a more accurate prognosis after the operation."

With the immediate crisis passed, Susan tried to turn more of her attention to her daughter during the next two days as they all waited. Donica was reeling, she knew. Scarcely had Susan ever seen her daughter so lethargic.

Susan tried to get her to talk about her feelings.

"I don't feel like there's any hope anymore," Donica finally admitted to her late Thursday afternoon. "With everything that's happened, I just don't see why we should keep trying."

"You and I are both going to survive," Susan said. "It doesn't help anybody — Daddy included — if we give up."

After a long silence, Donica said, "If Dad comes out of the coma and is able to be normal again, like he was before Chase was killed, *then* maybe I'll be able to survive."

Like he was before Chase was killed . . . Susan pondered the implications of her daughter's statement. To go back to life as it was before Chase's death — was such a thing possible? That life seemed so remote now, so distant. They were all different people. And Jordan . . . Was such a miracle really possible?

Didn't thousands of others pray daily for miracles, only to see God appear to be silent and unmoved?

Didn't 99.9 percent of the people have to live with their pain and adverse circumstances, regardless of what they desired or prayed for?

Still, Susan resolved to keep praying, remembering the Scottish missionary's story.

And to keep waiting.

At ten-thirty Friday morning, Dr. Pennington announced that all but a marginal amount of pressure had dissipated from Jordan's brain, and that the spinal surgery would take place at one o'clock that afternoon.

Everybody rejoiced, though a bit nervously.

Four or five times during the surgery, Susan's mother squeezed her arm and told her, "God's going to help you through all this, honey. I know He will."

Dr. Pennington came out of the surgical theater at around eight-thirty. Anxiously they all gathered around him.

"After removing the loose fragments of bone," he told them, "we were able to reconstruct the three broken vertebrae. But the best news is that the nerve roots leading from the spinal cord to the legs were not damaged as much as we had anticipated. Instead of being severed or cut, which would have caused irreversible paralysis, they were only pinched. My prognosis is that Jordan, if he comes out of the coma and has sustained no extensive brain damage, will eventually be able to walk again."

There were tearful smiles all around. "Thank you, doctor," said Paul Krueger, shaking Pennington's hand.

Thank You, God, Susan prayed, her eyes turned upward.

Seated aboard a Delta 767 on its final approach to Munich on a sunny, mid-January day, Susan reviewed the list of tasks she needed to complete on this final trip to Germany. She glanced over the notes she had made during the nine-hour flight:

1. Sell car.
2. Cancel car insurance.
3. Arrange for a freight forwarding company to collect, pack, and ship all furniture and household goods to the U.S.
4. Have telephone disconnected.
5. Pay final telephone bill.
6. Notify all utility companies of move.
7. Pay final utility bills.
8. Notify German school of Donica's withdrawal.
9. Ask post office to forward mail to the Chattanooga address.
10. Call U.S. military and Bad Aibling police departments. Tell them about Jordan's accident and the move back to the States. Ask for latest murder investigation report. Give them Chattanooga address and telephone number.
11. Clean apartment. Get deposit from landlord.
12. Notify city hall of move. Register out of the country.

She was already tired, contemplating everything she had to accomplish, but she was buoyed by the knowledge that she need never again return to Germany. In fact, despite the difficulties they still faced, she had much to be grateful for.

Jordan was still comatose, but his body had been repaired to the greatest extent possible. His respiratory functions were normal. He was no longer on any type of life support, other than intravenous feeding and catheterization. Three days ago he had been transferred to Erlanger Hospital in Chattanooga at Susan's request, so that she and Donica could live with her parents while they all continued to wait.

The mission board was being more than helpful and considerate. Paul Krueger told her repeatedly not to worry about Jordan's salary; they would continue to honor their commitment to him until he was back on his feet and able to decide what he wanted to do. Susan was even more grateful for the excellent medical coverage provided by the board. The ICU and surgical expense had already been staggering and the length of Jordan's convalescence was still impossible to predict.

And she was now living back home in

Chattanooga. It was such a comfort to be in her parents' home, receiving the love and support they were happy to give. Donica, too, was responding to the thoughtful and loving care lavished on her by her grandparents.

As she felt the landing gear being released in preparation for landing, Susan whispered a prayer of thanks.

Within the next eight days, thanks to the kind assistance of two of the missionary couples from Nürnberg, everything on the list was accomplished except for cleaning the bathroom and all the floors, visiting the police, and selling the car. The car had been advertised in the major Munich newspaper, but no one had responded to the ad. Susan decided that the automobile could just be shipped back to the States. One of the men agreed to place it with a freight forwarding company the next day.

When Susan awoke the next morning, the sunlight was shining through the crisp winter air, filling the room with the freshness of a new day. She remembered that today was the day she had an appointment with the German police authorities at Bad Aibling — the last big hurdle to cross before returning home.

She was anxious to get back. In their

telephone conversation last night, her mother had said that Jordan was still comatose. The doctors were not making any predictions. It was still just a matter of waiting.

But Susan felt that Donica needed her. Enrolled once again in her former school in Chattanooga, Donica was surrounded by old friends, and that was a big help. But her friends couldn't imagine the difficult feelings Donica was dealing with. Susan continued to be concerned for her.

During the train ride to Bad Aibling a few hours later, Susan stared out the window at the snow-covered countryside, and dwelt on her hopes.

When she was finally seated in the superintendent's office at the German police station and had informed him of the accident, his first statement in response shocked her.

"Your husband beat us to an eyewitness, and with the man's help possibly found out who the killer is," the superintendent told her matter-of-factly. "What he discovered undoubtedly led him to Detroit," he added.

The superintendent went on to explain that several investigators of the German police force were now working with the eyewitness, a Bosnian man, and with his help were trying to locate a silverish-gray BMW with an American military license plate. They hoped they would soon track it down, find the owner, and be led to the murderer or murderers. Maybe even to Detroit, with the military police's assistance.

With dozens of unspoken questions burning in her head, Susan gave the superintendent their Chattanooga address and phone number and asked him to keep them informed if any new facts came to light.

Riding the train back to Munich, Susan's mind replayed the same fearful realization over and over: Jordan had gone to Detroit to kill someone. The thought chilled her to the bone, but she knew in her heart that it was the truth. Her husband had been transformed into a would-be killer by his obsessive grief.

What would Jordan do if he came out of his coma and could be normal again? Would he realize how destructive he had become? Or would the insanity brought on by Chase's death still control him?

Two days later, when her flight departed for the States, Susan still wasn't sure she was strong enough to learn the answer.

★ ★ ★

On a downtown construction site in Chicago, standing with three other teenage boys around a scrap-wood fire burning inside a fifty-gallon drum, Ricardo tried to convince himself for the hundredth time that he had made the right decision.

On Christmas Day — more than four weeks ago — his mother told him she would be traveling to northern Italy with her husband for a month-long stay in a small village in the Alps. Mitchum's special forces team was participating in a winter training exercise with Italian troops.

Ricardo at first responded in anger. Abandoned again. Then he realized that this particular abandonment was the chance he had been looking for.

His near-death encounter weeks earlier with the man in the woods had left him petrified. The fear of being caught again by the big man and stabbed to death, or caught by the police and tried in a court of law for murder, had grown more burdensome with each passing day. He had awakened several nights in a cold sweat, dreaming about the imagined scenario.

Ricardo had finally decided that the only safe course was to run. But where? The complications of getting the money for an airline ticket had suppressed the thought of going back to the U.S. — until his mother's news sparked a plan in his mind.

Now standing by the fire warming himself, Ricardo was proud of his daring escape. He had already told the getaway story several times to several of his new friends in Chicago. He now relived the story again in the privacy of his own mind, trying to reassure himself that running away had been his best option.

The morning his mother and stepdad had driven out of Bad Tölz, he had set out to gather the $264 needed for a one-way ticket from Munich to Chicago on one of the daily military charter flights.

First, in a few deals with some German teenagers, he sold several of his compact disks, his stereo box, his new coat, and all of his mother's household booze. He made the prices irresistible — less than half of what the items would have cost in German stores.

Then he stole a hundred dollars in cash that he found while searching his stepdad's closet for something else to sell. The cash had been stashed away inside a money belt stuffed in a binocular case.

So within two days he had procured the money needed for a plane ticket. On the third day, he purchased the ticket. On the fourth day, he flew out of Germany.

Never to return.

He was now on his own. With the help of his new street friends in Chicago, he would somehow survive.

For a moment, as he stared at the flames of fire leaping into the air, he wondered how his mother would react when she returned to Bad Tölz in the next day or two and found him gone. His lingering response to that thought was one of disdain for her, more than pity.

He was just glad to be free. Free from her. Free from Mitchum.

Free from the big man with the knife.

Free from the German police and the military police.

And free from Germany.

Exulting in the newfound freedom, he made a vow that never again would anyone suppress, ruin, or control his life.

20

In a private room at Erlanger hospital in Chattanooga, Susan pulled up a chair and sat beside the bed where Jordan remained in a coma. Donica was seated on the other side.

It was now April. Susan's daily routine included visits with Jordan early in the morning and at noon, and again in the late afternoon. Donica joined her for the afternoon visits.

The visits were good for Donica. She would sit at Jordan's bedside and hold his hand while talking to him or reading aloud from her school textbooks.

"I've heard that people in a coma know when someone's talking to them," she told her mother several weeks ago, "and that talking to them a little bit every day can sometimes help them wake up."

For his fortieth birthday on February 3, Donica had even given him a party, complete with songs, gifts, and a cake she made.

Her enthusiasm had become so infectious that Susan had started reading to Jordan during her private visits. In fact, she had taken to reading from the Bible. Had Jordan been conscious, she suspected he might have scorned this as naive, but Susan persisted.

Since returning to Chattanooga, Susan had begun attending the church she had known as a child, the place where her parents were members. She found the atmosphere congenial. The congregation's frank acceptance of the power of prayer and the infallibility of the Scriptures did far more to strengthen her for her struggles than Jordan's lectures about how everyone is equipped with the inborn power to determine and control his own destiny.

She looked at him, lying in his bed, and sighed deeply. She thought she could almost put up with one of those lectures, if he would only sit up and talk to her.

She half-listened as Donica began reading to Jordan from her English literature book. She let herself stare out the window for a moment, then turned again to face the bed.

Jordan's right hand was moving.

Susan gasped.

Donica looked up, then allowed her eyes

to follow her mother's.

Jordan's fingers were slowly spreading and closing as his palm rested on the bedsheet.

"He's moving!" Donica shouted in ecstasy as she leaped to her feet.

Susan rushed over to push the call button, then turned back to Jordan.

The nurse quickly appeared in the doorway. "His hand is moving!" Donica said.

Susan was leaning over her husband, her face inches from his. She clasped his moving hand. "Jordan?" she pleaded. "Can you hear me?"

The nurse at her side watched closely for a response on Jordan's part. She saw none. "You say it was his hand that was moving?" she asked.

"Yes — this hand," Susan answered. "It was moving, but . . ." She slowly released her grip. "But it stopped."

"Squeeze it again and keep talking to him," the nurse instructed, as she threw back the top covers to look for any movement in Jordan's legs. She let her eyes scan his lower limbs, feet, and toes. She detected no movement anywhere in the lower part of the body.

"Donica and I are here with you, Jordan. Try to move your hand again," Susan urged while staring at his face, hoping to see his eyes open.

"Ask him to move his other hand," the nurse told Susan.

Susan reached across the bed and touched the hand that Donica was now holding. "Try to move these fingers, Jordan," she pleaded.

The fingers didn't move.

Susan urged him three or four more times. Then Donica tried. "Please, Daddy!" she prompted. Still there was no response.

The nurse then pinched his inner thigh. "I'm testing for a response to pain," she explained to Susan.

Jordan's leg didn't flinch.

The nurse then pinched him on the other thigh, the abdomen, the arms, and the neck. Susan and Donica stood in silence, watching. But still there was no reaction.

"Keep talking to him," the nurse told Susan, "I'm going to get my penlight to check his pupils. I'll be right back."

For the next couple of minutes, Susan and Donica tried to coach Jordan out of the coma.

When the nurse entered the room again, she lifted one of Jordan's eyelids with her thumb and shone the penlight into his pupil. The pupil contracted normally. She checked the other pupil. It contracted like the first.

"Good," the nurse said. "That shows that both sides of the brain are functioning without any trauma."

She paused, then looked up at Susan and said, "As I mentioned before, when a person stays in a coma this long and comes out of it, he normally doesn't just wake up, fully alert. He awakens slowly and progressively." She gave a sympathetic and hopeful smile. "Maybe this is the start."

When the nurse left the room a few seconds later, Susan embraced Donica and whispered a heartfelt prayer. "Please, God," she said with her eyes open and looking at Jordan's hands, "let this truly be the beginning."

Filled with new hope and new energy, Susan and Donica began spending more time at the hospital, trying even harder to talk, read, and touch Jordan out of his coma.

The following Saturday afternoon, they were both present in the hospital room when his hand moved again.

Donica had just finished a forty-minute session of nonstop reading. Susan was standing at the bedside. She was holding his hand, the same one that had moved earlier, when she suddenly felt the fingers fan open.

She spoke Jordan's name. Donica looked up from her seat on the other side of the bed.

"He's moving his hand again," Susan told her.

Donica stood.

"Jordan," Susan said loudly as she repositioned her hand to the inside of his palm, "you're here in the room with me and Donica. We're right here by your side taking care of you, honey. I want you to try to squeeze my hand if you can hear me, okay?"

She paused, feeling for a response.

"Try to squeeze my hand, Jordan."

Susan exhaled a deep breath when she felt her hand being slightly pressed.

"He's trying," Susan whispered. And then she nearly shouted, "He's trying, Donica! Get the nurse, quick!"

When the nurse entered the room on Donica's heels about two minutes later, she saw Jordan, eyes wide open, his head turned sideways on the pillow, staring into Susan's face. It was the first time since the accident that his eyes had been open without the help of outside manipulation.

Susan, her cheeks wet with tears, was

250

rubbing Jordan's hand, telling him, "It's going to be okay, honey. We're right here with you."

Donica was frozen in her tracks. Were her eyes telling her the truth? "Daddy?" She leaped to the head of the bed.

The nurse quickly walked to Jordan's other side. She stood for about twenty seconds, trying to assess what was happening. She saw Donica hugging her father and trying desperately to get him to talk. She saw Susan now looking away from Donica and Jordan, and looking at her, pleading with her eyes.

"Has he said anything?" the nurse asked Susan.

"No. He squeezed my hand once or twice when I asked him to, and he opened his eyes. But it's like he's looking right through me, and it doesn't even register that I'm here. And now, he's not even moving his hand anymore."

As Donica and Susan watched, the nurse turned Jordan's head to face her side of the bed. For three or four minutes she worked with ease and confidence, based on years of nursing experience, to determine a sign of coherency.

Her efforts, like Susan's, ended up being fruitless.

"Let's give him time, Susan," she said. "Already, we're looking at a small miracle."

Later that evening when everyone had left the room, Jordan's eyes opened again, this time just slightly.

"Can someone . . . get me . . . some water," he mumbled. His voice, weak and rough, would have been almost inaudible, even for someone listening from the bedside.

When no one responded, he closed his eyes and went under again.

Early the next morning, Susan received a phone call from the superintendent of the German police station in Bad Aibling. She was told that the car used by Chase's murder suspect had now been found, but that the suspect himself had apparently fled the country.

Susan was certain that these facts were somehow related to Jordan's secret trip to Detroit. But she refused to dwell on it.

For the next six days, she and Donica worked relentlessly to get some sort of response from Jordan. Susan somehow feared that if they didn't redouble their efforts, he would slip back from the brink of consciousness and into oblivion. Though she tried to keep her tone optimistic and assured, she felt herself becoming more and more disturbed, and in some ways desperate. She hoped Donica wasn't picking up on her mounting and unspoken fear: that Jordan was permanently brain-damaged. But with every day that passed without any further response from him, her dread became harder and harder to contain.

Her fears were heightened one morning when she came into Jordan's room and found a doctor and two nurses huddled around his bed. "What's going on?" she asked. "Has something happened?"

"Nothing has happened, Mrs. Rau," said John Evans, the doctor. "We're just getting him prepped for an EEG test, to see what kind of brain activity he's showing."

Sensing Susan's fear and apprehension, Dr. Evans stepped out of the way of the nurses and joined Susan at the foot of the bed. He knew that for Jordan to open his eyes without being coherent was a possible sign of brain damage. But he told Susan only about the EEG process, adding, "Hopefully the test will give us a better idea of what we're facing."

As the nurses removed the IV tube from Jordan's arm and released the brakes on the gurney, neither of them noticed the intermittent movement of his feet. They also missed the brief opening and closing of his eyes.

Jordan knew he was asleep. He didn't know for how long or where, but he felt as if he were at the bottom of a warm, dark pool. He knew he wanted to surface but wasn't sure how to go about it.

No — wait! Hadn't he managed to open his eyes? He was sure he had. Or was he? He didn't remember registering light, sound, or logic. Where was the real world? What was happening?

He tried to open his eyes again. He couldn't. His eyelids felt as heavy as marble tablets.

He suddenly felt panicky. He tried to shout, but couldn't seem to exercise any willful control over his voice or mouth. Why couldn't he operate the members of his body? Why couldn't he bring his thoughts into focus? Where was he? Was he sleeping? Was he dreaming?

His head hurt. He felt movement. Flashes of light started dancing across the top of his mind — or was he actually seeing light? As he tried desperately and painfully to capture the light, he remembered a thought: Someone had died. A girl. No. A boy. Who was it? Was it him? Was he dead?

Oh, his throat was dry!

He heard voices in the distance. Who were they? Where were they?

I need some water, he said aloud in his mind.

With his mind on a hit movie he had seen the previous evening, an orderly was pushing Jordan down the hallway toward the elevator. He had just turned the last corner when he thought he heard the patient on the gurney making some kind of sound.

Knowing a little about Jordan's case, he brought the bed to a stop and peered into the patient's face.

"I neeeeed . . . some . . . waaa . . . waaaterr," he heard Jordan whisper. His lips were barely moving, but he was indeed talking.

"Hold on, guy!" the orderly responded. "We're gonna get you some help!"

He wheeled the bed around and headed back down the hallway to the nurses' station.

Jordan was still making attempts at communicating when the orderly spotted one of the nurses behind the desk.

"I think our man is waking up here," he said to her, interrupting the paperwork she was doing. "You might want to call a doctor."

Within a matter of minutes, Jordan was surrounded in the hallway by three nurses and Dr. Evans.

"Can you hear me, Mister Rau?" Dr. Evans said in a loud voice, peering into Jordan's face.

Jordan's eyes were flickering, then squinting weakly. "I . . . heeear . . . you," Jordan whispered, his voice sounding slow and crackly like a ninety-year-old's.

Dr. Evans turned to one of the nurses. "Go darken his room." Nodding down the hallway, he ordered the other two, "Let's get him back in there."

Once Jordan's bed was rolled back into his now-dim room, Dr. Evans stood at the bedside near the patient's head.

Evans watched as one of the nurses gave Jordan a tiny sip of water through a straw. Jordan barely managed to suck the water to the top of the plastic tube as the nurse held the cup steady. When the cup was set aside, Evans put his face close to Jordan's.

"I'm Dr. Evans, and I want to ask you a few questions, all right? First I want to know if you can tell me your first name, Mr. Rau?"

There were about twenty seconds of silence. And then came the answer. "Myyy . . . naaame . . . I'm . . . Jooordan . . ."

"Good. Are you married, Jordan?"

More silence. "Mmmaaarrrried . . . yyyyesss."

"How many fingers am I holding up?" Evans questioned, holding up one finger within a foot of Jordan's face.

Jordan grimaced. His eyelids were straining to open wider. Finally his eyes closed as he whispered, "Juuuussst . . . one."

"Can you open your eyes again, Jordan?"

Jordan's eyes opened halfway.

"What is your wife's name?" Evans then asked.

"Sssssusan . . . Her . . . name . . . iiiiis . . . Ssssusan." Jordan said with concentration, his eyes starting to close again.

"How wide can you open your eyes for me, Jordan?" Evans asked.

Jordan's eyes came halfway open again. The muscles throughout his face slightly contorted as he strained to lift his eyelids higher. He managed to open them slightly wider.

"What do you see around you?" Evans inquired.

Jordan's eyes slowly moved up and down and from side to side as he tried to focus on the various objects around the room. He grimaced again. His eyes started to close.

"What did you see?" Evans asked.

Closing his eyes all the way this time, Jordan ssaid, "A . . . couple of . . . laaaadies . . . uhhh . . . TV . . . uhhh . . . wiiindow . . ."

Missing the exchange of smiles between a couple of the nurses, Evans continued his questioning. "Can you open your eyes again and tell me where you are?"

As Jordan's eyes reopened, the gears of his mind were turning. "I . . . I'm . . . no . . . I don't knooow . . . where," he finally answered. "Youuu . . . tell . . . me."

Evans, now smiling broadly, explained to him that he had been injured in an automobile accident in Detroit, and that he was now recovering in a Chattanooga hospital.

When Evans finished answering Jordan's question, without mentioning the coma or the duration of it, he paused to see if Jordan would respond.

He didn't. He just lay there in silence, his eyes now almost fully open.

The doctor wasn't certain if Jordan had comprehended the scope of his answer or not. For the moment, he didn't want to press the issue.

"Can you move your right hand for me, Jordan?"

Jordan's head rolled to the right, his eyes shifting to focus on his right hand. Staring at it, he coughed three or four times. The coughs sounded like those of a weak, elderly man.

Evans turned to the nurse who had earlier served Jordan the sip of water, and asked her to give him another drink.

Jordan didn't hesitate to suck on the straw when the nurse placed it to his lips. It was obvious he was thirsty.

When Jordan finished drinking, Dr. Evans said again, "Let's see if you can move that right hand for me."

Once again Jordan focused on his hand. Everybody else in the room focused with him.

As Jordan closed his eyes and wrinkled his face with strain, his right hand lifted slowly from the bedsheet and rotated left to right, then right to left. Jordan produced the same pattern of movement several times.

"Great!" Evans exclaimed. "Now, can you make a fist?"

The fist was made, but it was a loose

one. Evans then put Jordan through fifteen minutes of movement drills, watching his patient successfully — if weakly — lift, bend, and rotate every movable part of his body until he was convinced that Jordan's lack of quick and tight movements was due to muscle atrophy, not partial paralysis or brain damage.

"Janine, why don't we get some broth or soup for Jordan to sip?" Evans suggested.

"I'll put a special rush order on it," Janine said, smiling.

As she headed out the door, Dr. Evans looked down at Jordan and told him, "Your wife stepped out of the ward a little while ago. She should be back pretty soon. She's going to be one happy lady."

He then asked Jordan one more question.

"Before I leave, is there anything you would like to ask or say?"

Jordan exhaled a small breath, looked Evans in the eye, and said, "I had a terrible dream . . ." He coughed another weak cough. "I dreamed that my boy was killed."

The doctor breathed deeply himself. He had heard about Chase's murder from Susan. He decided that the resident psychiatrist could best help Jordan deal with this issue.

"Okay," Evans responded in a neutral voice, "why don't you tell that to Dr. Rosenberg? He'll be introducing himself to you either sometime this evening or tomorrow morning. He'll spend some time talking with you about it." Evans paused, then squeezed his shoulder. "We're going to do everything we can to help you. You're in good hands."

21

At the nurses' station less than an hour later, Janine and another nurse intercepted Susan before she reached Jordan's room.

Janine told her that Dr. Evans had requested to meet with her prior to her visit with Jordan.

"He wants you to wait here for him while we page him," the second nurse added.

"Susan," said Janine, grinning, "Jordan woke up. About an hour and a half ago."

Susan's eyes widened, and her hands came up to her face. She slid down the wall where she was leaning, sat on the floor, and wept.

While the second nurse paged Dr. Evans, Janine knelt beside Susan and hugged her. "We're so glad for you," she said in a voice choked with happiness.

Janine helped her to her feet. "Is he in his room?" Susan asked. "I want to see him."

The nurses could barely convince her to

meet with the doctor first. Fortunately, Dr. Evans appeared in the hallway. He flashed her a triumphant grin. "Well, it looks like you heard the good news already!"

Susan gave him a grateful hug.

"Now, Susan, I need to tell you some things," he said. "Jordan is still pretty fuzzy. His speech is somewhat slurred and his eyes don't always focus as he wants them to. He's very weak, as you can imagine, since his muscles haven't been doing anything at all for the last four months."

Susan nodded, hanging on every word.

"I'm telling you this not to discourage you, but to prepare you. I believe that neurologically and physically, Jordan is on the road to recovery. But it's going to be a long, difficult road.

"Susan," he concluded, taking her by the shoulders, "Jordan's recovery, as badly as he was hurt, is little short of miraculous. He beat some very tall odds. I want you to remember that, and appreciate it."

"I do, Dr. Evans," she said, her eyes shining with tears. "Believe me, I do." *Thank You, Lord. Thank You, thank You, thank You* . . .

"Two more things before you go in to see him," Evans said. "We haven't yet told him how long he stayed in a coma. We wanted to steer away from subjects that weren't positive, so unless he asks outright, don't offer that information to him right now.

"Also . . ." Evans paused, studying her face. "I need to let you know that Jordan told us he had a dream. He . . . said he dreamed his son had been killed."

Susan flinched.

"That's a very heavy issue, so I'd like our resident psychiatrist, Dr. Rosenberg, to work with him on that, starting tomorrow. So try to avoid talking about your son until Rosenberg has had a chance to make some headway."

She once again nodded her understanding, but with less confidence than before.

"And now," Dr. Evans concluded with a grin, "I believe you have an appointment in Room 1202."

Susan walked toward the room, trying to keep from running. She opened the door and saw him.

Jordan's bed was in an upright position. He was staring with half-closed eyes out the window at a beautiful spring morning.

"Jordan?"

He slowly turned his head toward her. She sprang across to his bedside, throwing herself across him in a fierce embrace.

Jordan tried to return the hug as well as he could. His hands reached upward only to the middle of her back, but for Susan, it was a moment of emotional ecstasy.

"Thank God you're alive," she managed to whisper into his shoulder.

"I'm . . . ssssssorrrrry . . . Sssusan," Jordan whispered, breaking his silence.

Susan wasn't sure what he might be apologizing for. But right now, it didn't matter.

"Forget it," she told him. "I'm just glad you're still with us."

"I . . . almosssssst . . . didn't . . . make it . . . huh?"

"It's a miracle you're here. God has been so good."

"Hhhow long . . . have I been . . . in the . . . hhhhosssspital?"

Susan remembered Evans' instructions: Don't offer that information to him . . . But he had asked! How could she avoid telling him without sounding evasive?

"For . . . four months," she answered after a slight pause, watching him for any response.

His eyes twitched this way and that, from her face to the room and back again. His brow furrowed. He appeared to be troubled or confused by what she had said.

265

To her relief, Jordan changed the subject with his next question.

"What were . . . my injuries?" he asked.

In brief form Susan recounted the accident, the brain concussion, the broken back and other fractures, the surgeries, the long wait, and now the extraordinary victory.

"Against all the odds, Dr. Evans thinks you're going to be able to walk out of here on your own," she finished. *But why were you in Detroit?* she heard a voice ask inside her head. Quickly she buried the thought.

She gripped his hand and gazed fondly into his face. He looked up at her and tried to smile.

"I'm going to go get Donica at school," she said. "She's been reading and talking to you just about nonstop for the last four months. She'll be overjoyed to know how well her therapy worked," Susan laughed. Reluctantly, she backed toward the door. "I'll be right back, I promise."

Jordan's brow wrinkled again. He looked as if he wanted to ask a question.

"What is it, honey?" she asked him.

After a moment, he shook his head. "Nev . . . never mind," he said.

"Are you sure?"

He nodded, and smiled again, faintly. "Beee . . . caaarrreful," he said huskily.

She grinned. "You got it. I'll be back as fast as I can."

Fifteen minutes later, Susan was signing Donica out of school for the day.

When Susan broke the news to Donica in the school hallway, Donica stood motionless for about two seconds. Then she started jumping up and down. "Yes!" she shouted. "Yes, yes, yes!" Susan, despite her own exuberance, felt compelled to quieten her there in the school corridor. Then they rushed outside to the car.

The prolonged family reunion that took place in Jordan's hospital room twenty minutes later made them almost forget the pain and uncertainty of the last four months.

After a lot of hugs, tears, and I-love-you's, Jordan turned to his wife, with Donica still hanging from his neck, and asked, "Where . . . where's . . . Chaaase?"

Susan, absorbed in her emotional high, was caught off guard by the question, even though Dr. Evans had given her a fair warning. Not knowing what to say, she regarded Jordan with a troubled stare.

His eyes were begging to know the answer.

Susan saw Donica, looking confused, slowly pull away from him. Susan had failed to tell her about Jordan's "dream."

Susan's desperate pause lasted too long.

"It . . . wasn't . . . a dream . . . was it?" Jordan asked, more to himself than to them. A look of painful revelation burst into his eyes. "That's why . . . I was in Detroit . . . wasn't it?"

This time he looked at Susan, waiting for an answer.

"I don't know why you were in Detroit, Jordan. You . . . you never told me," Susan replied.

Suddenly it all came back to him with a horrifying rush.

The move to Germany . . . the murder . . . the hatred . . . the hunt . . . Ricardo . . . the three Jamaicans . . . the trip to Detroit.

It was all clear again, as clear as fresh blood on a white shirt. As clear as the razor-sharp pain and relentless agony.

Closing his eyes, he felt his emotions twist together in a crippling knot of rage and despair.

"Why did they have to kill him, Susan?" he heard himself whimpering. "Why would anyone kill my son?"

"Jordan," Susan said, fear rising again in her throat. "Please! You can't deal with this right now. You've got to get well. You've got to —"

"Why? Why? Why did they have to kill him?" His voice, still weak from disuse, was breaking with strain and emotion. His chest pumped convulsively as the frenzy grew on him. Pressing down on the mattress with both hands, he strained to lift his legs off the bed.

"Jordan, don't!"

"Daddy, please stop it!" wailed Donica.

After three or four seconds, he collapsed back onto the bed. He was breathing as if he had run up two flights of stairs.

He refused to look at Susan and Donica while he caught his breath.

Susan felt as if she were falling down a dark well. She felt as if daylight and warmth were vanishing behind her, and ahead lay only darkness and silence. *He's giving in to it,* she realized with despair. *The hatred is taking him back. He can't fight it. Maybe he doesn't want to.* With her worst fears materializing before her eyes, she sank into a chair and sobbed.

Donica looked on, her moment of triumph turning to ashes.

Jordan lay in his bed, staring at the wall and grinding his teeth as he contemplated the day he would be mobile again. The day he would be able to return to Detroit and finish the job.

♦ Part 4

Part 4

22

Jordan strained to lift his legs as high and as fast as he could while pushing himself through the chest-high water. His physical therapist had just stepped out of the pool, having been summoned to the telephone. "Take a break; I'll be right back," he had said as he exited the water.

But Jordan chose not to slow down. Relentlessly he exerted himself. Six weeks had passed since his awakening, and the prognosis from Dr. Evans had been proven correct.

"All of Dr. Rosenberg's psychiatric tests show that you are 100 percent lucid," Evans had said to him five days after he awoke. "You've suffered no loss of memory, your reading comprehension is above average, your mental reflexes are quick and sharp, and you're coping satisfactorily with your situation. The bones in your back, knee, and shoulder have healed beautifully, and there are no signs of paralysis anywhere in your body. With the help of daily physical therapy sessions, there's no foreseeable reason why you shouldn't be able to walk out of here in a couple of months and be on your way back to a normal lifestyle."

Jordan smiled as he reached the end of the pool. Tomorrow he would be released from the hospital — two weeks ahead of schedule. Evans had given the official word earlier this morning. "You've surprised us all with the speed of your recovery," the doctor had added. "You've reached the point where you'll be able to finish your recovery on your own."

Jordan's lungs swelled with air as he began another trek down the length of the forty-foot pool.

Susan, of course, was characterizing his rapid rehabilitation as a miracle from God.

That's fine if it makes her feel better, he thought as he shoved himself through the water. But he knew his recovery was due to hard work — day in and day out, sunrise to sunset. He had pushed himself throughout every physical therapy session. Even in the wheelchair during his free times, he had done leg lifts, arm lifts, shoulder lifts, neck rolls, and seated body lifts — anything he could to build his strength and endurance.

The number of repetitions for each exercise and the degree of movement had been painfully limited in the beginning, but he had driven himself mercilessly. Even when he was supposed to be lying in bed resting, he had done sit-ups; he was now up to five.

Eleven days ago, he progressed from the wheelchair to arm-support crutches. Yesterday the therapist told him he would probably need both crutches for another two or three weeks, then graduate to a single crutch for an additional few weeks to complete the rehabilitation.

Cutting his way slowly through the warm water and puffing heavily, Jordan decided he would be independent of both crutches within three weeks.

He drove himself, willed himself back into shape, because *they* were still out there, waiting for him — in Detroit.

Images of Susan and Donica loomed before him. Again he recalled Donica's look of defeat as his grief for Chase had spoiled their moment of reunion. Again he saw the expression of wounded disappointment on Susan's face. But he stifled the thoughts of doubt and guilt rising in the back of his mind.

I'm getting back on my feet ahead of

schedule. Why can't they at least be happy about that?

Reaching the end of the pool, he jerked angrily around for another lap. I don't need this conflict, he thought. I've got to do what I've got to do. They'll just have to deal with it.

The therapist came out of the office and rejoined him in the water.

"Everything okay?" Jordan asked, trying to get his mind off the troubling thoughts he'd been having.

"Yeah, just a last-minute shuffling of my afternoon schedule," the therapist explained. He began to coach Jordan into the next exercise.

But Jordan had a question to ask.

"When do you think I'll be able to drive again?" he asked in an offhand manner.

"I'd say you should be able to start taking short trips two or three days after you stop needing crutches," the therapist replied. "But we'll just have to wait and see what kind of progress you're making."

Jordan grunted. Then it wouldn't be a very long wait. He'd see to that.

At four-thirty the next afternoon, Jordan was released from the hospital.

Approaching the car with Susan and

Donica at his side, he was both excited and relieved. Over five months of his life had slipped behind him since his initial confinement. This was the first time he had been outdoors in nearly half a year. He couldn't remember when the early summer air had ever felt so fresh.

He inhaled deeply and appreciatively, savoring the smell of freshly clipped lawns and blooming honeysuckle. Though he still had to lean heavily on his arm braces, he felt liberated. He wanted to jump up and down and dance.

Almost as if Susan and Donica had read his mind, they both grabbed him when they reached the edge of the parking lot and yelled, "Surprise!"

Jordan was staring at an automobile parked in a handicap parking space. It was the automobile Susan had shipped from Germany, but it was almost unrecognizable. Big yellow ribbons were tied on the antenna, on all four door handles, on both windshield wipers, across the front grill, and all over the front and rear bumpers. And marked in shoe polish across the windows were the words *Welcome Back, We Love You.*

The sheer joy of the moment brought mist to his eyes. Awkwardly shifting his weight, he reached for his wife and daughter and embraced them.

Twenty minutes later, Susan pulled to the curb in front of the new apartment she had rented three weeks ago in anticipation of Jordan's homecoming. A giant plywood sign — with the words *Home Sweet Home* hand-painted in white — was staked prominently in the front yard.

"Thank you, guys," he grinned, "but you didn't have to do all this!"

"It's okay," Donica explained. "Granddaddy made the sign and put it in the ground for us. All Mom and I did was paint the letters. I did most of them."

Susan squeezed his thigh. "It's just a token of our gratitude to God. We love you."

"It looks like Chase's handwriting," Jordan said softly.

In the backseat, Donica's smile faded. Jordan didn't notice.

They got out of the car and went inside.

Their family furniture, having been shipped from Germany, now looked shiny and new from Susan's shampooing, dusting, and polishing. It looked fresh and different, positioned neatly in the new surroundings. Everyone's favorite pictures and posters were hung on the walls, and their personal things were placed in cabinets and on shelves. Everything was in place.

All except Chase's furniture. And Chase's favorite pictures and posters. And Chase's personal things.

Jordan noticed the omission immediately.

As he stood in the doorway of the bedroom he would share with Susan, Donica spoke up at his side. "Daddy, do you like the way everything's laid out? Look — I picked out some new slippers for you —"

She broke off as he turned away. In his preoccupation, he hadn't even heard her. He turned to Susan and said, "Where are Chase's things?"

As Donica fled the room, Susan told Jordan, "I've had his things put in storage until we decide what to do with them. I thought it was best that —"

"What's that supposed to mean?" he demanded, pointing at a handmade decoupage standing atop Susan's dresser. It was made with a colorful variety of letters cut from magazines and newspapers. It read:

OUR NEW HOME

OUR NEW FAMILY

OUR NEW LIFE

Susan stared at him, uncomprehending. "Donica made that. I . . . I guess it means that she hopes we can start over . . . Start better."

"Better than what?" he retorted, his anger beginning to master him. "Better than when Chase was alive? Better than before some criminal stole the rest of our family?"

"Please, honey," she coaxed, trying to remain calm. "It's going to be okay. God is going to help us. He's already worked one miracle —"

"I'm sorry, Susan," he said, looking away from her. "Don't lay that stuff on me. I can't accept it. I can't lie down and roll over about this."

"Jordan, I don't think trusting God means lying down and —"

"I don't see how in the world you can expect me to just —" he gestured angrily in the air, searching for a word — "to just start over, like a kid playing a game of hopscotch or something. I lost my son, Susan! Somebody just reached out and yanked him away from me, and I can't ever forget that!" His voice was getting louder and louder.

"I lost my son, too, Jordan." She spoke quietly, her eyes never wavering from his. "I hurt, too."

He stared at her for several seconds, then turned away. "I'm going to get a hot bath and be alone for a while."

"I'll start supper," Susan responded despairingly. She started to walk toward the kitchen, then turned back and said, "We're going to make it, Jordan. With God's help, we're going to make it."

"Yeah, sure," he answered, moving toward the bathroom.

Soaking in the hot water, Jordan grudgingly admitted to himself that he had treated Susan insensitively just now. Something deep within him recognized a new strength inside her, and felt indicted by it. Pressed into a corner by the unfavorable comparison, he had responded with hostility.

He ruminated uneasily for some time, until he drifted off to sleep in the warm water.

Susan awakened him about thirty minutes later. Supper was almost ready.

As they sat down to the homecoming meal, Jordan attempted an apology. "I know I've probably ruined the afternoon for you . . . I guess I was a little out of line . . ."

There was an uneasy silence, broken by

Susan. "Well, we're all a little uptight, honey. Why don't we eat, before the food gets cold." She glanced at Donica, who sat listlessly in her place, her eyes red-rimmed and downcast. Donica looked up at her mother. Without meeting her dad's eyes, she mumbled, "Yeah, Dad. It's okay."

Then Susan told Jordan she wanted to say a blessing.

"Go ahead," he said in a monotone. For some strange reason, the ritual nettled him. He didn't feel like participating, but having just apologized, he felt compelled. He bowed his head.

"Lord, we thank You for faithfully providing for us . . . even in miraculous ways," she whispered. "We're indebted to You for this very special homecoming. May we always be grateful for this and all Your blessings. In Jesus' name, amen."

They were almost finished with their meal when the phone rang. Susan answered it.

"Hi, Paul . . . Yes, we've been home for about an hour and a half . . . Okay — it might take just a minute, but I can get him to the phone."

Jordan had already started reaching for his crutches. He got up and slowly maneuvered himself around the dining room table, then over to the kitchen bar. He picked up the phone.

"Hello?"

"Jordan, this is Paul Krueger. I wanted to call and let you know how happy we are in Chesapeake to know you're back home."

"Thanks, Paul. It's . . . great to be here."

"We've believed in you all along, Jordan," Paul told him. "We've all felt that if anybody could fight back and overcome a situation like this, you could do it. I just want you to know we're all really proud of you."

"Thanks, Paul," Jordan responded without enthusiasm. "That's great to hear."

"At the end of September, we'll take a fresh look at your situation," Paul stated. "By then, you'll probably know more about your desires and capabilities. We'd love to keep a man with your grit and determination, but you don't have to make that decision until you're ready."

"I appreciate that."

Paul's voice rose a half-tone as he continued. "To help all of us work toward that time and that decision, we'd like to recommend a counselor to meet with you and Susan."

Jordan had never sought the help of a

professional counselor at any time in his life. As far as he was concerned, he had never needed one — he had always managed alone. And though he was somewhat uncomfortable with the thought of going to a counselor now, he would probably go along. The last thing he wanted to do was aggravate the mission board. He wasn't exactly in a position to bargain with them, just now.

"Her name is Dr. Maureen Kinskey," Paul told him. "She's with Bradach and Kinskey Psychiatric Associates. Their office complex is in the same downtown building that houses the First Tennessee National Bank."

"Maureen Kinskey . . . Bradach and Kinskey Associates . . . First Tennessee building," Jordan repeated. He knew the location, no more than twenty minutes from their apartment.

"Would June first — that's a week from Monday — be a good day for you both to see her? If so, I'll call and set up the first appointment."

They don't think I'll go on my own, Jordan thought. "Yeah. That will be fine."

"Good. After I speak with them, I'll have someone in their office call you and let you know the time. We'll stay in touch," Paul told him, bringing the call to a close. "In the meantime, if there's anything we can do to help you, don't hesitate to call. And don't forget: We all still believe in you."

Jordan hung up the phone and looked at Susan. "They want us to start meeting with a psychiatrist downtown."

Susan toyed with her spoon. She was no more thrilled by the prospect of a psychiatrist than Jordan was — but for entirely different reasons, she suspected.

23

That night Jordan's mind was as restless as a bear in a cage. He lay in bed and stared up at the ceiling, unable to drift off into the restful sleep he so badly needed. Tangled thoughts rushed through his brain — thoughts of Chase, Ricardo, the Jamaicans, Detroit . . . and Percival Blake.

He was following the doctor when the wreck happened. He had been hoping to learn where the Jamaican doctor lived, and perhaps to get a lead on where to begin his search for the gangsters who had killed Chase.

His thoughts shifted to the All People's Church, and to Jason Faircloth.

Listening to the older pastor's incredible story of pain, loss, and self-discovery, Jordan had come as close as at any time in recent memory to believing someone else might understand the suffering he himself was experiencing. Listening to Faircloth's gentle voice, and hearing of the incredible difficulties he had faced, Jordan had forgotten — if only for a few minutes — the hateful quest which had first drawn him to that meeting in the shabby inner-city church building.

Jason Faircloth. Undeniably intelligent. Under no illusions about the fairness of life, and yet a devout believer. A man he had seen and heard only once, but whom he strangely respected.

For a moment, Jordan considered writing a letter to Faircloth, to discuss the issue of "personal faith." He remembered that night how he had been tempted to seek out the older man after the missions meeting, only to be distracted by the need to keep track of Percival Blake.

He could call the All People's Church and, most likely, obtain Faircloth's mailing address. It wouldn't hurt anything. In fact, if he got the address and wrote such a letter, nobody else would need to know.

Then another idea, a more relevant one, struck him. By calling the All People's Church he could probably also get the address for Percival Blake, the Jamaican doctor.

He played with the thought until after midnight, when sleep finally overtook him.

★ ★ ★

The next morning, after Donica left for school and while Susan was running errands, Jordan dialed directory assistance for Detroit and requested the number for the All People's Church. Jotting it down, he hung up the phone and stared at the receiver.

He thought of Susan and Donica, fought back the guilt, then picked up the phone again and dialed. He heard the ring on the other end. Three times. Five. Seven. Just as Jordan started to hang up, someone answered.

"Hello?" a male voice panted on the other end of the line. "All People's Church. Can I help you?"

"Yes, I'm calling long-distance from Tennessee. My name is Jordan. I want to know if anyone there can give me the address of Reverend Jason Faircloth, the featured speaker at your missions conference last December. I was in Detroit during the conference and was able to attend one of the services. And for the last five months now I've been intending to write a note of thanks to tell him how much I appreciated his ministry. I know this is a little late, but I've promised myself I wouldn't put it off any longer."

"Yes, let me look that up for you. Fair . . . cloth. Jason. Here it is."

Jordan copied the address. In what he hoped was a casual tone, he then asked, "And is it possible also to get the address of another speaker that same night? His name is Percival Blake — he works with the Jamaican youth there in the inner city. I'd like to write him a letter of thanks as well."

"Sure. I've got it . . . right here."

After penciling down Blake's address, Jordan repeated both addresses aloud for confirmation, then thanked the man.

After hanging up, Jordan stood there a moment. He now knew he would find the three Jamaicans. And destroy them.

Dear Reverend Faircloth,

Last December while on a business trip to Michigan, I attended one of the mission conference services at the All People's Church in downtown Detroit.

On the particular evening I was there, you were the primary speaker. You shared your observation concerning the lack of openness and honesty in the typical American church. Then you led the congregation in a time of sharing some of their past pains and struggles.

It was one of the most unusual and heart-touching church services I've ever witnessed . . .

Jordan stared at the screen of his word processor. It was Sunday morning, and Susan and Donica had gone to church. He had excused himself on the grounds of fatigue. They had been gone less than ten minutes when he sat down to compose this letter to a man he had never met, a letter he still wasn't sure he would end up sending. Again he reached toward the keyboard.

I just want to tell you how much I appreciated your openness and honesty and also your fresh approach to ministry. I would have thanked you earlier, but due to an automobile accident soon after the meeting, I was unable to write or type until just recently.

Therefore, please accept this belated word of thanks.

And now that I'm finally able to compose this letter, I also have a question I would like to ask you. It pertains to a statement that was made and a philosophy that was alluded to during one of the testimonies given on the night I was there at All People's Church. I'm almost certain it was shared by a black man. He said that someone there at the church — I believe it was the pastor — had taught him that "the just shall live by faith."

My question is this: Is blind faith in a "personal" God a legitimate option for an intelligent and resourceful person in the twentieth century?

I realize "the just shall live by faith" is a quotation from the Bible. But at the time in history when it was written, man didn't possess the same accumulation of strength, resources, and knowledge we have access to today. Therefore, was not this verse written out of man's weakness? Wasn't it written because of man's inability to do centuries ago what we, his descendants, can manage today without needing or expecting "divine" help?

If you have the time to answer these questions, I would greatly appreciate your insight. Your response will either reconfirm what I already believe, and thus give me needed determination in life, or else it will challenge some of my strong doubts and perhaps provoke a new perspective for me. Whichever, I'm sure your thoughts will be enlightening and helpful.

Thanks again for your ministry, and for your openness and honesty.

I look forward to your reply.

Sincerely,
Jordan Rau

Jordan reread the letter several times. He decided that it accurately raised the questions he was pondering without revealing the details of his struggles or his intentions.

After printing the letter, he folded it and put it in an envelope, then addressed and sealed it. He stared thoughtfully at the letter, ready to mail. Should it be sent? Or should it be torn up and tossed in the trash? What difference would either choice make?

After another minute of contemplation, he reached into a drawer and pulled out a book of stamps. He affixed a stamp to the envelope and placed the letter in his desk drawer. He would give it to the postman tomorrow.

When Susan and Donica arrived home from the morning church service, they found Jordan lying on the bed, asleep with his clothes on. They quietly closed the bedroom door and left him undisturbed.

Ricardo's stepfather, Sergeant First Class Neal Mitchum, was nervous and mad. Nervous because of the impending threat to his military standing. And mad at Ricardo for putting him in this position.

It was early Monday morning in Bad Tölz, Germany. Mitchum was sitting before the American military's Family Member Conduct Board, which was in essence a lower military court. Also present were the community commander, a family advocacy representative, and the battalion commander — a lieutenant colonel whose authority could affect Mitchum's career.

Ricardo was now wanted by the American military police and the German police, and was being searched for by police in the U.S. He was wanted as a prime suspect for the double murder of Chase Rau and Heather Anne Moseley.

Under oath, Mitchum once again explained, while trying to maintain an upright and stalwart composure, that neither he nor his wife had driven his BMW to Bad Aibling on Friday evening, 25 October 1991, the night of the killings. He himself had been in another part of the country on a field exercise, an airtight alibi that various military authorities had already verified. His wife had spent the evening hours of October twenty-fifth at the base club, also an airtight alibi, supported by a host of witnesses, including two of the club's bartenders.

"Unless some unidentified person stole the car for a joyride," Mitchum addressed the board, "a possibility for which there has not yet been any evidence, then my seventeen-year-old stepson, Ricardo, was the one driving the car that evening. As my wife has already testified, she found out about a month after the teenage murders that Ricardo had illegally driven the BMW on repeated occasions when I was away on field exercises. That's all we know, sir."

Sergeant Mitchum's testimony and confession had already been recorded for military records, but was once again officially noted.

Now, after two months of thorough investigation, bureaucratic red tape, and embarrassing press coverage, it was time for the colonel presiding over the board's deliberations to make a decision.

His pronouncement came with military forthrightness. "Whatever your stepson's involvement in the murder of the two teenagers, Sergeant Mitchum, your negligence to keep him within the limitation of the German driving laws, and your negligence to insist that your wife report her son's violation of those laws, has brought this base under a lot of damaging publicity and political embarrassment. In the event your stepson is apprehended and proven guilty of the murder charges, the political and public damage will be even worse.

"Therefore, as a public statement of our effort to execute and restore base discipline, I charge you with failure to control a dependent. Your duty at this base will be terminated next month. You will be reassigned to stateside duty, most likely at Fort Bragg. This disciplinary action will be noted on your official records.

"Any questions, Sergeant?"

"No sir," Mitchum answered, and saluted.

As he walked outside the building, Neal Mitchum knew that the upward momentum of his career had just been halted.

He felt his anger toward Ricardo intensifying.

He wanted the boy to hurt.

Jordan sat in the passenger's seat while his wife drove. They were approaching downtown Chattanooga for their first appointment with Dr. Maureen Kinskey.

Susan drummed on the steering wheel with her thumbs as she contemplated the upcoming session. Her greatest fear was that Dr. Kinskey, like Jordan, would scoff at her determination to trust God and the Bible as a divine source of strength — both for healing her marriage and for continuing to heal her own heart and emotions.

The abyss into which Chase's death had plunged all of them had finally made her realize that, despite all the determination and resourcefulness in the world, there were times when she couldn't cope by depending on human resources alone. She knew, with a certainty beyond words, that her revival of intimate trust in God had been the only thing sustaining her through all the horrible things she had endured. She knew her life would be impossible without that confidence, that trust.

As Susan prayed for God to help her relax and be courageous, she glanced over at Jordan, seated listlessly on the other side. She knew he wasn't at all enthused about this morning's appointment either. But his reticence had more to do with his determination to be self-sufficient, to be strong, to be in control. "Never admit the need for outside help" was a cardinal rule in his life.

Susan shuddered. Why couldn't he see how impoverished he was? His obsessive response to Chase's death had crippled him, had shrunk his universe down to a single theme, a single wish. She didn't see how anything or anyone could deflect him from the destructive course on which he'd set himself. She was afraid for him, but she couldn't talk or reason with him — her words just didn't seem to penetrate. She wondered if Maureen Kinskey would be able to persuade him to face reason.

Susan glanced in her rearview mirror, then pulled into the parking garage of the First Tennessee Bank building.

Inside the lobby, they scanned the building directory. "Fifth floor, room 510," she said. There was a small knot of tension in the middle of her forehead that was quickly broadening into a headache.

They walked into Dr. Kinskey's office at 10:24. The receptionist gave Jordan some forms to fill out, then asked them both to seat themselves in an adjacent waiting room. A young woman was sitting alone in the room when they entered. She glanced up at them, then went back to leafing through the magazine she held.

After she and Jordan were seated, Susan glanced around at the abstract oil paintings hanging on the four windowless walls. A tall potted plant sat in the corner. The narrow room had a relaxed look, but to Susan it still felt clinical.

A few minutes later, a door opened from the office area. A trimly built lady, about five-feet-eight in height, stepped briskly into the room. She had short, dark hair, wore glasses, and was expensively dressed. Carrying herself confidently and seriously, she reflected a strong professional presence.

"Good morning," she said, approaching Jordan and extending her hand. "You must be Jordan and Susan Rau. I'm Dr. Maureen Kinskey."

Jordan levered himself from his seat and shook her hand.

"Well, it's exactly 10:30," Kinskey said. "Let's get started, shall we?" She ushered them inside.

They entered a spacious hallway which opened into five or six offices. Dr. Kinskey directed them to her door.

Kinskey's oak desk was positioned in one of the corners, flanked by a floor-to-ceiling oak bookshelf filled with various volumes, and impeccably organized.

"Have a seat there on the couch," the doctor instructed them.

While Susan and Jordan tried to make themselves comfortable on the long couch, Kinskey pulled up an armchair about five feet away.

"Well, I'm glad to see you," she smiled. "Paul Krueger, from your mission headquarters, has briefed me somewhat on your background and on your circumstances of the past year." Her face took on a more serious cast as she continued.

"The quantity of stressful situations you've been through during the last twelve months," she told them, "would be enough to scar most people emotionally for many years.

"Depression, bitterness, reclusion, insomnia — those are just a few of the emotional disorders that would normally arise."

Susan looked down, toying with her wedding ring. Jordan's gaze roved somewhere over the doctor's left shoulder.

"Therefore," Kinskey continued, "over the course of the next three months as we meet together, I want you to feel free to share with me your deepest thoughts and feelings. It's important for you at this point to be as honest as you can.

"In the beginning, it will be my job to pinpoint the emotional disorders you might be facing in your lives right now, knowingly or unknowingly.

"As we continue to dialogue, I'll ensure to the best of my ability that you understand what you're dealing with and how to release yourselves from it.

"At the end of the three months, I'll share my assessment and recommendation with Paul Krueger. And, as I understand it, he will at that time decide if it's best to continue the sessions."

Dr. Kinskey leaned back in her chair, stopped talking, and looked at them, waiting for a response.

Neither Jordan nor Susan turned to look at the other. Instead, they both stared straight ahead at Kinskey. Jordan nodded his head. Susan, still filled with doubt and apprehension, only stared.

"All right, let's jump into it," Kinskey told them.

First she asked Jordan to tell her how he was doing physically and how he was feeling about his recovery. She then gave him a series of advanced flashcard tests — identifying geometric shapes, calculating various math equations, and defining a mixture of political and biological terms —

to assess his mental agility after the coma.

Then, without breaking her pace, she asked Jordan to evaluate the present condition of his marriage relationship.

Caught off guard by the question, Jordan crossed his legs, cleared his throat, and said, "Uh . . . we have our minor problems like every couple . . . but I don't think the problems are so complicated that we can't work them out on our own, with a little time." He then delved into a five-minute monologue of how much he loved his family, how much they meant to him, and how he fully intended as a husband and father to be emotionally strong and optimistic, and to lead his family to a permanent victory over their adverse circumstances.

Kinskey made a few notes on the pad she was holding in her lap, then asked Susan, "How do *you* feel about the marriage at this point?"

Struck by the untruthful answer Jordan had given, Susan had already decided she wasn't going to hide anything.

"His intentions might be good and well-founded," Susan answered, looking straight ahead at Kinskey. "But the truth is, he's locked up in his own secluded world of bitterness. There's no meaningful communication between us at all right now. So I would say our marriage is under a tremendous load of stress."

Kinskey looked carefully at both Susan and Jordan. Then she said to Susan, "From your perspective, what do you think is the root of this perceived problem?"

Susan braced herself and answered from her heart. "Jordan has never learned to trust God. If his life starts to get out of control, he panics. And when he panics, he uses every possible resource, and will run over anybody who gets in his way, to wrestle back into the driver's seat. In essence, he can't function if he can't be the master of his own life."

"So," Kinskey interjected, "you're saying that when your family's life spun out of control during the last twelve months, it was *wrong* for Jordan to try to wrestle things back into order?"

"I'm saying," Susan explained, "that as a person who claims to be a follower of God, Jordan needs to stop fighting circumstances and start relaxing and trusting God. Or else anxiety will destroy him — and all those around him."

Kinskey paused, then continued: "We're down to the last fifteen minutes of this session, so we need to start drawing things to a close. Susan, don't answer out loud, but I would like to ask you a closing question just to provoke a different angle of thinking on your part. Are *you* relaxing, or is it possible that you are subconsciously trying to manipulate Jordan to be under *your* control?"

The question caught Susan off guard. She forced herself to take a deep breath. A tear managed to escape down the curve of her cheek, and she quickly wiped it away.

Kinskey redirected her attention to Jordan. For nearly ten minutes she encouraged him to be more open and communicative with his wife and daughter, reminding him that communication at this point was vital to their healing process. She wrote down the titles of three different books dealing with the subject, gave Jordan the list, and urged him to go to one of the city's libraries, check out the books, and read them. "They will be helpful if you will use them," she prompted him.

Turning then to give her concluding remarks to Susan, Kinskey said, "You've been through a lot. And I believe you're more fatigued than you realize. Therefore, I'm going to prescribe an antidepressant for you. It's called Fluoxetine. It's an extremely safe drug that will give you some relief from the stress you're feeling."

The doctor went on to explain that during times of stress and anxiety one of the major enzymes in the brain is depleted, thus causing depression. "Fluoxetine will synthetically restore that particular enzyme to the brain, and alleviate the depression," she continued. "It's like a splint. It will give your brain some temporary and needed rest so that it can replenish its own natural supply. I'll go ahead and prescribe a bottle of one hundred capsules. Each capsule will contain a mild dosage of twenty milligrams. Take a couple of those each day, one in the morning and one in the evening."

A few minutes later, Jordan and Susan stepped outside the building. Jordan, instead of heading in the direction of their car, started walking across the street in the opposite direction.

Susan didn't feel like talking at the moment, but not knowing what Jordan was doing, she called out to him and asked him where he was going.

"To the drugstore," he yelled back to her, nodding toward a pharmacy just across the street.

Susan wanted to call out that he would be wasting his money; she had no intention of using any antidepressants. But not wanting to embarrass herself by getting into a public shouting match, she let him go.

She went back to the car and waited — and prayed.

When Donica arrived home from school that afternoon, she overheard her father and mother arguing in their bedroom about whether Susan would or would not take the drug. Donica thought her father sounded cruel, unwilling to let up on Susan. Then she heard her mother scream. It was a scream of pain.

Running into her parents' bedroom, she saw her mother lying twisted on the bed with blood dripping from her mouth.

Her dad was standing beside the bed, propped on one crutch, breathing heavily. His other crutch was leaning upside down against the corner of the mattress.

Donica felt something inside her break. She wanted to strike out at her mom and dad and hurt them both. Instead, she fled in the opposite direction. Away from their bedroom. Out of the apartment.

Finding a quick hiding place behind an apartment dumpster, she sat down and wept. For the first time in her life, in the rush of her erratic breathing, she contemplated suicide.

Later that night as she lay in her bed — in a house filled with so much tension, darkness, and uncertainty — she regretted that she had not carried out her afternoon wish.

When Jordan awakened the next morning, he could feel with his body that Susan was no longer in bed. Turning on a lamp in the darkened room, he looked at the alarm clock. It was already nine o'clock.

The house was quiet. Donica would have already been at school for nearly an hour, on her last full day of the school year.

But where was Susan? What was she doing?

He maneuvered himself out of the bed, collected his crutches that were propped at the headboard of the bed, and went to look for her.

He wanted to apologize to her again for yesterday — for his out-of-control rage. His hurtful words. His . . . physical . . . abuse. He still couldn't believe he had jabbed the heel of his crutch into her face. What had gotten into him?

He called out her name. He wanted to reassure her that nothing like that would ever happen again. Ever.

But there was no answer — only the low-volume hum of the air conditioner vibrating through the central air vents.

Finally, on the kitchen table, he found a note: "Gone to spend some time with Mother today."

That was it.

Maybe he should call her.

No. If she wanted to be out of his presence and out of his sight, he would just have to deal with it.

He sat down on one of the kitchen chairs and tried to take stock of the situation.

Until he carried out his mission in Detroit, things were only going to get worse, he decided. He had to go north, and he had to go soon.

With a new surge of determination, he stood to his feet, this time taking only one crutch.

Concentrating with all his might, he slowly lifted his right foot and placed it forward. Feeling unsure and unbalanced, he gritted his teeth and fought to stabilize himself. Moving parallel to the wall, he managed three steps before he had to catch himself against the wall.

But three steps was a start.

For the next twenty minutes, he grunted

and strained, pushing himself through the same exercise several more times. For the next few days, he decided, he would push himself even harder.

Feeling sweaty, he took a shower and got dressed for the day.

He had just sat down at the table to eat a bowl of cereal, and was wondering again if he should call Susan, when he heard the postman outside the door filling their mailbox.

Jordan moved to retrieve the mail. There were three pieces: a phone bill, a sweepstakes promotion, and a letter. The letter was addressed to him. Looking at the return address, he saw the name Jason Faircloth.

Back at the table, he slid the bill and the promotional material to the side and placed Faircloth's letter beside his cereal bowl. He stared at it.

He wondered if he should have even wasted Faircloth's time. After hearing Dr. Kinskey deride Susan yesterday for putting her trust in God, instead of capitalizing on the resources of the human will, he wished he had never written to Faircloth.

It was simple, undeniable: Faith was the religion of the emotionally weak.

Curious to see how Faircloth had responded to the question, though, Jordan put down his cereal spoon and removed the letter from the envelope.

The twice-folded letter was typed on plain white paper with no letterhead. Jordan began to read.

Dear Jordan,

Thanks for your letter and for the positive and encouraging words concerning the evening service in Detroit. I wish I could have had the opportunity to meet and speak with you in person. As I thought about your lengthy recovery following the car accident, my heart went out to you. Even though I know none of the details, I do rejoice with you that there has been some progressive healing.

However, judging by the comments and questions in your letter, it sounds like you're a strong but desperate individual who is struggling with severe loneliness and uncertainty.

Had Jordan not already seen Faircloth in person and witnessed the man's heart and mind in action, he would have stopped reading at this point. He would have viewed the last paragraph as the judgmental, out-of-line opinion of a cocky and narrow-minded individual.

But he had witnessed Faircloth's heart and mind in action. He had sensed the self-abasing spirit and the sincere, heartfelt concern for others. The man was not a slick, power-hungry ministerial jockey. He was genuine — a serious, brokenhearted man who had demonstrated convincingly that he understood people, and that he cared.

Maybe the fact that Faircloth had read between the lines of his letter so well was what made Jordan feel so uncomfortable. Or maybe it was the fact that Faircloth, a man who should know him the least, instead seemed to know him the most.

Annoyed and intrigued, Jordan kept reading.

Therefore, before I attempt to answer your questions, I first want to say that I am no stranger to such pain. I've been there. I know what it's like to struggle alone. And I know the need for nonjudgmental friends you can share openly with. If there aren't any potential prospects who can be that kind of friend for you, then I would like to make myself available. You have my address. Feel free to write to me anytime. Or, if you prefer, just call.

The phone number was written in the margin.

Jordan was oddly moved. He was forty years old and he couldn't remember anybody ever making that kind of offer to him before.

He kept reading.

Now to your questions. Instead of trying to answer them dogmatically as you might have wished or expected, I'm going to share a side fact with you that I hope will challenge you to think your way through your questions to your own answers. Let me begin by saying there are many people who in their entire lifetimes never approach the Scriptures. For many, it's a willful choice; for others, it's due to an absence of exposure. On the other hand, there are millions of others who do approach the Scriptures — some by choice, others by parental, educational, or religious coercion. Obviously, you are one of those who have approached the Scriptures, but whether by choice or by coercion, I'm not sure. And since you are one of those in the "approach" category, I think you will understand when I say there are only three basic ways the Scriptures can be approached:

(1) They can be accepted as they are, without being added to or subtracted from — the literalist approach.

(2) They can be accepted in their entirety, then added to — the far-right or legalistic approach.

(3) They can be critically dissected, and then deleted from — the far-left or liberal approach.

To the extremes are the legalists and the liberals. The legalists, of which in the past I was one of the most devout, add to the Bible their own set of denominational prejudices, their favorite teachings by idolized leaders, and the particular preferences of their native culture. All this "tradition" becomes embedded in their definition of Christianity. The legalists will then elevate these man-made teachings to the very level of Scripture. They preach them dogmatically and universally in the name of God, and imprison people with them.

This approach is destructive in the sense that it gives people a wrong concept of what Christianity is. (For example, Christianity is not physical cleanliness, nineteenth-century hymns, unfaltering patriotism, and 100 percent Sunday school attendance.) It also ladens people with an unnecessary load of false guilt, and turns its adherents into merciless and self-righteous judges who think that they and they alone have developed Christianity to its maximum potential.

To the other extreme are the liberals, of whom I've also been a part. They conveniently delete passages and teachings from the Bible, not because the passages have in any way been scientifically proven false, but simply because they are the cause of personal offense, or are difficult for the logical mind to believe (for example — the teaching of the lake of fire, or the physical resurrection of Christ, or His exclusive saviorhood). This approach is also destructive in that it reduces Christianity to a personalized religion of subjective relativism, implying that finite and mortal man is his own god who can decide what is or is not divine revelation. In this setting, man will never believe any teaching that would uncomfortably regulate his lifestyle, thus rendering Christianity ineffective and creating a spiritual anarchy.

Inevitably, a person who becomes his own god tends to fuel his own basic selfishness. At a great expense to others, he ends up respecting no one but himself.

Having personally experienced the destructiveness of both the legalistic and liberal extremes, I now take the third approach, Jordan. I am a literalist. I accept the Bible as it is. I don't purposely or consciously add to its teachings, even if I think it should speak out on an issue about which it is silent. Likewise, I don't purposely or consciously subtract from it, even if some of its pages cause me personal offense and are hard for me to understand. I trust that it is what it claims to be — the inspired and preserved Word of God, irrefutable, sufficient, and trustworthy in its entirety.

Therefore, based on my belief system, supported by many years of diverse experiences and observations, I can tell you unequivocally: Yes, the one God of the universe is personal. Very personal. To become His follower and trust Him on a daily basis is a very legitimate option. In fact, it's the only wise and safe option for any man in any culture in any generation — past, present, or future.

But if you take the liberal approach to the Scriptures, as you indirectly confess in your letter, then no scriptural answer I can give you will change or affect your thinking. Your beliefs about God will be determined solely by your approach to the Bible, not by anyone else's. Therefore, you've got to decide what you really believe about the Bible, Jordan. And then you'll find answers you can accept and hold on to.

To stimulate your thinking, you may want to take a fresh look at Luke 21:33.

God bless.

And remember, if you need someone to be your unconditional friend while you search for answers, I'm available. I mean it.

Sincerely,
Jason Faircloth

When Jordan finished reading the letter, he continued to hold it in his hand and look at it. He wanted to dismiss it as simpleminded and off the mark, but he couldn't. He was irritated that Faircloth's letter disturbed him.

Was he trying to be his own god?

Who was this man who could read through his soul?

Was faith the religion of the emotionally weak, as he had convinced himself for so many years? Or, as Faircloth had just advocated, was it indeed the only wise and safe option for any man?

Dropping the letter, Jordan hit the table two or three times with his palms.

For a reason he couldn't explain or understand, he continued to feel drawn to this older man he didn't really know. And yet Faircloth was only echoing what Susan had already been trying to tell him.

Feeling more distraught and confused about the "faith" question than ever before, he tried to block Faircloth's letter from his mind. But no matter how hard he tried, he couldn't.

He left his cereal bowl behind at the table and went to his computer. When the PC was booted up and the word processing program was ready, Jordan typed out a soulful plea.

Dear Reverend Faircloth,

Since you believe God is personal, and that He hears the prayers of faith, will you please pray for ME?

I don't even know who I am anymore, much less what I believe about God or the Bible.

All I know is that my life is out of control, and I'm quickly destroying what's left of my family.

I'm supposed to be a strong individual, but as you accurately perceived, I am desperate.

My whole life has become a pursuit of vengeance. Only my wife and daughter know this fact, yet not even they know all the details.

I have no one to share with. For the first time in my life, I am lonely. Maybe even going mad.

Please pray,

Jordan Rau

When Jordan finished typing, he didn't know if he had impulsively typed out the letter as a therapeutic release, or if he was genuinely reaching out toward the help Faircloth had offered.

After rereading the letter several times, he almost decided to throw it in the trash.

Instead, he addressed it to Faircloth, and gave it in secret to the postman the next morning.

24

Nine days later, two letters arrived in the Rau mailbox. One was from Donica's junior high school. It was addressed to both Jordan and Susan. The letter informed them that Donica, due to failing grades during the last four and a half months, would be held back next fall to repeat the ninth grade.

When Susan read the letter aloud, Donica reacted numbly to the news — *until* Jordan lost his temper with her. He cursed her for her stupidity and ripped the letter in half. Donica burst into tears and ran from the house. Susan followed on her heels to try to comfort her.

Jordan cursed again in his fury — this time to himself — then tore open the second letter addressed only to him.

It was from Jason Faircloth in New York.

Faircloth wrote that he wanted to respond to the contents of Jordan's last letter, but that he preferred to do it in person instead of in writing. "I'll be in Atlanta from the nineteenth through the twenty-fourth of this month for a week of ministry and to visit the graves of my wife and daughter," the letter stated. "If your schedule will allow for it, maybe I could drive up from Atlanta on the morning of either the twenty-fifth or the twenty-sixth and meet with you in your home." The letter was signed, "Your friend, Jason."

Jordan crushed the letter in his hands and stuffed it into the kitchen garbage pail. He never looked at it a second time, and never mentioned it to Susan.

With his eyes now on Detroit, he took his single crutch — to which he had now graduated — and walked away like a foaming mad dog.

On the following Monday, Jordan and Susan met with Dr. Kinskey for their second session.

Jordan managed to conceal his destructive and obsessive behavior pattern simply by being withdrawn. He answered only the questions Kinskey asked, with the shortest answers possible.

Viewing depression as his predominant ailment, Kinskey prescribed a bottle of Fluoxetine capsules for him as well. Again she urged him to find and read the books she had recommended on family communication.

Susan, now looking forty-nine instead of thirty-nine, likewise withdrew during the session. When she did talk, she mainly expressed her belief that the root of her and Jordan's struggle was a spiritual one. And no, she had not been taking the Fluoxetine.

Somewhat agitated, Kinskey stressed to Susan the importance of the anti-depressant, exhorting her to take it both for her sake and her family's. Finally, Kinskey admonished her not to take the Bible too seriously. "To do so," she told her, "can add needless pressure, confusion, guilt, and false expectations to your life. Perhaps worst of all," she concluded, "to put all your hope in a book like the Bible can distract you from capitalizing on your own inner resources. It's a passive approach that promotes what I call the 'lazy-self syndrome.'"

Susan didn't argue; she only nodded.

But in the days ahead — just as she had purposed in her heart — she still refused to take the Fluoxetine.

So did Jordan, though he had gotten the prescription filled. So caught up in his urgent goal, he forgot about the yellow-and-green capsules he had placed in the medicine cabinet above the bathroom sink.

Sweat rolled down Jordan's face as his lips twisted into a horrid smile.

Outside the apartment building alone in the dusk, he was leaning breathlessly against a large birch tree on the backside of the apartment complex. He had just walked a hundred yards unassisted. Today, Friday the nineteenth, was the second day since throwing down his last crutch. The distance of his hourly walks since then had been increasing with each new effort.

But nobody knew. And he didn't plan yet to tell anyone.

Susan and Donica would be arriving home late Monday evening from a five-day getaway trip into the Smokies with Susan's parents. Before they returned, he planned to be driving.

And by late next week, he thought to himself, *I'll be ready for Detroit.*

Walking down a well-worn fishing path through the trees and brush that surrounded a lake in the Smoky Mountains, Susan was struggling in the brilliance and heat of the summer sun to make a decision.

For the first time in twenty years of marriage, she was contemplating a separation.

Should she and Donica move out of the apartment and in with her parents? Or should she stay with Jordan in spite of his ever-increasing verbal and emotional abuse?

She didn't know if she could trust him anymore. After recently being struck by him again, this time by his hand, she wasn't sure how much more of his psychopathic behavior she could endure. Not only did she fear for her own safety, but also for Donica's. Jordan had not yet hit Donica, but he *had* threatened her. He was now completely unpredictable.

It looked as if their once-normal lifestyle was over.

She had talked with Jordan, reasoned with him, and pleaded with him until she was now empty. Her husband was no longer a rational human being. He had evolved into a monstrous contortion of bitterness and insane ugliness.

She didn't want her marriage to collapse. She wanted God to help save it. *Needed* Him to help. *Trusted* Him to help. But Jordan, contrary to her prayers and trust, had grown steadily worse.

Had her faith been too weak? Had she

waited too late in life to turn back to God? Was she not good enough to be heard? Had God not forgiven her for her past faithlessness?

Or was "faith in God" an emotional cop-out, as Jordan had been telling her for so many years, and as Dr. Kinskey had communicated during the last two visits?

Straying off the path, she sat down in some high grass, then lay back and wept. She tried to pray but was emotionally too tired. Looking up into the sunlit sky through watery tears, she suddenly felt all alone.

Perhaps she should try to talk to Pastor Rawlings at her church . . .

While a small butterfly fluttered around her tennis shoes, she faded into a needed sleep. Her thoughts became a kaleidoscope of darkness, dim flashes of light, and incomplete thoughts that never registered.

And then only nothingness.

Sweet, blissful nothingness.

25

Walking directionless at midday along the apartment complex streets, Susan was still shaking with fright.

She had tried to stop Jordan, but to no avail.

She was certain he had just left for Detroit. The checkbook and the suitcase he took with him convinced her. That, plus the look of total obsession in his eyes.

"I don't know *who* or *what* is in Detroit," she told him while following him out to the car, "but if you're going there to . . . to do something illegal —"

Jordan had turned on her like an aggravated lion. Grabbing her wrists and squeezing tightly, he had thrust his face into hers and growled, "I'm not going to Detroit, Susan! Now get out of my way!" Then he pushed her aside.

"If you get into any kind of trouble with the law, I will not stand behind you. You will be on your own," she had shouted at him as she watched him crawl into the car. The door slammed on her words as she added, "Do you understand me?"

Now, several minutes later, she was trying to calm down. But her fears, her uncertainty, and her inner threats of divorce were like a strong drink, intoxicating her.

Since Jordan sped away, she had just walked aimlessly. She hoped eventually to calm down and be able to make some quick and sensible decisions. Should she move in with her parents this afternoon and declare an indefinite separation? Should she call the church and try to talk with Pastor Rawlings? Should she go ahead and file for divorce?

She thought of Donica, who was spending the day with her grandparents. What would be best for her?

She rounded the corner facing the front of her apartment building and saw someone standing at her front door. It was a man, someone she didn't recognize.

When she saw him walk next door and ring the doorbell there, she dismissed him as a door-to-door salesman. But when she drew closer to her apartment and glanced that way again, she saw her neighbor in her open doorway, pointing the strange man in her direction.

As he started to walk toward her, Susan felt irritated by the intrusion. As he approached to within fifteen feet of her, she grimaced and lifted her hand in silence to signal her lack of interest, and to wave him away.

The man stopped.

Susan started to walk on inside when she heard him say, "You're hurting, aren't you?"

The power of the question and the guileless tone of his voice caused her to stop in her tracks.

Unsure of what to say or how to respond, she turned and for the first time looked into the man's face. The deep brown eyes, staring from a gentle and bearded face that looked to be about sixty years old, seemed to be on the verge of tears, as if the man somehow was sharing with her in her agony. *Am I supposed to know this man? How does he know who I am? How does he know I'm hurting? Why would he care?*

At that moment he held out a couple of addressed envelopes to her, as if he had heard her questions.

Susan took the envelopes into her hands and looked at them.

They were addressed to a Reverend

Jason Faircloth in Queens, New York.

The return address was . . . *theirs*. In Jordan's name. And in Jordan's handwriting.

She once again looked up at the man.

The sensation was awkward, unlike any she had ever felt before. She had heard the man speak only four words, yet she was already feeling the striking strength of his presence.

He looked at her from the heart — tears cresting in his eyes — and said with assertive compassion, "I would like to be your friend, Susan."

He made the statement with the unmistakable sound of *give,* not *take,* as if he had both the will and the ability to be just that kind of friend.

Susan felt touched, but confused.

"Are you Reverend Faircloth?" she asked. Her voice quavered with fatigue.

Faircloth smiled softly. "Jason."

"How does Jordan know you?" Susan asked as she sniffed and wiped away an emerging tear.

"Why don't we sit down so we can relax?" Faircloth replied after a thoughtful pause. He nodded downward toward the warm grass.

Feeling drawn to the stranger for a reason she couldn't explain, Susan nodded a slight okay. When he sat down on the freshly mowed grass with his legs stretched out over the parking lot curb, Susan sat down beside him.

"I think the letters will answer some of your questions," Faircloth prompted when they were seated.

Susan looked at Faircloth curiously, then removed the letters from the envelopes and started reading.

When she finished both letters, a part of her felt numb. Another part felt angry. Another part felt pity.

The letters partially answered her questions about Faircloth — when and where Jordan met him, and how Faircloth had attracted Jordan's confidence. But it was Jordan's emotional revelations, written from the secret parts of his soul — the desperate plea for answers concerning faith in God, the hurting confessions of being out of control, being lonely, going mad — that reached Susan's heart.

"I knew nothing about these," she told Faircloth, gesturing with the pieces of paper in her hand. "I knew nothing about you either." She paused. "Even though it's probably too late for him, I'm glad he was at least able to . . . open up . . . to someone."

"Too late?" Faircloth asked.

Susan sighed. "I'm assuming from what's in these letters that you've never met Jordan."

"No . . . I haven't."

"And yet," she asked with honest confusion, "you've come all the way here to Chattanooga to be able to meet with him?"

Without hesitating, Faircloth told her, "I've driven up from Atlanta where I've been staying for the last week. Not only to meet with Jordan. But also to meet with you."

"I don't understand," Susan said. "Why would you come all the way here to meet with strangers? How could you possibly care about our situation?"

Faircloth shifted his focus and looked into the distance as if he were conferring with someone. "Do you have time to hear a story?" he asked, turning to look her in the eye again.

Susan could feel the man's compassion by the way he asked the question. "Sure," she said.

Faircloth hesitated, then once again looked into the distance.

"I never knew the pain of loneliness, desperation, anxiety, and fear," he began, "until I was forty-two years old. In the span of only five days, I watched both my daughter and my wife lowered into their graves. I killed them, Susan. With intolerance, insensitivity. With emotional abuse . . ."

At those words, Susan felt a tenseness swell within her spine.

She listened intently as Faircloth told his story. As she listened, Susan found herself asking, *Why would he, as a minister, open his life up to a stranger and share such revelations?* She became so absorbed in his painful odyssey that she momentarily forgot her own pain.

Not until he finished did she realize she had been crying.

As she raised her hand to rub the teardrops from her face, she heard Faircloth speak the most powerful words that anyone had said to her during the last year of her emotional, mental, marital, and spiritual upheaval.

"To answer your question," he told her, "I care about people like you and Jordan *because I choose to care.* Because I *know* the loneliness. And because God never intended for any of us to struggle alone . . . and you *are* struggling alone, aren't you?"

Susan started crying again. She suddenly understood why Jordan had been so drawn to the man.

In one sense, she felt that Faircloth was an angel sent from God. The strong and reassuring peace she had started to feel in his presence was undeniable. Yet in another sense, she found herself trying to deny the fact that such concern could come from a stranger.

"What makes you think we're struggling alone? You don't even know the details of what's happened."

Faircloth bowed his head. "I don't have to know the details. I can read between the lines of Jordan's letters." He paused, then said, "Pain is like language, Susan. It comes in many different sounds, dialects, and accents. Once you learn a spoken language fluently, you can understand and communicate with others who speak that same language. It's the same for those who experience mutual pain. They understand each other."

Faircloth once again looked up at her. "I speak your language of pain, Susan — and Jordan's, too. I understand the loneliness, the desperation, the disillusionment, the tiredness, the emotional destruction. And my heart breaks for you. I don't know if you're a believer in Christ or not, but I came here to say that God cares, and that there's also a Christian brother out here who cares."

Susan wondered if it wasn't already too late. Could a new friend — even someone who had experienced common pains and was willing to listen — really make a difference now?

As if Faircloth understood her tiredness, he said gently yet urgently, "I want you to know — from someone who's been where you are, Susan — that it's always too early to give up."

Susan threw her caution aside and blurted out through tears, "I *am* a believer! And yes, I *do* need someone to talk to!" Then she added, "But can I trust you?"

"I'm here only to be a friend . . . an unconditional friend . . . Not anything less," Faircloth assured her.

Susan could hear in his words that he truly felt her pain. And cared.

"Do you have any idea," she asked, "why Jordan was in Detroit?"

"I only know what he said in his letter."

Susan swallowed. "I haven't told anybody . . . but I'm sure he went there to . . . uh . . ." Susan sighed. "Maybe I should just start from the beginning."

Frequently wiping away tears, she unbottled her story. She told about her conservative Christian background, about her profession of faith in Christ at the age of fourteen. About her gradual erosion of faith once she married Jordan. About the birth of their epileptic son, then the birth of their daughter. And about Jordan's wonderful orientation toward his family, especially toward Chase.

"He was one of the greatest husbands and fathers I'd ever seen," Susan stated.

She then told about Jordan's pastoring — about his persuasive theology that hailed "self" as the all-sufficient resource for a positive and victorious life.

Then came the turning point — for everything.

It was the hasty loan of $21,000, which they borrowed for an irresistible investment . . . followed by the sudden and complete loss of the entire amount when the investment crashed overnight.

Then the debt. And the letter from the denominational headquarters about the seminary project in Germany, with its financial enticement. Jordan applying and being accepted for one of the professorship slots. Resigning his Chattanooga pastorate and moving his family against their will to Germany as a means to recover their financial loss. The traumatic adjustment and emotional breakdown of their family. Her efforts to rebuild her own personal faith, which had withered through the years.

Susan tried to fight back tears as she told about the mysterious and nightmarish murder of their son and his girlfriend. Then Jordan's devastating guilt, bitterness, and reclusiveness. Donica's chronic depression and withdrawal. Her own weak and struggling faith. The unsuccessful investigation by the police. Jordan's daily and unexplained disappearances, which she later learned were due to his personal search for the killers. Then his quick departure for Detroit.

For the first time, Susan spoke aloud of her most troublesome fear: "Nobody else knows, but I'm almost sure he went there to . . . to . . . to try to get revenge for Chase's death. To try to . . . kill someone."

When Faircloth showed no sign of surprise or condemnation, Susan concluded by telling him about Jordan's automobile accident and injuries, about his lengthy but miraculous recovery, his continued obsession with revenge, the final breakdown of their family, and Jordan's obvious and destructive intent to go back to Detroit to finish his "business."

She looked at Faircloth, the blistering toll of her journey embedded in her face and eyes, and said, "About fifteen minutes before you came, Jordan and I had a fight. He left with a suitcase. I'm almost sure he's on his way to Detroit. When you showed up, I was just getting ready to go in and pack suitcases for my daughter and me, and move out. I've decided that . . . that our marriage —" she broke down and started sobbing — "has reached the point of divorce. I've prayed, and I've tried to have faith, but I guess I've failed."

For nearly forty minutes Faircloth had sat with undistracted attention, hearing Susan's every word and feeling her every pain. He was touched deeply by the complexity of her family's wounds.

But in response to her last words, he straightened up and turned his whole body around to face hers.

"Susan," he said, "are you familiar with God's words in the book of Galatians, where He says, 'A man reaps what he sows . . . the one who sows to please his sinful nature will reap destruction, but the one who sows to please the Spirit will reap life'?"

It had been years since Susan had read the verses or heard them quoted, but she did remember them, at least in a vague kind of way. "Slightly," she replied.

"Do you mind if I show them to you?"

"No, I don't," Susan whispered.

Faircloth excused himself to go to his rental car to retrieve a Bible from his briefcase.

When he returned and sat in the grass with her again, with his Bible already opened, he pointed to the verses in the sixth chapter of Galatians and invited her to read.

Susan focused on the words where Faircloth was pointing. She cleared her throat and read.

When she finished reading the verses, Faircloth spoke again. "When someone ignores God, intentionally or unintentionally, he or she is sowing bad seed. According to these verses, what kind of harvest will that person reap?"

Susan saw the initial point to which Faircloth was leading — that she and Jordan, according to their own testimony, had practically ignored God for years. But she could tell by the tone of Faircloth's voice that his question was not posed from a condescending or judgmental position. Rather, it was simple truth telling.

"A harvest of destruction," Susan answered, as she thought about the last twelve months.

Faircloth responded with a second question. "When someone pursues God, as you've done throughout the last year, what kind of seed is that person sowing — good or bad?"

Susan hesitated. "That would be good seed, I suppose," she finally answered, a little uncertain.

Faircloth turned to other New Testament verses confirming that the pursuit of God was indeed equivalent to sowing good seed.

Going back to the book of Galatians, Faircloth then presented a third question: "If you sow good seed, what kind of harvest will you reap?"

Susan looked at the verses again. "A harvest of life," she read. But even as she quoted the answer, she realized that it must be more complicated than she understood. If she had been sowing good seed over the past year, as Faircloth said, she wasn't reaping a harvest of life.

Faircloth continued, "Let's read the next verse." He pointed to verse 9.

Together they read the words: "Let us not grow weary while sowing good seed, for in due season we shall reap if we do not lose heart."

"According to this verse," Faircloth asked, "why do you suppose people who sow good seed, such as yourself, some-times grow weary and lose heart?"

Susan considered thoughtfully. "Because we expect the harvest to come sooner than it sometimes does, and we lose patience." Even as she spoke, the truth of the verses began to strike her like a flash of lightning.

"And while we're just beginning to sow good seed and are longing for the good harvest," Faircloth continued, "we're still reaping what kind of fruit, if we sowed bad seeds earlier?"

"A bad harvest." Susan's eyes sparkled with embryonic hope. "You mean I'm caught in between harvests?"

Faircloth nodded. "While sowing your good seed, you may *still* be reaping from the old harvest. The good harvest, the har-vest of life, hasn't yet come to fruition. Therefore, you're living under the false il-lusion that your efforts to sow good seed are ineffective."

New tears formed in Susan's eyes. "Is that why you told me earlier that it's too early to give up?"

Faircloth again nodded in consent. "That's why it's also too early to *feel* hopeless," he added. "If you give up now, you start sow-ing bad seed again. And that will destroy the production of the good harvest."

Susan hung her head. She wanted to believe. But how could she?

"Don't give up, Susan," she heard Faircloth tell her. "Keep sowing good seed."

"But Jordan has already gone to Detroit; I'm sure of it," she cried out in anguish. "There's nothing *I* can do to bring him back. There's nothing good I can do now that's going to change anything."

Faircloth looked at her, the pain and agony of her soul reflecting in his eyes. "Don't try to *track* God, Susan. Just *trust* Him. He *will not* . . ." Faircloth stopped when he saw Susan turn from him. He waited until he was sure he had her attention again. "He *will not* and *cannot* lie. He promises He will reward those who diligently seek and trust Him. That includes *you*, Susan."

"But you don't understand!" Susan cried from her heart, turning to face Jason again. "I'm tired! I need someone to help me! I can't keep going on, all by myself!"

"Then I'll help you!" Faircloth said.

Susan didn't know what to say. How could he help her? Especially living hundreds of miles away in New York?

"When I say good-bye to you, I will stay here in the car for the next hour and pray for you. I'll sit here so you can look out your window and see me. And when I leave here, I'll drive down the street, check into a motel, and I will pray for you around the clock for the next twenty-four hours. I'll call you every hour between sunup and sundown to remind you that I'm here and that I'm petitioning God on your behalf. And when I fly back to New York, I'll call you once a day to encourage you, to remind you that God cares and that there's a Christian brother who cares."

Susan was dumbfounded. Never once in her entire life had anyone, for any reason, ever made such an offer. Or anything similar. She was so moved, she started choking on her emotions. She understood Faircloth's words, but *how* could he mean them? *Why* would he mean them? He hadn't known her for more than two or three hours.

"I . . . don't understand," she spoke between gasps. "Why would you do such a thing for a stranger?"

Faircloth locked eyes and hearts with her. "Because I've *chosen* to," he answered.

Suddenly it registered with Susan that the man sitting beside her indeed had been where she was, had felt what she was feeling. He did understand her pain, her loneliness, her need. And as odd as it sounded, he really did care.

Before Faircloth left her to return to his car, he encouraged her for another twenty minutes or so, gave her his New York address and phone number, then prayed out loud there on the lawn with her.

When Susan finally said good-bye and watched him head for his car, she felt a new kind of strength, unlike anything she'd ever experienced. She just prayed to God that it wasn't a prelude to another letdown. If so, she felt it would destroy her faith altogether.

Inside the apartment, she went to the kitchen window and peered out. Faircloth was indeed sitting in his car praying. She could see his head bowed, and a slight movement of his lips.

She watched him for a few minutes, her tears flowing freely. He really was a friend, wasn't he?

Never in her life — not during her conservative Christian upbringing, nor during her years as a minister's wife, nor even now in the evangelical church she was attending — had she witnessed this type of Christianity.

It was odd, but she wondered if she wasn't for the first time seeing a genuine representation of Christ.

Yet as deeply as she was touched, she fought the appeal to hope again. How could it *not* be too late?

Just when she started to turn from the window and get a cold drink of water from the refrigerator to cool her contracting and hurting throat, the phone rang.

The noise caused her to jerk.

But within a second, she moved toward the kitchen bar to pick up the receiver.

"Hello," she answered after clearing her throat.

There was silence on the other end.

"Hello," Susan said a little louder.

Still there was silence.

Just when Susan started to hang up, she heard a voice speak her name. The voice, dull and heavy, sounded like death.

It was Jordan.

"Jordan!" Susan said. "Are you —"

"I've changed my mind," Jordan's voice interrupted her.

"You . . . you what?"

"I won't be coming home today, Susan. I'm going to Detroit . . . I have to do it . . ."

Susan realized there was no emotion in Jordan's voice. Neither was there any sound of defensiveness. The deathlike sound frightened her.

"Jordan?"

Again there was silence.

Susan tried to get control of her emotions. "Jordan . . . I know I told you earlier that if you went to Detroit again, you wouldn't be welcome back here. But I've changed my mind, too." She stretched the phone cord and walked back toward the kitchen window. "I decided I'm going to love you, Jordan," she said with her heart in her throat. "I'll be here waiting."

After another slight moment of silence, Jordan broke the void. "I love you, Susan. Tell Donica . . . I . . . uh . . ." He started to choke up. "I know I've been a poor father, but . . . I . . . uh . . . love her . . . too."

"Jordan?" Susan raised her voice, now trying to reach out to him. "What's happening? What are you . . . ?"

Jordan started to weep.

Susan's fear intensified. Jordan wasn't planning to come back, was he?

Looking out the window, she saw Faircloth still sitting in his car, still praying.

Susan now broke into tears.

"Jordan . . . just a minute . . . there's someone who wants to talk with you."

"Susan . . . I don't have —"

"It's Jason Faircloth — he's here. He came up from Atlanta to visit with you."

"Faircloth?" Jordan responded softly through his sniffling. "Here in Chattanooga? What's he . . . ?"

"He wants to be our friend, Jordan. He wants to help us. Will you please just let him say hi for a moment? Please?"

"It's too late, Susan . . . nobody can help now." Jordan's voice sounded final.

"Hold on, Jordan . . . please . . . just a moment . . . I'll be right back . . ." Susan laid down the phone, now praying as hard as she'd ever prayed in her life, and ran outside.

She threw open the front door, banging it against the inside wall.

She ran out as fast as her legs would take her, to where Faircloth was sitting in his car. "Can you come inside — quickly?" she shouted through gasps of air. "Jordan just called — he's still on the phone. Will you please talk with him? He's crying — he needs help!"

Faircloth moved hurriedly out of his car and followed Susan into the apartment.

Susan, shaking nervously, pointed him to the phone. She prayed to God that Jordan had not hung up.

"Hello? Jordan?" Faircloth said as he picked up the receiver.

Susan waited anxiously.

When Faircloth said, "Yeah, this is Jason," Susan let out a breath that she wasn't even aware she had been holding.

To keep from pacing, she forced herself to sit down in one of the chairs at the kitchen table. She looked at her hand and saw that it was shaking.

She heard Faircloth responding with an occasional "Yeah," and, "Uh-huh." She continued to pray.

She heard Faircloth confirm that he had come to Chattanooga in response to the letters, that he wanted to give Jordan some support.

"Yes," he added a moment later, "she's already told me the whole story. But it's okay . . . I still want to be your friend — *now* more than ever."

As Susan asked God to give Faircloth special wisdom, she heard him say, "What if I told you, Jordan, that you're not re-acting to your son's murder, but to your own interpretation of the murder? I'm not minimizing the sorrow and the grief or the need for justice, I know what it's like. As I told you before, I lost an eighteen-year-old daughter and a wife. But think with me for a moment: How have Heather's parents dealt with Heather's death? How has Susan dealt with Chase's death?"

Susan saw the intensity of Faircloth's expression as he paused to listen to Jordan's reply.

She kept praying.

"They've reacted differently," Faircloth stressed, "because their interpretation is different from yours. As disillusioned, sorrowful, and hurt as they've been, they've interpreted the murder as an event that somehow happened within God's control. You, on the other hand, have interpreted it as something that happened without *any* control, without any reason.

"They've also interpreted that God in His own time and in His own way will make the criminals face justice. You've interpreted that justice lies solely in the hands of man."

There was a pause.

"I understand," Faircloth replied, "but what if *you're* the one who's believing lies? In that case, all of your actions and emotions are being misdirected. The hurt you're causing yourself and your family is needless.

"Believing lies destroys, Jordan. Only the truth sets you free."

There was another pause.

Judging by the waiting look on Faircloth's face, Susan guessed that Jordan had gone silent.

Was Jordan getting ready to cut Faircloth off? Was he not willing to listen to the wise and strong words of a man he respected?

When Faircloth began to respond again, Susan breathed a sigh of relief.

For the next several minutes, Susan listened as Faircloth quoted verses from the Bible and explained to Jordan the definition of a true believer.

"Stripped down to the basics," he was saying, "the heart of Christianity is the *heart,* Jordan. If a man is locked away in a prison cell and has no Bible to read, no money or material goods with which to be generous, no freedom to attend any kind of worship service, no pulpit from which to preach, and no tradition to define his Christian expression, he can still be a Christian. Because the heart of Christianity is the heart. It's having a personal relationship in the heart with Jesus Christ — confessing Him as Savior, accepting His forgiveness, communing with Him, worshiping Him, loving Him, believing Him, obeying Him, honoring Him.

And if that heart-born relationship cannot be expressed outside the prison cell, the man can still express his Christianity from the heart — through a supernatural peace of mind, a loving kindness toward his enemies that's contrary to human nature, an inner joy that can't be explained logically, a willingness to trust God regardless of the situation, and a self-control that reflects God's surpassing strength. It's the *heart*, Jordan. The heart."

When Faircloth handed the phone back to Susan, she was hoping beyond herself that Jordan would now change his mind and come home. Maybe Faircloth's love and concern had made a difference.

But all she heard Jordan say from the other end was, "Pray for me, Susan. I love you. More than you'll ever know." Then he hung up.

Susan stood almost in shock, the dead receiver suspended in her dangling hand.

"He's still planning to go to Detroit," Faircloth reported. "All we can do now is pray."

Reaching out, he took the phone from Susan's hand and placed it back on the hook. He then took Susan's hands into his palms and bowed his head. His prayer for Jordan was strong, loving, and full of faith.

Susan had never heard anything comparable. The presence of Christ that seemed to blanket the room arrested her runaway heart and kept her from losing hope altogether.

"Remember, Susan," Faircloth told her when he finished the prayer, "I'm going to call you every hour for the rest of the afternoon and evening, and again throughout tomorrow morning."

Then he added: "Just now, Jordan said he recently realized that he's never been a true believer in Christ, that he's been deceiving himself since childhood."

Realizing that Jordan had never in their twenty years of marriage made such a confession, Susan understood the magnitude of its importance, especially when Faircloth reminded her that a man will never choose to be healed from his blindness until he first realizes he cannot see.

As she followed Faircloth to the outside of the apartment's front door, he turned and said, "Whatever happens, Susan, I'll always be a friend. Remember that."

She thanked him as best she could, then watched him drive away.

At least for a while longer, she told herself, maybe God would grant her the strength to keep sowing good seed.

★ ★ ★

In his car heading north on I-75 toward Detroit, Jordan was watering his shirt with tears. He knew now that he would probably never see his family again.

He knew he was driving to his own death.

26

Jordan sat in his car under the cloak of night-time darkness about a hundred feet from the main entrance of a high-class Detroit discotheque. Inside the dance club, Jordan knew, was a Jamaican drug dealer.

The dealer was inside the dance club, and had been for about forty minutes. Jordan was waiting to trail him.

From the moment he arrived in Detroit nine days ago, Jordan had worked with un-tiring diligence to reach this point. He wasn't about to let it slip through his fingers now.

Jordan had penetrated the inner city of Detroit like a virus, with only one thing on his mind: to end the life of those who had destroyed his, and to go down with them. Then his wife and daughter — who had been put through hell because of his foolish insensitivity — could start their lives over again in peace, without his own selfish and destructive interference.

With his every move haunted by visions of his family life in ruins, and by images of Chase lying in the morgue, he had lost all faith in himself — in his wisdom, knowledge, and strength . . . in his "fail-safe" human spirit . . . in his ability to shape his own destiny.

He felt only the unmerciful and crushing weight of guilt: pure, painful, life-defying guilt. All he wanted now was to accomplish his mission, then close his eyes in peace for the final time.

He had begun his search in the neighborhood of Percival Blake's address, in a section of the city known as Cass Corridor.

He found out from a gang of teenagers that Jamaicans indeed lived in the neighborhood, but not in any concentrated area. They were scattered among the mixture of other minorities.

He had then staked out Percival Blake's apartment, believing that Percival would at least lead him to groups of Jamaican teenagers.

But after watching Percival's apartment for two full days, he lost patience. Not one person left or entered the apartment during that whole time. Jordan decided he would try to find some other lead.

There were always the prostitutes.

Finding four of them working the Cass Avenue district, he selected the one who had the most abused and anemic look about her — the one who looked most like a drug addict. He picked her up and paid for thirty minutes of her time.

Parking on a nearby main street in a well-lit area, he tried to convince her that, as an out-of-towner, all he wanted to buy was a little coke. Could she tell him where he could find a dealer?

At first hesitant, she eventually talked when he handed her an extra hundred-dollar bill. She wouldn't give him the dealer's name, but she told him he could find the man working a particular bar where the prostitutes hung out on Cass Avenue. He was there on location at least once every night. He was a short black man in his mid-twenties who, due to a pigmentation disorder, had a large white blotch on the side of his face. He was unmistakable.

Jordan thanked the girl and returned her to the street. With the help of her directions, he then drove directly to the bar.

Not until the next night, however, did he spot the man. Jordan was sitting at the bar drinking a cola, when the man came in and started circulating smoothly among his buyers. At the opportune moment, Jordan approached the man in the confinement of the rest room, where they would be alone.

As the man stood at the urinal, Jordan moved to the sink, tried to look and sound harmless, and said, "Excuse me, but do the Jamaican names Martin, Tito, and Ottey mean anything to you?"

As the man turned and zipped up his pants, he stared at Jordan with eyes of intense uncertainty. He then started to casually reach inside his suit-coat pocket.

Quickly Jordan told him, "I'm not a cop. I'm just a businessman from out of town who needs to take care of some personal business with my three Jamaican friends. They're dealers like you are. I thought maybe you could help me." Jordan unfolded his hand and nodded in the direction of the cash he was holding.

The black man removed his hand from his coat pocket. "You're a brave man to do business with the Jamaicans," he told Jordan, as he reached out and took his money. "I don't know any Martin, Tito, or the other man you mentioned, but I can tell you the names of six or seven clubs where the Jamaicans deal their business."

Glad for any bit of information he could get, Jordan wrote down the club names on a paper towel, thanked the guy, then left.

For the last five nights, he had gone from club to club on the list, mingling with the patrons, trying as inconspicuously as possible to represent himself as a cautious buyer. He tried to find someone who could help him locate and identify the local Jamaican dealers.

He had met with no success, and was wondering if the man in the restroom had lied to him — until forty-five minutes ago.

He had been sitting inside the discotheque that he was now staring at through the windshield of his car. For over three hours he had sat at several drink tables, enveloped in cigarette smoke, trying over the loud and pulsating music to find someone who could give him the information he needed.

He had been sitting at a table with two white guys — rich, young girl-hunters — when luck extended its hand to him.

After talking in general with the two guys for thirty minutes or so, he expressed his need for some cocaine.

Drunk enough to be loose-tongued, one of the guys leaned over to Jordan and said, "You need to go talk to that man over there." The guy was pointing across the dance floor, his finger held close to his chest.

"The brown fellow with the braids — sitting next to the blonde?" Jordan whispered, looking in the direction through the dancing crowd where the guy had indicated.

"He's Jamaican," the guy told Jordan with a lowered voice. "Sells good stuff."

Neither of the guys knew the Jamaican by name, only by face.

Without allowing himself to be noticeable, Jordan made sure he got a memorable look at the brown-skinned face.

Now sitting in his car waiting to trail the Jamaican when he came out, Jordan was fantasizing about the moment he would meet Ottey, Martin, and Tito face-to-face. When the Jamaican exited the dance hall a little after eleven, Jordan almost missed him.

A hard rain had started to fall and was obscuring his vision.

It was the presence of the platinum blonde that caused Jordan to make the identity.

A black, late-model BMW had pulled up next to the curb in front of the disco and stopped. About thirty seconds later, the Jamaican ran out of the building with the blonde on his arm and jumped into the waiting BMW.

The car pulled away slowly, flashing its blinker for a right turn at the next block.

Jordan waited until the car made its turn at the corner, then pulled out to follow.

Jordan had barely made the right turn at the end of the block when he saw the taillights of the BMW turning left at a major intersection ahead.

Now Jordan was thankful for the hard rain. It should make it easier for him to follow unnoticed.

As he approached the intersection, he slowed down to let a couple of cars coming from the opposite direction turn into the traffic behind the BMW. Jordan executed the turn and followed.

He then reached over and opened the glove compartment. He pulled out both guns — the gas-operated, .44-magnum, semiautomatic Desert Eagle with a nine-round magazine, and the Austrian-made, .45-caliber, semiautomatic Glock with its extended thirty-round magazine. He had purchased them both in Chattanooga, just before coming here. One at a time, he laid them on the seat beside him. His hunting knife and rope were on the floorboard beneath the front seat on the passenger's side.

Now he was ready. It was just a matter of time and opportunity.

They had gone no more than six blocks through a heavily trafficked downtown business district when the BMW, about two hundred feet ahead, began pulling over to the right curb. Above it, a large, flashing neon sign marked another nightclub.

As Jordan started to pass the BMW with the rest of the traffic, he zoomed in on the car's license plate number — BBR 704 — and kept moving.

He started repeating the number aloud as he cut his eyes upward to the rearview mirror, making sure he kept his face positioned straight ahead.

In the mirror, he saw the Jamaican and the blonde getting out of the BMW. Under an umbrella, they hurried across the sidewalk and into the club.

Jordan wondered if the blonde was the Jamaican's girlfriend, a one-night stand, or a conspirator who worked with the posse as a decoy to give the Jamaican drug dealer a look of innocent companionship. Whoever she was, Jordan was thankful for her presence. Her long, platinum-blonde hair made the two of them easy to spot, especially on such a rainy night.

After going a couple of blocks farther, Jordan made a left turn, circled a four-block area, then turned back onto the four-lane street that approached the club.

As he expected, the BMW was now gone.

He wondered who the chauffeur was. A paid laborer? Or another Jamaican posse member?

He switched on his blinker and turned left onto the first street past the club. He bypassed the parking spaces on the right, drove the length of the block, turned around, drove back, and selected a space on the opposite side of the street near the corner. From there he could see the front of the nightclub across the four-lane street ahead of him. It wasn't the most ideal spot, but it would work.

The rain was coming down harder now, rolling down the slanted windshield. Once Jordan had the engine cut off, he placed his guns on the floorboard and slid over to use the side window as his observation point.

He looked at his watch. The time was 11:25.

He slid down in the seat and glued his eyes to the disco's front entryway.

Thirty minutes slowly passed.

He carefully screened all the people coming and going. The Jamaican and the blonde were not among them.

Then another thirty minutes.

Had he not been so pumped with adrenaline, the strain to his eyes would have caused him to take a break. But he kept watching, refusing to let the front door of the club out of his sight.

It was nearly a quarter to one when he was suddenly moved by a new rush of adrenaline.

It was the black BMW.

The black sedan pulled up to the front of the discotheque and stopped.

Jordan fought the urge to straighten up in his seat. He remained slumped, forcing his eyes to remain steady.

Every muscle in his body was now ready to move. His heartbeat accelerated. He started breathing hard.

The BMW was motionless, its warning lights flashing.

A dark-skinned man exited the dance hall under an umbrella. Alone, he jumped into the back of the waiting BMW.

Was it the Jamaican?

He had braids, didn't he?

Where was the blonde?

When the black car pulled away and

passed the side street where Jordan was parked, Jordan launched himself over to the steering wheel, cranked the car, turned on the headlights, and moved quickly up to the intersection.

Before he could turn, he had to wait for an oncoming car approaching from his left. "Come on!" he shouted at the strange car.

When he turned left across two lanes and entered the flow of traffic behind the BMW, he tried to replay the sight of the man leaving the building. It had to be the Jamaican.

He was tempted to pass the three cars now in between him and the BMW, to see if it carried the BBR 704 license plate. But he didn't want to draw quick attention to himself. He couldn't take that risk.

Ahead, the BMW veered right onto an expressway entry ramp.

Jordan followed at a distance.

The sedan went south for three exits, then turned off the expressway.

To remain unnoticed, Jordan decreased his speed so the BMW could reach the bottom of the exit ramp and make its turn just as he himself started down the ramp.

But when he entered the ramp, the BMW was already out of sight.

In a panic, Jordan stomped the accelerator and sped to the end of the ramp. There was some light traffic to the right, but he didn't see the BMW.

He looked to the left. A block away, three cars were stopped at a traffic light. He breathed again. The BMW was the last in line.

Fighting rain, traffic, and traffic lights, he trailed the BMW for six more blocks. Then, unexpectedly, his concentration was ambushed.

To his left was the All People's Church.

Jordan jerked his head away, trying to forget the sight. The memories. And the unsettling and disturbing reminders.

He didn't want to dwell on them now. Not now, of all times. *Now* was when he needed to concentrate.

But it was too late.

As he stared ahead, trying to focus with renewed determination on the BMW's taillights, the insistent thoughts — like a body of water that couldn't be restrained — started seeping through his mental resistance, one drop at a time.

The evening service last December. The open and honest expression of hurts and struggles. The black man's testimony of losing his sister to thieving murderers, and then forgiving them — choosing to let God

362

deal with them instead.

Jordan shook his head from side to side.

Not now, he told himself.

Then there was Jason Faircloth, the one man in the world who had challenged him to question his liberal views. The compassionate, wise old man in whom God — the God who wasn't supposed to be personal, or visibly involved in the details of people's lives — seemed to manifest Himself so royally and irresistibly. The man who had known the helpful touch of God through prolonged pain and loss. The man who proclaimed the deceit of the human heart. The man who knew the truth. The man who wanted to be his friend.

Once again, the thought of Jason Faircloth made Jordan feel slapped by the harsh hand of truth.

He clenched his teeth. Again, he tried to force the thoughts of light into the dark side of his mind, to be quenched.

Again he failed.

He really was a *believer of lies,* wasn't he?

Monstrous, odious, destructive lies.

If only he had listened to his family during the last year.

Or to Faircloth during the last six months.

It's too late, Jordan. Forget it! Concentrate on the BMW.

He restretched his fingers around the steering wheel and squeezed it with force.

Maybe if he had been a believer of truth like Faircloth, or believed in the personal God whom Faircloth and Susan believed in, perhaps his son would still be alive.

He squeezed the steering wheel tighter.

Why, why, why had he moved his family against their will to Germany? *Why* hadn't he been willing to trust God for his family's financial needs?

It was clear, wasn't it? Undeniably clear. Because of his "self and self alone" theology, and his unwillingness to believe in God and in truth, *he* — Jordan Rau — had killed his own son.

No! I don't want to think about it now! Follow the BMW to the right.

He shook his head again.

He had also destroyed his own marriage.

His wife.

His daughter.

Even himself.

The truth was, he was a pathetic individual who had been deceived by his own heart.

"NOOOOOOO!" he screamed.

Tears started watering his eyes.

For the briefest of moments, he had a burst of thoughts he had never had before:

Maybe it's not too late . . . Maybe if I believe . . . Faircloth said the heart of Christianity is the heart, and that Christianity is a personal relationship with Jesus Christ, God's Savior for man . . . Can Christ really save me from myself and from my sin? After all I've done? After all my unbelief? Would He even want to? Even if He'll do it, will trusting Him now make a difference?

Will believing truth at this point really set me free?

Would I first have to forgive the Jamaicans?

"No!" he stopped himself. That wouldn't be possible.

Not now. Not in the past. Not in the future.

He could never, *ever* forgive the Jamaicans for what they did.

Enraged by the direction of the unwanted thoughts, he reached out and twisted the radio knob to the on position.

The blissful noise of music — loud, distracting, hard music — filled the interior of the car, helping create a different mood, a mood that brought him back into the rainy pursuit.

He could breathe again.

Soon it would all be over.

Splashing through torrents of water on a straightway, he reached over, retrieved his guns from the floorboard, and placed them on the seat again.

A minute or so later, the BMW, four cars ahead, turned left. When Jordan reached the turn, he could see the blackness of the Detroit River out in front of him, the hazy lights of Canada far on the other side.

He suddenly felt lonely.

Let's just get it over with, he told himself.

The BMW's brake lights illuminated.

Jordan looked ahead. It was another nightclub. Off to the left. The BMW turned into the parking lot.

Overcome with impatience, he was tempted to rush the BMW with his guns drawn.

Instead, Jordan decided to keep driving. He drove past the nightclub's parking lot entrance for about a hundred yards, then did a U-turn.

He parked on the side of the road and waited. Waited for the BMW to leave.

Three minutes passed.

Then five minutes.

The BMW didn't leave.

Jordan took the .45-caliber from the seat and stuffed it down into his pants. He put the .44-magnum under the seat on the driver's side.

After ten minutes passed, Jordan put his

car in gear and drove down the road and into the parking lot. It was still more than half-filled, even at 1:10 in the morning.

As Jordan cruised the lot, he kept his eyes peeled for the BMW.

He was moving slowly down the last row when he saw the black sedan through a tall, swinging gate at the rear corner of the building. Along with a Porsche and a Mercedes, it was parked face-on against the back wall of the club.

Still in the parking lot, Jordan pulled his car into a space on the last row. From there he could see the back half of the BMW through the open gate.

Looking around to see if anyone was taking notice of him, he saw only a group of three men — swaying as if they were drunk — who were leaving the club's main entrance. They got into a parked car and drove away.

Not seeing anyone else, Jordan chose to sit tight for a few minutes.

Judging by the location of the BMW, he now wondered if this particular nightclub was a special business connection for the Jamaican, or maybe even an operating base or headquarters of some kind.

After sitting for ten minutes and seeing no activity around the BMW, Jordan decided to go inside.

He entered the building, paid the cover charge, then moved to one of the two bars. He ordered a ginger ale, and started scanning the crowd.

After eyeballing every person two or three times, he decided the braided man he'd seen earlier wasn't in the room. Was the Jamaican in the back somewhere? Or had his eyes and his mind made a mistake?

Jordan decided to go out to the rear of the building and look at the BMW's license plate number.

Outside in the now slackened rain, he walked briskly across the parking lot toward the last row of cars, in the direction of the open gate.

He was halfway there, with every vein in his body carrying a full load of adrenaline, when he heard a burst of music coming from a car boom box.

He turned. Two cars were swinging into the parking lot. As they passed him, they turned through the open gate into the back lot.

With his mind and heartbeat thrown into overdrive, Jordan sprinted to his car and jumped in.

He saw at least eight men pile out of the two cars on the other side of the gate.

They were Jamaican — it was obvious by the hairstyles and color of skin. But were Ottey, Martin, and Tito among them? He had to know for sure before he went shooting his way through their gang. He had come too far to waste his life on uncertainties.

He tried to think quickly and carefully through his options.

After three or four minutes, long after the Jamaicans had disappeared into the rear of the building, he decided what to do.

The plan wasn't going to give him the immediate gratification he wanted, but at least it would provide him with the certainty that Ottey, Martin, and Tito were present when he struck.

Cranking his car, he backed out and returned to his downtown hotel.

27

For the next four nights, Jordan hung out at the two nightclubs where he saw the "first" Jamaican, along with the blonde, supposedly carrying out his business.

Jordan's goal was to find the Jamaican in one of the clubs again, and confront him alone.

But the four days of fruitless waiting had lifted his heart and soul to new heights of misery. The reason: He couldn't get Christ off his mind. The Christ of Jason Faircloth. The Christ of the All People's Church.

The truth about the person of Christ, as radiated by Faircloth's life and words, kept speeding through his thoughts like a ghost locomotive.

For the first time in his life, he was experiencing a spiritual pull at his heart, a pull to *believe.*

Christ *was* real, wasn't He? Just like the Bible proclaimed. He was God revealing Himself to His creation. God dying for man's sin, offering Himself as the one and only Savior. God resurrected from the dead.

The weight of the realization that he had been pitifully blind was pressing down on him. He didn't feel he could bear the pain anymore.

The pull to admit his wayward direction and to confess Christ as real and personal was unrelenting. But he kept fighting it, more now from guilt than pride.

Determined to see his plan of retribution reach its end, he kept stubbornly waiting for the Jamaican.

As he waited, he also spent time monitoring the third club, the one where the Jamaicans had gathered during the early morning hours. Convinced that the location was an operating base, he wanted to find a pattern of activity around the area, if there was one.

There was.

He now planned to use to his full advantage what he had learned during the last four nights of observation: Up until midnight, there was always one car parked at the rear of the building, on the other side of the gate. It was always *after* midnight when the other cars showed up. And they always did, filled with Jamaicans.

The plan he developed was rudimentary, but it was the best he could come up with. If he had to, he would wait indefinitely to be able to execute it.

But the uncertain waiting quickly came to an end.

On the fifth night, Jordan spotted him. In one of the discotheques. This time the Jamaican was attached to a redhead.

As Jordan monitored him, he felt adrenaline tighten his body like a pumped muscle.

Everything was set.

It would all be over soon. The kill he had lived for during the last ten months was now so close he could smell it.

The instant the Jamaican made a move toward the men's room, Jordan started working his way through the crowd in the same direction.

The restrooms were located off a dimly-lit hallway that ended with an exit to the outside.

Jordan waited till the Jamaican disappeared into the men's rest room, then entered the hallway. He looked at his watch. It was a little after ten.

With his blood burning with anticipation, he traced the Jamaican's steps down the hall and entered the room.

A young white man passed him, going out. Ignoring him, Jordan visually swept the room, and saw no one. Then he scanned the floor beneath the three stalls. There was one pair of legs.

Jordan moved in front of the stall, and said out loud, "Caribbean Parade . . . Ottey . . . Tito . . . Martin." He hoped the guy would react.

He did.

When Jordan crashed open the stall door, the Jamaican was already holding an open switchblade in his hand, scrambling at the same time to get his pants pulled up.

With his six-foot-four, 245-pound frame, Jordan stood facing him, breathing fire like an unstoppable dragon. A year's worth of hate was showing in his eyes.

As the Jamaican lunged at him, Jordan with one swift and powerful move intercepted the man's knife arm and stopped it motionless.

Then, with a hideous grunt, Jordan grabbed the drug-dealing criminal around the neck with his free hand and slammed him back against the wall.

The Jamaican, with fear in his eyes, was instantly fighting for his next breath.

Pressing on the jerking body with all his weight, Jordan said, "I'll give you one chance. What's your name?"

The Jamaican spit in Jordan's face.

Jordan sighed, and for a split second stared into the Jamaican's brown eyes, with a look that told him he had just made the greatest mistake of his life.

In an explosion of hateful pleasure, Jordan took the Jamaican's knife arm that he was still holding tightly at the wrist, and in one violent movement wrenched it backwards, breaking it at the elbow.

As the switchblade dropped to the floor, the Jamaican's eyes and mouth stretched wide in a detonation of breathtaking pain.

Jordan cupped the face with his big hand and squeezed to muffle the initial cry.

When the Jamaican's eyes rolled back in his head, Jordan removed the 45-caliber from underneath his belt and closed the stall door behind him.

He placed the end of the barrel between the Jamaican's eyes and waited for his eyes to focus again.

"Sit down," he ordered him when the presence of the gun was acknowledged.

Gasping and groaning, the Jamaican slid down the wall to a sitting position on the open toilet.

Jordan held the gun in the Jamaican's

face with one hand and searched the man's coat pockets with the other hand.

When he found a wallet, he pulled it out, flipped it open, and looked at the driver's license.

He once again stared into the eyes of the panting drug dealer. "So, Stuart Ashley, do you think you can manage to take a personal message to your friends Ottey, Tito, and Martin for me?" he asked calmly, trying to bait a telltale response.

Holding his broken arm and still grimacing in pain, the Jamaican responded with a loathsome and mocking gaze. "You can tell it to dem yourself, mon, when dem come to kill you."

That was all Jordan needed to hear. The connection was verified.

"Good, then," Jordan told him as he kicked the Jamaican's knife across the floor into the other stall, "you can tell them I will be here in the parking lot tomorrow night at midnight waiting for them."

With that, he put his gun away, pulled from his pants pocket a two-foot piece of thin nylon rope, and tied the Jamaican's legs together at the knees. He pulled the knot so tight that it jerked the knees together and cut the skin.

"You be a dead mon," the Jamaican said.

"I'm prepared to die," Jordan said. "How about you?"

The Jamaican started to spit at him again.

Replaying the image of Chase lying dead in the morgue with his throat slit, Jordan grabbed the Jamaican's broken arm and twisted it.

The Jamaican swallowed his saliva. As he screamed out, his entire body going tense, Jordan said to him, "I guess you are, too, huh?"

Jordan didn't wait for a response. He stood up, opened the stall door, and stepped out.

Before he left the room, he turned to face the Jamaican one more time. "By the way," he told him, "my name is Jordan. I'm from Germany. Remember to tell your friends: *Here . . . tomorrow night . . . midnight.*"

Then he left the building through the rear exit.

As he sprinted to his car, parked on a curb two streets away, he now knew that Ottey, Tito, and Martin were among the group who gathered every night at the third club.

He would now go straight to that location and wait. There would be no meeting tomorrow night. After midnight tonight, when the group was all gathered, he would surprise them all.

When he reached his car, he crawled in and turned on the engine. He switched on the headlights, then the overhead interior light. He checked his watch again. It was 10:40. He turned off the overhead light and put the car in gear.

Then he saw it.

Displayed across the bottom of the back car window in front of him was a window sticker proclaiming the message, "God Does Exist, and You Are Not Him."

It was as if God, in His revealing mercy, was reaching out to him one final time, with one final reminder.

Once again, his lifelong self-delusion resounded in the forefront of his brain, along with Faircloth's inescapable proclamation that believing lies destroys lives, while only the truth sets people free.

As Jordan drove away, the foundation of God's eternal and unchangeable truth broke free like an avalanche, and came crashing down on him. The TRUTH he had foolishly and pridefully criticized all his adult life as a "Christian minister" was suddenly plain. Alive and real.

As the Bible so clearly explained, he,

Jordan Rau, was a sinful being, both by birth and by choice. He was a fallen part of God's creation who stood in need of a divine Savior. God, in His unconditional and perfect love for His fallen creatures, *became* that Savior. Became Jesus — God among us — who walked in human skin. Sinlessly. Yet willfully felt all our pains and temptations. Died sinless on the cross for our sins at the punishing end of His own divine justice. Was resurrected as the death-conquering, one and only God. And offered His gift of saving grace to the whole world.

But it all had to be *believed*. Had to be personalized in the heart by crying out to God and trusting Him with simple, childlike faith.

As he sped through the city streets, heading toward the third club, he once again felt the temptation to believe, felt that God was whispering urgently to his heart to give up.

"I can't," he whimpered out loud. "I can't give up now!" He smashed his hand into the ceiling of the car. "I've come too far. I've . . ."

He started crying.

He started thinking of Susan and Donica.

As a foolish man and false teacher, he

had misled them. By his pathetic pride he had destroyed the lives of his wife and daughter. And also his son.

It was too late for him. Too late to surrender.

The killers of his son had to die.

The Jamaicans. And himself.

Both equally guilty.

Both deserving to die.

Feeling pulled into a war of depression and euphoria, he reached for the radio knob.

The loud, hard music that rocked forth from the speakers once again provided a distraction from thinking.

He was now moving on impulse.

A mile from his destination and his destiny, the music station he was listening to broke for a few commercials.

He reached out through the darkness and touched the scan button. When the automatic scanner stopped at the next incoming signal, Jordan heard a man's voice say, "You've been listening to the weekly broadcast of the All People's Church in midtown. The guest speaker via a prerecorded sermon has been the Reverend Jason Faircloth from New York City . . ."

Jordan shook his head. Was he dreaming?

But it was too late. His thoughts once again jerked him back into the arena of truth.

He tried to force his mind to go blank.

As he reached out to touch the scan button again, his hand froze.

"And now, Faircloth's closing remarks," the radio announcer said.

Then came the voice of the nontraditional old man whom God had used as a catalyst to point him to truth. It was Jason.

"Without forgiving those who hurt you — your enemies *or* your friends — you give away your right to personal peace," the gentle voice said.

"Leave me alone!" Jordan shouted.

But his hand, only inches away from punching the scan button, still wouldn't move. The part of him that had been humiliated and broken would not grant his hand the freedom.

"All those who choose to fight God and His Word will lose," Faircloth's voice continued. "If you fight Him through disbelief, defiance, disregard, apathy, or any other self-imposed or outwardly imposed reason, you *will lose*. Nobody fights God and wins. Nobody . . ."

By the time Jordan drove his car into the nightclub parking lot, the broadcast from the All People's Church was over. Faircloth's words had vanished from the airwaves.

But Jordan was now the one being pursued. By the light of forty years' worth of spiritual blindness.

And now, as hard as he tried, he couldn't even find a shadow in which to hide.

When he pulled his car into the parking space next to the fence gate and turned off the engine, he was shaking under the pressure of what was now clear.

But he was *so* close.

He took hold of the steering wheel as something solid, and tried through concentration to calm himself.

Just ten feet in front of him, through the brick and cement-block wall, was the place. The place where he could end it.

The final domino.

The outside darkness seemed to echo Jason's words: *Nobody fights God and wins, Jordan. Nobody . . .*

He closed his eyes and took a deep breath. He looked out the windows. The front lights of the building illuminated the other end of the building and some of the parking area. He saw a group of six or seven people walking toward the main entrance. Otherwise, he appeared to be alone in the car-filled lot.

He reached under the passenger's seat and removed the hunting knife, the rope, and the .44-magnum.

He tucked the knife under his belt, opposite the .45. He tied the rope around his waist, underneath his suit coat. The magnum he would carry in his hand.

Before he got out of the car, he took another deep breath. He thought over the last year again:

The misguided move to Germany.

Chase's tolerance toward the move because of finding his first-ever girlfriend.

The murders. The dark day that altered their lives forever.

The hunt.

Gagic.

Ricardo and his confession.

The first trip to Detroit.

The automobile accident. The injuries.

The healing of his body. The emotional demolition of his family.

Now, back here in Detroit again.

The end of the search. *Here* at this club.

And Faircloth.

Jordan opened the door and got out of the car.

"Believing lies destroys, Jordan . . . Nobody fights God and wins. Nobody."

With the magnum in his hand, he walked through the eight-foot-high gate toward the rear door of the building. One car, a Mercedes, was parked inside the back fence.

"Without forgiving your enemies, Jordan, there will be no peace of mind . . . The heart of Christianity is the heart — a personal relationship in the heart with Jesus Christ . . . a relationship that will change your life from within."

The door to the rear of the club that the Jamaicans used to enter and exit the building was metal. The bottom part of the door frame was about six inches above the asphalt parking lot, requiring a step upward.

Walking up to the door, Jordan stood for a few seconds in the moonlight. Was it *really* too late for him?

Once again, he wanted to believe.

But again, "self" failed him.

He reached for the doorknob and tried to turn it. His flow of adrenaline accelerated.

The door was locked.

Holding the magnum in his right hand, he knocked on the door with his left. He hoped the person or persons inside would assume he was one of the posse members coming in early.

Jordan then stepped to the left and held his gun hand to the doorknob.

He waited.

But no one was answering.

He knocked again, this time louder.

Several seconds passed. There was still no answer.

Just when he started to knock again, he heard the lock on the inside of the door being opened.

The sound of impending contact with the "enemy" transformed him back into a human machine, a machine fueled by the bloody and vengeance-producing images of his slain son.

Seventeen years old.

Epileptic.

Innocent and harmless.

Senselessly and callously murdered.

Hate!

In less than a second after the door opened, Jordan's peripheral vision registered the Jamaican's lifted gun.

Before the Jamaican could assimilate what was happening and pull the cocking bolt to fire his weapon, Jordan threw the door open wider, pulling the Jamaican for a split second off balance.

The Jamaican's right hand, holding the 9 mm machine gun, was jerked out of control toward the upper part of Jordan's stomach.

In that brief moment, Jordan clutched the incoming gun with his left hand and slung the Jamaican, still holding the gun, facedown to the asphalt.

Pulled into a swirl by the force of the movement, Jordan swung his left leg over the falling Jamaican to keep his balance. Driven by hate, he drove the butt of his magnum down onto the back of the Jamaican's head.

The Jamaican went limp, his attempted yell fading into a sickly groan. Then there was silence.

In almost a nonstop move, Jordan, emotionally strung to the max by his determination to survive until he reached his prey, shifted with lightning speed to once again face the open door. His magnum was pointed and ready to fire.

His eyes ran the length and width of the lighted hallway he was now looking into. The hall was empty, with no sign of human presence.

Jordan stepped backward and looked down at the immobilized Jamaican lying on the ground bleeding. He picked up the machine gun from the man's hand.

Then, for no apparent reason, he started crying.

Refastening his sight to the inside hallway, he used his shoulder to wipe the sweat and tears from his face. He then slung the Jamaican's machine gun over the fence into the vacant lot on the club's southwest side.

Facing the inner corridor with his magnum aimed in that direction, he bent down, never shifting his eyes from the hallway, and groped until he found a handhold underneath one of the Jamaican's armpits.

He heaved the man's limber body up from the pavement and wrestled his arm around the chest, the body's head and arms drooping down like a rag doll over his forearm.

Without forgiving your enemies as Jesus forgives His, you will never find peace.

NOOOO! he told himself, and swallowed hard.

With his trigger finger tense, he cautiously entered the building, holding the Jamaican close to his side.

Still moving like a programmed machine, he scanned the hallway for doors. There were two on either side, then the hallway disappeared around both corners, forming a T. Three of the four doors in view were closed and appeared to be metal, like the door leading to the outside. The fourth, the farthest door on the right, was open, with light coming from it. It must have been the room where the Jamaican was staying.

But had he been alone?

Or was there someone else?

Maybe several.

If there were others, would they have heard the episode at the back door?

When he reached the open door, he gripped the limp body in his arm and took a deep breath. Envisioning another person or two in the room, he jerked the Jamaican's body to his front side as a shield and stepped into the doorway with his gun sweeping back and forth.

But no one was in the room.

A quick glance told him the room was a hangout. In the forefront were three long foldout tables set up side by side, with a number of folding chairs surrounding them. A large refrigerator stood against one wall, next to a small kitchen bar with cabinets and a sink.

On the far end of the room were couches, lewd pictures on the wall, a stereo system, and a giant projection-screen television.

The room was littered throughout with

beer cans, ashtrays, and food scraps.

He laid the Jamaican in one of the nearby corners and tried to ignore the young man's blood all over the front of his own suit coat.

He returned to the back door and locked it again from the inside.

He then checked the other three doors, keeping an eye at the same time on the other end of the hall, expecting someone to walk around either corner at any second.

All three doors were locked. He knocked on each one and waited. There was no response.

He then made his way to the other end of the hall, where it joined the two others to make the T. His gun still drawn, he stepped forward to look down each of the other hallways. Each of them ran about forty feet out, then turned another corner. There were no doors on either side.

He moved down the right section first.

When he turned the next corner in the direction of the nightclub part of the building, he was staring at another door about ten feet in front of him. There was another door immediately to his left.

He tried the left door first. It was locked.

Then he tried the one at the end of the short hall. Judging by the increased loudness and vibration of the nightclub's music, he figured the door must lead right into the club somewhere.

It, too, was locked.

He retraced his steps to the T, and was getting ready to check the hallway going left when he heard a groan from the "hangout" room.

The guy was alive.

Jordan caught himself weeping again. He felt that the inner turmoil of his conscience was on the verge of causing his heart to explode. But he kept pushing.

Going back to the room, he found the guy rolled over on his stomach, trying to get up.

Jordan pulled his knife from his belt and turned him over.

When he moved the knife toward the Jamaican's stomach, the guy closed his eyes and tried to speak. But his words came out as mumbles and moans.

With the knife, Jordan sliced off a piece of the guy's shirt. He tied the piece of cloth around the face and the back of the Jamaican's head and gagged him with it.

Jordan then removed the thin nylon rope from around the upper part of his waist and cut off two pieces, about three feet each.

With one piece, he tied the Jamaican's hands together behind his back. With the other, he tied his feet together at the ankles.

Jordan then lifted his captive and moved him over into the kitchen area and laid him on the floor, out of direct view from the hallway.

He was about to search the guy for a wallet and identification when a sudden percussion of music from the nightclub flooded the back part of the building. The wave of music lasted for about five seconds.

An inner door from the club had been opened.

Somebody was coming.

Jordan moved quickly, trying to silence his rapid breathing. He scooped up the rope he had left lying on the floor, then positioned himself against the wall just inside the doorway.

He heard footsteps.

He strained to listen. There seemed to be only one set.

He readied his magnum and inhaled long and slow.

When the Jamaican stepped through the door with a six-pack of beer in his hand, it took less than three seconds for him to spot his comrade tied up on the floor.

Jordan had waited out those seconds to confirm that the man was alone.

When the Jamaican pivoted, it was too late. In midswing, he felt the burning jerk of a rope around his neck.

Wrenching the rope with the momentum of hate, Jordan kept pulling it tighter until the gasping and flailing Jamaican started losing consciousness. When the man's head started to bob, Jordan released the rope and let him drop to the floor.

Jordan then rolled him over onto his stomach.

While the Jamaican fought to breathe again and gather his senses, Jordan cut a piece of rope, forced the guy's resistant hands behind his back, and tied them. The Jamaican made a sudden attempt to fight with his feet, but Jordan ground his own knee into the base of the guy's spine and pinned him hard to the floor.

Ignoring the eruption of agonizing groans and cursing threats, Jordan tried to keep an eye on the doorway as he sliced off another section of the rope.

He then grabbed the Jamaican's ankles and doubled his legs behind his back. He pressed the heels downward till they made contact with the buttocks. Then he tied the feet together. With the loose ends of the knot he bound the roped feet to his roped hands. Then he gagged him.

He dragged the guy across the floor to where the other Jamaican was lying. Then, with gun in hand, he returned to check out the other section of the hallway.

It, too, ended with a doorway around another corner.

Jordan carefully pulled the handle.

The door opened. It had to be the one the last Jamaican had used.

Peeking through, Jordan saw that the door led into an unfinished room that looked like a storage area for the club's bar.

Were there other Jamaicans up front who would be returning at any moment via this route?

Jordan closed the door and locked it with the dead bolt on the hallway side.

The only way into the back section of the building now was through the rear outside door, with a key. He would wait for the other Jamaicans to enter through that door.

Feeling momentarily secure enough to give his full attention to his two captives, he rushed back to the "hangout" room.

Both Jamaicans were struggling to get

free. And both were offering up guttural protests. Strenuous, but indecipherable.

First, Jordan frisked them for weapons.

The one with the head injury was clean. The other one was carrying a knife.

Jordan disposed of the knife under the refrigerator, sliding it deep to the back of the wall so it would be unreachable.

Jordan then went through their pockets. He found a driver's license on one. The name showing on the plastic card was Ras Bogle.

Jordan sliced up the card with his knife and threw the pieces across the floor toward the base of the sink cabinet.

On the other Jamaican, who was older, Jordan found a passport along with some plane tickets. The name in the passport was Martin Garvey.

"It was the one they called Martin; he's the one who knifed her" — Ricardo had screamed the confession at him.

Jordan closed his eyes. He thought about Heather, about Ralph and Lynn. About their pain.

He cupped his hands over his face. As a new rush of hatred and disgust assaulted his emotions, he felt his entire body start to shake.

Behind that rush, however, was another,

an unwelcomed one. *Without forgiving your enemies, Jordan, as Jesus forgave His, there is no peace . . . The Moseleys reacted differently because their interpretation was different . . . They've interpreted the murder as an event that somehow happened within God's control . . . You've interpreted the event as something that happened without any control, without any reason . . . They believe that God will in His own time make the criminals face justice . . . You believe justice lies solely in the hands of man . . . Believing lies destroys, Jordan . . . Believing the truth will set you free.*

Clenching his fists, he could not hold back the scream of confusion that burst from the core of his soul. "NOOO! NOOOOO!" he bellowed.

In a fit of emotional reaction, he grabbed Martin by the back of his arms and yanked him straight up into the air and slammed him face-first into the refrigerator. He let him drop to his knees, leaving a smear of blood on the refrigerator's white door.

With new tears in his eyes, Jordan pulled out his hunting knife.

Again, he picked up Martin, dazed with pain, off the floor. He positioned him on top of one of the nearby folding tables.

He waited until Martin's visual focusing

was complete, then looked him in the eye. "Munich, Germany," he said. He paused to give the words time to be absorbed. Then he continued. "Two teenagers. Rape. Murder."

He didn't have to say anymore. The surprised reaction in Martin's face and eyes said everything.

Jordan felt the urge to end the guy's life with one quick plunge of the knife.

But he resisted. As much as anybody had ever deserved anything, this guy deserved to suffer for a while. He deserved to feel the approaching pain of a premature death, just like Chase and Heather.

Just out of curiosity, Jordan picked the plane tickets off the floor where he had dropped them and looked at the destination. It was Jamaica. For a three-day trip, leaving tomorrow morning.

Then he noticed the names of the ticket holders: Martin Garvey, Ottey Grant, and Tito Manley.

Jordan ripped the tickets and scattered the pieces onto the dirty floor.

He had found the killers.

But the confirmation left him with an overpowering taste of personal waste. It was as if God, Faircloth, Susan, and Donica were all standing there saying, "We told you this pursuit was useless . . ."

Trying to shake it off, he returned his attention to the table. Staring at the exhausted but determined Jamaican, he took his knife and moved it toward the guy's throat.

The man tried not to show any fear. But when Jordan held the razor-sharp blade against the skin of his neck and started applying pressure, he gulped and tried to hold his head motionless by ceasing to breathe.

"I wonder how many others you've killed," Jordan asked, as if speaking aloud to himself.

The Jamaican closed his eyes.

"You're a pitiful piece of scum — you know that?" Jordan queried. He wasn't sure if he was talking to the Jamaican or to himself.

At that particular instant of dark reflection, he heard the back door opening . . . followed by voices.

Jordan saw the Jamaican's eyes pop open with a look of defiant victory.

Without wasting a second, Jordan lifted the Jamaican off the table into a headlock with his left arm. Squeezing the Jamaican's neck with all his might to keep him as quiet and distracted as possible, he backed them up against the wall and behind the door.

But the other Jamaican, still lying on the floor, had also heard the welcomed noises at the back door. Perking up, he started forcing guttural warnings through the piece of shirt wrapped through his mouth.

At the same moment, the two phones located in both ends of the room started to ring.

Contending with the Jamaican who was locked in the grip of his arm, fighting to breathe again, Jordan at the same time hustled the .44-magnum from beneath his belt.

Jordan heard a male voice. In the loud thumping of his own heartbeat, he couldn't seem to understand the words. Either they were being spoken in a foreign language, or else his mind was racing too fast in other directions to comprehend the accented English.

Had the guy coming in heard the strained grunts of the Jamaican tied up on the floor? Was he now yelling questions? Or was he shouting commands?

When the third Jamaican stepped into the room, Jordan was already aiming at his back, below his long and knotty rust-colored hair.

Then, almost ghostlike, a woman walked in between them. It was the platinum blonde he had seen over a week ago with the other Jamaican.

When the standing Jamaican spotted his bound-up comrade on the floor, he started to whirl.

Jordan took the man still gripped in his arm and rammed him into the back of the opened door, slamming it closed. Dropping him at the foot of the door, Jordan reached out for the blonde, who was facing away from him.

When he pulled her into his grasp, he saw a machine gun being pulled from inside the coat of the Jamaican who was now facing him.

Hardly hearing the girl's scream, Jordan aimed his magnum at the Jamaican's heart.

28

Jordan started to issue his order for the Jamaican to put down the weapon, but he never had a chance. Piercing him with dark, fearless eyes, the Jamaican never retarded his progressive motion of lifting his gun and pulling the cocking bolt.

The blonde burst into another scream.

Fully intending to accomplish his objective, Jordan allowed the nozzle of his magnum to slightly drop as he pulled the trigger.

The screaming, the gunfire, and the abrupt look of horror and pain on the Jamaican's face seemed to all occur in the same split second.

Jordan had shot twice.

One bullet had passed through the Jamaican's leg just above the knee. The other went through his upper thigh near the groin.

As the Jamaican recoiled, he held on to his gun. But when the man faltered on the bullet-ridden leg, Jordan, with the girl in tow, moved in on him. Not knowing if the guy had been able to cock his gun, Jordan this time pointed the magnum toward the man's head.

"Drop the gun, or you're dead," Jordan demanded.

The Jamaican, agonizing in pain, hesitated.

"Help me, Ottey," the blonde begged, sounding uncertain about the Jamaican's loyalty to her.

"Ottey . . ." Jordan heard himself echo the name.

At that pivotal moment, when the next move would be a final commitment, Jordan saw the Jamaican make his decision and try again to cock the gun.

With a monumental sense of triumph, Jordan made his decision as well. Propelled by a name that had put him through eight months of sleepless hell, he shoved the girl into the Jamaican with so much force that both of them were knocked off their feet.

As they went crashing onto the floor and into the tables, Jordan went down on top of them.

With flailing arms, Ottey managed to spray a few wild bullets into the ceiling. But before he could fight through the explosive pain in his leg and regroup, Jordan already had the barrel of the .44-magnum buried under his chin.

Everybody froze. Heavy breathing was all that broke the silence.

"Now, let go of the gun, Ottey!" Jordan snarled.

Ottey's eyes blinked, and his arm tightened.

Jordan pushed the gun barrel deeper into his neck until he started choking.

"*Now*, Ottey!" Jordan barked.

The moment Ottey released his grip on the machine gun, Jordan seized it.

With both guns now in his hands, he stood carefully to his feet.

He knew those up front in the club had undoubtedly heard the gunfire. How they would respond was anybody's guess.

Jordan moved quickly.

Never letting the magnum's aim veer from Ottey's upper body, Jordan ordered the blonde, "Stay lying down — back-to-back with him."

Shaking with fear, and fighting the pain from the fall, the girl obeyed.

With both guns pointed at his prey, Jordan moved sideways for about four feet and retrieved the rope from the floor.

With Ottey now incapacitated because of

the leg wounds and severe bleeding, Jordan found only verbal resistance as he tied the Jamaican's feet together with the girl's.

Moving to their heads and stepping between them, Jordan forced Ottey's hands behind his back.

As he tied the Jamaican's hands and then the girl's, he heard her say in a pleading whisper, almost as if talking to herself, "Please . . . don't kill me!"

Hearing and seeing her terror, Jordan found himself back in Germany in the wooded area where Chase and Heather's bodies had been found. His mind, playing the role of Heather, tried to feel her horror, her pain, her nightmare.

Once again, he started crying.

Looking over at Martin, still lying at the base of the door, he wanted the animal to hurt now with the same hurt Heather had felt.

Then he thought of Chase.

His son.

The son to whom he had given his fatherly love for seventeen years.

The son he had fought for all his life.

The handicapped son, outnumbered, who never had a chance.

Now gone.

At the hands of — Ottey.

"So you're the one they call Ottey," Jordan spoke aloud with a strained voice, giving the Jamaican beneath him a devouring stare.

Quickly becoming lost in his thoughts, Jordan ignored Ottey's bursts of threatening curses. He shifted his stare and his concentration to the pair of hands bound together behind the Jamaican's back.

These were the hands he had searched for, for eight months.

The hands that had trespassed human rights.

The hands that had ended a family.

The hands that had taken the life of his only son.

With his haunting thoughts reaching their peak, Jordan suddenly felt as if he would mentally choke — more from confusion than victory.

Removing the knife from his belt and kneeling down at the Jamaican's side, he wanted more than anything in all the world to cut out the savage heart that had ordered the Jamaican's hands.

With Ottey lying captive and helpless beside him, he was now free to do it.

Nothing was stopping him.

As Jordan gripped the knife handle in his hand, he closed his eyes.

Why was he hesitating? To get here, he had crushed everybody who had gotten in his way.

Feeling his throat growing so tight that it hurt, he opened his eyes and brought the knife around to the front side of Ottey's body.

At that moment, the phone started to ring again. He ignored it.

Go ahead, he told himself. *This is what you've lived for. You've triumphed. You've won. Now do it.*

He positioned the tip of the blade over Ottey's shirt-covered heart.

The pain swelling inside his throat, combined with the pain that was sucking the surety from his mind, was now almost unbearable.

He gripped the knife even tighter.

He knew it could all be over in just a matter of seconds.

Why was he stumbling?

What was wrong?

Closing his eyes in utter frustration, he lifted the knife for the final plunge that would culminate his revenge.

His hand started shaking.

As he inhaled a deep breath and readied himself, he suddenly saw Susan, Donica, and Faircloth standing there in the darkness of his mind, looking at him with tears in their eyes.

He wanted to tell them to go away, but couldn't.

It was as if time froze. In the inner ear of his soul, he thought he heard a familiar voice call out to him — a cherished voice he had not heard for the last eight months.

It couldn't be.

But it was. *Chase's voice.*

"It's okay, Dad," he was sure he heard the voice say. "I'm safe. It was just my time to die, that's all. Forgive them, Dad."

Then came what sounded like a plea: "Mother and Donica need you at home now."

Jordan tried to reach out and touch the voice, but the darkness of his mind turned to light. A brilliant light. Hot. And piercing.

Immediately, Susan, Donica, and Faircloth were not alone. Chase was standing with them, along with Heather . . . and her parents. And the black man from the All People's Church.

And behind them . . .

Behind them stood . . . the Source of the light.

When the image appeared, like a reverse silhouette it cast everything around it into utter darkness.

Then Jordan knew.

He tried to close his inner eyes. But against his shame, they were forced to stay open. He watched as the image extended His hands.

Hands of love and tenderness.

Scarred hands belonging to an only Son who had been nailed to a deadly cross.

Hands that *understood.*

"Your son is safe, Jordan." Like streams of light, the words of compassionate authority burst forth and conquered more of the darkness.

Jordan started weeping aloud. "But . . . but I . . ."

"Just believe, Jordan . . . just believe!"

As if returning from a dream, Jordan opened his eyes.

Staring across the room into the distance, he heard himself saying, "Just believe, Jordan . . . just believe."

He bowed his head. Then his eyes saw Ottey staring up at him, saying something with an expression of pain.

Again, Jordan shook — violently this time.

At the apex of twisted emotion, he cut loose with a scream that commandeered every cell of his body. Stretching the knife upward to the ceiling, he held it there until his scream had died. Then, with fury, he plunged the weapon downward with all his might.

The tip of the blade broke off and exploded outward, like sparks off an anvil, as it struck the tile floor.

On all fours, Jordan dropped his head in tense silence. His only movement was his massive chest heaving in and out with his breathing. His shirt was soaked with sweat.

Then, before he finished breathing hard, he started gathering up his belongings.

With the knife and .45 secured beneath his belt, the rope in one hand and the magnum in the other, he stood over Ottey and emptied the remaining four bullets from the magnum onto the floor.

He then placed the end of the empty gun barrel against Ottey's forehead, between his eyes, and slowly pulled the trigger.

"Click," Jordan said, watching Ottey flinch from head to toe.

He walked over to Martin and did the same.

He didn't know if the visual-aid ceremony was to placate his own sense of could-be victory, or to demonstrate to the murdering Jamaicans that they were *not* beyond the reach of justice.

With blood all over his clothes, and

sweat and tearstains on his face, Jordan looked at Ottey and Martin one final time.

"I've got a message for both you pieces of trash," he told them with the voice of a broken man. "You can pass it along to your friend Tito as well." He paused as new tears seeped from his eyes. "God saw what you did to the two teenagers in Munich, Germany, on October 25, 1991. He was there. He was watching. And in His time, He is going to make you pay. And when that time comes, just remember: The father of the boy you killed . . . is the one who told you so."

He turned from the Jamaicans and their stunned expressions, and walked away.

29

Hiding deep inside the half-filled garbage dumpster, nestled behind empty cardboard boxes and bloated garbage bags, Donica ignored the searching calls of her mother and her grandparents.

She didn't want to talk anymore.

She didn't want to hear anybody else tell her for the millionth time that life would eventually get better.

She just didn't believe it any longer.

Hope, she had come to realize, was only a cruel and meaningless word.

Her mom's talk about faith and prayers had changed nothing.

The fact was: Her dad had now abandoned her, had proven that she, as an only daughter, was unloved and unwanted, a reject and a misfit.

Well, she would show them.

She would just go ahead and make it easy for everybody.

With the desperate shouts of her name

now fading in the distance of the night, she continued to open each of the Fluoxetine capsules one at a time, then empty their contents into the coke bottle.

Ninety-eight.

Ninety-nine.

One hundred.

She then broke open the second bottle.

One hundred and one.

One hundred and two.

She continued emptying capsules until she reached one hundred and thirty.

Satisfied at that point that a sufficient amount of the medication had been mixed with the coke, she closed the soft drink bottle and held it to her chest.

In the darkness and quietness of the night, she closed her eyes and tried to psych herself up.

It wasn't as difficult as she had anticipated.

The overwhelming sense of loneliness and depression she was feeling was going to make it easy.

As she shook the bottle and opened the cap, all she had to do was think of the betrayal of her dad.

Placing the bottle to her lips and tipping it upward, she gladly drank, eagerly looking forward to her escape.

At around 2:45 a.m. a pair of uniformed policemen arrived at the Raus' apartment in response to Susan's 911 call.

With her parents at her side giving her needed support, Susan explained anxiously to the leading officer that Donica had disappeared around 11:30 p.m.

She replayed the evening's events to him. "I took a late shower. When I got out, it was about a quarter past eleven. About fifteen minutes later, when I was ready for bed, I went into Donica's room to kiss her good night. She wasn't there.

"I called for her, thinking she was probably in the living room or the kitchen. When she didn't answer, I tried to find her. But she was gone."

Wringing her hands together, Susan went on to explain to the officer that she had spent the next thirty minutes or so walking around the apartment grounds calling out Donica's name, but still hadn't been able to find her.

"At that point, I started to get worried."

Almost with guilt, Susan told how Donica, during the last year, had become withdrawn and depressed because of family problems, and that she had often run out of the house to be alone for an

411

hour or so. But never for this long. And never in the night.

"Shortly after midnight, when I still couldn't find her, I called my parents." Susan gestured toward her mom and dad. "They got here sometime before one. We've searched everywhere for more than an hour," Susan emphasized as her voice started to break.

"Then I called 911."

After asking Susan several questions, the officers filled out the initial pages of a case report and procured a few recent photographs of Donica.

Around three-thirty, they radioed Donica Rau's case and description to the central police dispatcher. The information was relayed to all units on duty, instructing them to be on the lookout for the fourteen-year-old brunette.

"If she hasn't been found by late morning," the leading officer advised Susan as he and his partner started to leave, "I'd suggest you start contacting her schoolmates. Maybe she's gone to one of their homes. In the meantime, we'll get a couple of detectives to make inquiries at the city's bus depots and the cab companies."

Feeling too fearful and uptight to just

wait out the remainder of the night, Susan and her parents chose to go back out and keep searching. They decided to check out the twenty-four-hour grocery stores, convenience stores, and gas stations on their side of town.

Before walking out, however, Susan's mother suddenly stepped back toward the phone. "I'm going to call Pastor Rawlings," she announced.

While Susan's dad went ahead to start up the van, Susan stood inside waiting for her mother so she could lock up the apartment.

As she heard her mother get Rawlings out of bed and ask him to pray, she thought of Reverend Faircloth. True to his word, he had called her once a day from New York for the last two weeks. With his astounding wisdom and insight, and his once-in-a-lifetime friendship, he had helped breathe life into her hopes again.

But now?

She was starting to feel afraid again. She didn't know if her faith could take another devastating blow.

She just wished Faircloth was here in person to stand by her side.

When her mother got off the phone and told her the whole church would be praying for them by morning, Susan took a slow, deep breath and determined, with God's help, to be strong.

As she walked out into the night and locked the apartment door behind them, she glanced up into the nighttime expanse of endless stars.

"I'll keep believing in You," she proclaimed with watery eyes, "until You completely destroy my faith. That's all I can do."

Throughout the night, Donica laid unconscious among the stinking bags of garbage.

As the sweltering summer temperature rose with the morning sun, a multitude of flies began swarming the contents of the dumpster.

Donica had no sensation of the pesky insects as they crawled on her skin.

Neither was she aware of it when her body, now having absorbed the antidepressant drugs, jerked into the life-threatening throes of a grand mal seizure.

Two hours later, Donica's body started gasping for breath because of an irregular heartbeat that was not allowing a sufficient amount of oxygen to reach her vital organs.

It was these nightmarish gasps that drew the frightened attention of Susan's next-door neighbor as she was throwing garbage into the bin.

Thirty minutes before noon, Jordan pulled into a gas station about twenty-five miles north of Chattanooga.

Kept awake through the night by his urgent longing to be reunited with Susan and Donica and to beg for their forgiveness, he was refusing to let up on himself. He was pushing to get to Chattanooga as quickly as possible.

Plus, he now wanted Susan's help — desperately.

After filling his car's gas tank and paying for the purchase, he picked up a pay phone to try once more to contact them.

He had already tried calling twice this morning — once from Cincinnati, then from London, Kentucky. No one had answered either time, neither at his house nor his in-laws'.

Using a long-distance credit card, he once again punched out his home number.

The phone on the other end started ringing.

One ring. Two rings.

Maybe they had all taken another trip somewhere.

Three. Four.

He had just started to hang up after the fifth ring when he heard the click of someone picking up the phone on the other end.

Jordan swallowed and took a quick breath. The tension of layered nervousness raced through his body. What if Susan had changed her mind and wasn't waiting any longer? What if she wouldn't believe him? What if she decided the marriage was over?

But his burdensome questions were forgotten when someone snapped the word "Yes?" with a voice of weeping fear.

"Susan? Is that you? What's wrong? What's happened?" he blurted.

"There's no time to explain now!" he heard the voice reply with high-pitched panic — it was his mother-in-law — "We've just found her! She's almost dead! We're rushing her out the door to Erlanger!"

"Wait!" he shouted, fearing she hadn't recognized his voice and was about to hang up on him. "This is Jor—"

But he was too late. She was already gone.

Jordan stood looking at the now silent

phone. Found her! Almost dead! Hospital!

"Oh God, no!" he shouted, as adrenaline filled him.

As he punched out the number again, his mind started tripping over itself. *Who* was almost dead? Susan? Donica?

"Come on! Come on!" he shouted when he heard the line on the other end start to ring again.

Five. Six. Seven. Eight. Nine. Nobody was answering.

"Come on!" he implored as he tightly closed his eyes and tried by the sheer force of will to get somebody to answer.

Twelve. Thirteen. Fourteen.

It was no use.

Slamming the receiver back onto the hook, he ran and threw himself into his car.

Racing the automobile up the acceleration ramp onto I-75, he mashed the accelerator into the carpet and held it there.

"I'm coming!" he tried to tell them.

Donica was lying on an emergency room gurney, surrounded by a medical team.

Her mother and grandparents stood just a few feet away, praying.

"Not detecting a pulse!" one of the members reported as he held his fingers to Donica's neck, and then to her wrist.

While one medic inserted a ventilation tube down her throat for oxygen, another began connecting cardiac-monitor leads to her chest, and another checked her blood pressure. A fourth medic prepared one of her arms for the insertion of an IV tube.

Susan's dad handed one of the doctors the antidepressant bottles found in the pockets of Donica's shorts. One bottle was empty, the other half-empty. Knowing that the doctors had already been informed that it was a suicide attempt, he stepped out of the way as he hurriedly emphasized, "Both bottles were full when she got them out of her parents' medicine cabinet."

"A pulse of twenty. And it's dropping," shouted the medic watching the first reports of the cardiac monitor screen.

"Blood pressure is sixty over zero," another one followed.

"Insert one milligram of atropine, now," the lead medic ordered.

The medic responsible for administering the heart stimulant injected it into the IV on cue.

"A pulse of seventeen," the medic watching the monitor shouted.

"Come on, work for us now!" the lead medic entreated in a stern whisper, as if he were negotiating with the medicine.

"Blood pressure: forty-five over zero."

"All right," the lead medic interjected, "let's pump the stomach!"

As the lead medic, with the help of an assistant, began inserting the nasal-gastric tube through the mouth to the stomach cavity, he shouted to the others, "Get ready with the defibrillator and a repeat of the atropine!"

Susan stood to one side, her arms locked with her mother's. Her head was now throbbing with near hysteria. She stopped breathing.

One of the medics relayed the first positive report: "Pulse is holding!"

"Blood pressure holding!" another one shouted.

Seeing and hearing everything, Susan exhaled slowly as her head continued throbbing. *Is the medicine working?* she wanted to shout.

The medic operating the stomach pump released the saline solution through the gastric tube into the stomach.

"Pulse still holding!"

Everyone waited.

The medic with the defibrillator had it ready in his hands. Another was standing by, ready to inject the second milligram of atropine.

★ ★ ★

At that moment, Jordan was entering the city limits over Missionary Ridge, doing almost twice the 50-mph speed limit.

As never before in his life, he was *praying*.

A fourth batch of saline solution was pumped into Donica's stomach, then sucked back up.

The pulse was still holding, but only around eighteen.

The wait continued.

Four minutes. Five minutes.

Then suddenly: "We're losing her again!" came the dreaded report. "Pulse is dropping!"

"Atropine!" instructed the lead medic.

The second dose — one milligram — was injected.

"Still dropping!"

"Set the defibrillator at two hundred watts, and get ready!"

Susan threw her hands up to her mouth and closed her eyes.

"No, God!" she shouted through her fingers.

"Come on! Kick in!" the lead medic whispered again at the atropine.

"Pulse is at ten!"

"Defib, now!" shouted the lead medic.

420

In a breathless thirty-second stop at the emergency ward's front desk, Jordan found out that it was his *daughter* the doctors were trying to save — that she had attempted suicide with a drug overdose.

As he launched himself toward the emergency room, with a nurse jumping up to follow on his heels, he screamed inwardly, *Not Donica! Not suicide! No! It can't be! You got it all wrong!*

Seconds later, when he burst into the tension-filled room, he saw the body of his only child jerking on the gurney beneath the pads of the defibrillator.

His insides froze.

"No response!" he heard one of the medics shout.

"Three hundred watts . . . now!" the medic holding the defibrillator pads demanded.

Donica's body jerked again.

In that microcosmic moment, it suddenly registered with him: It was *his* fault. Whatever Donica had done, she had done it because . . . of *him*. He was the one who had stolen away her hope and her will to live. The girl who at one time trusted him and idolized him. Foolishly abused and neglected by a delinquent father who had wasted a year of his life being obsessed by a wrong passion. By a father who had chased lies.

"My fault!" he whispered to himself.

"Still no response!"

Feeling his insides burst with unbearable guilt, he dropped to his knees as if he had been shot through the heart.

"No, God, don't let her die!" He begged through the tears in his throat while clinching his fists. "Please . . . not because of me . . . not because of my sin . . ."

Then he heard the unforgettable words that ripped out the last remaining parts of his heart.

"She's flatlined!"

While the medics started administering CPR — compressing her chest with the heels of their hands and pumping the ambu bag to fill her lungs with artificial breath — he went inward, desperately trying to reach God.

Only when he heard Susan burst into a scream of agony did his attention snap back to the room.

The medics had stopped the resuscitation attempt.

"I'm sorry," he heard the lead medic pronounce with genuine sincerity. "Your daughter's dead."

Slowly looking up at Donica from his bended knees, he paused in a moment of delayed shock, then stood straight up with a loud shout: *"Nooooo! I'm trying to believe. I'm trying! Don't You understand?"*

When a couple of the doctors stepped close to confine him, he started crying aloud to God, "I beg You . . . just one more chance . . . just one . . ."

And then, in the midst of all the tense agony . . . it happened.

It was the bleep on the cardiac monitor that drew their attention.

"My God, we've got a heartbeat again!" exclaimed one of the medics.

When the others scurried back around the table, Jordan at first was confused.

When he finally understood what was happening, a sob of joy rippled across his face with so much force that it blocked his entire peripheral vision.

With an almost instant heartbeat of seventy strong pulses a minute, Donica was alive again.

Jordan stood motionless, transfixed in awe.

Covered in the tears of euphoria, he watched as God, the Master of life and death, the Master of universal as well as *individual* details, worked a miracle.

Amid the tears and shouts of celebration, Jordan finally moved and threw himself at Susan's side. He overheard one of the doctors say to a colleague, "It must have been the atropine. It must have kicked in late."

Moved with elation, Jordan wept aloud and unashamedly.

For the first time in his life, he knew the TRUTH.

As the doctors finished working with Donica, Jordan — not waiting another second — led Susan out into the hall. He threw himself into her arms, begging for her forgiveness.

There in the hallway, with Susan's tearful help, he prayed aloud, reaching out from his heart to once and for all take hold of God's outstretched hands — the nail-scarred hands that understood.

In the clutching embrace of his wife, Jordan Rau was born-again.

With sudden alertness, people throughout the hospital wondered what was happening as they heard a shout echoing through the corridors: *"I believe! I believe!"*

Epilogue

Jordan spent the next forty-eight hours sharing with Susan and Donica the story of Gagic, Ricardo, Faircloth, the Jamaicans, and Detroit. He told them everything, answering any and all their questions.

Over and over again, as a new and broken man, he wept in their presence, pleading for their forgiveness, telling them how much he loved them.

Donica, however, had been hurt more deeply than he had ever imagined. Several times during her three-day hospital stay, he let her know that if it took months, or even years, to win back her love and trust, he would never stop trying.

On the other hand, he was humbled to the point of painful guilt at how quickly Susan lovingly forgave him.

Her merciful treatment and willingness to take him back was further evidence of the life-changing effect of her pure Christianity. He thanked her again and again for having never outgrown her evangelical faith.

He knew it would take a long time, perhaps, to heal many of the hurts he had inflicted on their marriage. But he promised Susan that, with God's help, he would sacrifice and do everything possible to make up for the destruction he had caused.

As hope began to grow in his heart, he couldn't help but think of Jason Faircloth, the wise, white-haired man whom God had used as a primary instrument to bring about his spiritual conversion — and the restoration of his family. He decided to phone him in New York and express his heartfelt indebtedness.

On Sunday afternoon, he asked Susan to join with him in the call from a hospital pay phone.

"Jason's not at home," Susan told him. "He's in Norway. A police friend of his in Oslo was shot last week and hospitalized. He flew over to be with him for a while."

With surprise in his voice, Jordan said, "But . . . how do you know —"

"He called me the morning before he flew out of JFK," Susan continued. "It was the day before Donica tried to take her life." Susan then backtracked and gave her husband the details of Faircloth's visit on the day Jordan left to go back to Detroit.

She told about his powerful encouragement, his twenty-four-hour prayer vigil, and his promise to call and encourage her every day from New York.

"It was a promise he honored," she said. "It's because of his special friendship and encouragement that I decided to wait for you and not walk out."

Jordan bowed his head, understanding that he owed Faircloth more than he ever realized. Lost in his feelings, he didn't know what to say.

Susan reached out and took his hand. "Until he comes back into our lives again," she said, "we'll just have to be Jason Faircloth to each other. We'll work together. We'll build each other up, and help each other to never ignore God or disbelieve Him again. We'll make sure we *love* Him, *trust* Him, *obey* Him, and *believe* Him. Even . . ."

"Even if He slays us," Jordan said.

On the following Sunday morning, after having resigned as a minister from his denomination earlier in the week, Jordan stood publicly, at his own request, in Pastor Rawlings' church with Susan and Donica tearfully at his side. Before a congregation of five hundred people, he openly confessed his new faith in Christ and in the Bible.

"It has taken me forty years — fourteen of those years as a minister," he testified with the quiet voice of brokenness. "But I have finally learned that I'm not God, and that the God who is God is not as small as my personal understanding of things. All my life I've taken major risks, but never — until nine days ago — was I ever willing to take the risk of completely believing God's Word, the Bible. And now I've learned, almost too late," he concluded, as he squeezed Susan and Donica to his side, "that it's the most wonderful risk a person can ever take."

Jordan would never know, but on Wednesday of that same week — in God's time and in God's way — Ottey, Martin, and Tito, along with eleven other members of the Caribbean Parade drug posse, were jailed without bond.

The Drug Enforcement Agency of Detroit, with a patiently executed "buy-bust" operation led by Nick Baldwin — the Stinger — apprehended the fourteen while they possessed both illegal guns and drugs.

Ottey, Tito, and Martin — now off the streets — would soon face the justice of an airtight prosecution. They would each be sentenced to a minimum of twenty years behind bars.

In Chicago, Ricardo Alvarez was now part of a local Hispanic drug ring. He was unaware that his mother and stepfather were now living in North Carolina, and that they had already made two trips to Chicago to try to find him — for vindictive reasons.

Neither was Ricardo aware that the Chicago Police Department, working in collaboration with German police, had listed him in their active "wanted" files as a primary murder suspect in the Munich slaying of Heather Anne Moseley and Chase Rau.

In His time.
And according to His justice.

On Thursday, July 23, an envelope addressed to Jordan Rau showed up in the Raus' mailbox.

It was from Jason Faircloth. The postmark was dated a week and a half earlier, from Norway.

The letter read:

Dear Jordan,
    Receiving correction — whether from God, a peer, or a nine-year-old — is

never easy. But it is a quality that God, in the book of Proverbs, associates more than a dozen times with wisdom, honor, safety, understanding, and peace.

I've observed that, of all people, pastors seem to lack this quality the most.

Let's you and I, however, be different.

Let's learn to listen to God's truth, no matter how it is delivered to us.

And then believe it — even when it isn't easy.

Your unconditional friend,
Jason

PS — Knowing your quest of the heart, I'm praying for you, especially as it relates to your understanding of God's personal salvation.

PPS — Please don't feel uncomfortable with the monetary gift. God has richly blessed my investments through the years.

Enclosed was a check for twenty-one thousand dollars — the exact amount of the Raus' financial debt.

Tears were drying on Jordan's cheeks when he fell asleep that afternoon on the warm grass next to Chase's grave.

With peace now reigning in his heart, it was clear to him:

He had finally crossed over — to the truth.